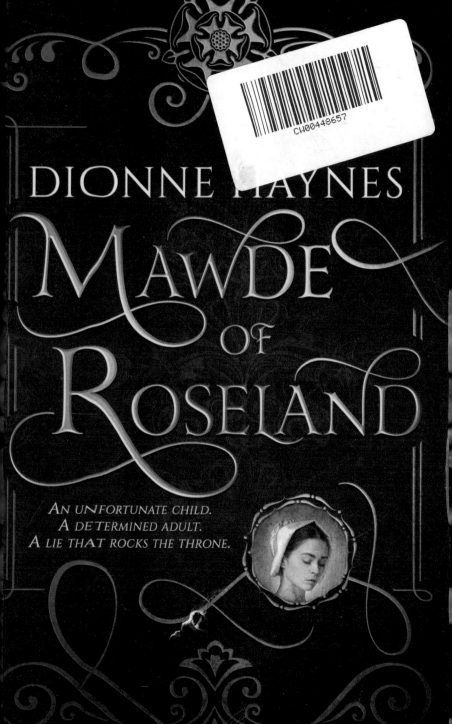

DIONNE HAYNES

MAWDE
OF
ROSELAND

AN UNFORTUNATE CHILD.
A DETERMINED ADULT.
A LIE THAT ROCKS THE THRONE.

ABOUT THE AUTHOR

Dionne Haynes spent most of her childhood in Plymouth, England. She graduated from medical school in London and enjoyed a career as a doctor for over twenty years. After returning to Plymouth, she traded medicine for a career writing historical fiction.

ALSO BY DIONNE HAYNES
Winds of Change
Running With The Wind
The Winter Years
The Second Mrs Thistlewood

For more information and updates:
www.dionnehaynes.com

MAWDE OF ROSELAND

DIONNE HAYNES

Allium

Published by Allium Books 2022
22 Victoria Road, St Austell, Cornwall, PL25 4QD

First published by Allium Books in 2022
www.alliumbooks.com

A CIP catalogue record for this book is available from the British
Library

Paperback ISBN: 978 1 9162109 9 8
Hardback ISBN:978 1 9156960 0 7
Ebook ISBN: 978 1 9156960 1 4

Book cover design by Dee Dee Book Covers

*This book is dedicated to
the family members, friends and villagers of St Mawes
who made my childhood summer holidays so magical.*

CONTENTS

PROLOGUE
MARCH 1513

CONSTANCE CROSSED herself as Margery drew a deep
breath between contractions. The morning light dimmed,
erased by a disc of darkness that slid across the sun until
only a thin rim of silver remained. The chickens fell silent
in the yard. The screech of herring gulls faded. Constance
muttered a quick prayer. She was a good person, charitable
to her neighbours and more generous than most with alms.
Surely the Lord would intervene?

Constance pressed her palm against the baby's
crowning head. 'Not yet, little one. Not yet. Wait for the
darkness to pass. Nothing good comes from a child born
during an eclipse.' She knew that from her own family
history. Her great-great-grandfather was born during a
darkening of the daytime sun and the timing had proven to
be a bad omen. There was no other explanation for his
dark moods and ferocious temper which had been noto-
rious across Roseland, driving him to commit murder and
plunging the family into poverty and shame. It had taken
three generations to rebuild their reputation. Such misfortune must not happen again.

Margery groaned, unable to resist the urge to bear down.

'No, no, no!' Constance clenched her jaw and swallowed her tears. God had forsaken her. She slapped her daughter's thigh, hard, leaving a red imprint of her hand on Margery's pale skin. 'Stop pushing!' She wrestled with the cord coiled around the baby's neck, then looked on helplessly as the baby slithered onto her lap. Daylight returned, slinking between the ill-fitting shutters and illuminating the small bedchamber. A lone gull cried out in the distance. A cockerel crowed to announce the start of a new day, confused by the interlude of a brief night sky.

'A darkling child,' Constance muttered as she cut the cord. 'Whatever did we do to deserve this?'

Margery struggled to raise herself up on to her elbows. 'What's wrong, Mamm? Why isn't the babe crying?'

Constance stared at the limp form strewn across her lap, the tiny child's blue-tinged skin slippery from her passage through the birth canal. 'Your daughter hasn't drawn a breath,' she said, battling an impulse to save the child's life.

'Daughter?' Margery heaved herself up further and blanched. 'Mamm, do something!'

Constance stroked the baby's forehead. Margery and Simon had waited years for this moment, but the timing was inauspicious. ''Tis best to let her slip away. The sun was eclipsed at the time of her birthing, a sure sign this child is cursed. No good will come from saving her.'

'No, Mamm! Give her to me!'

Constance passed the newborn to Margery. The baby's skin was cooling and turning a darker shade of blue. A little girl, perfectly formed, with hair as black as soot. Constance glimpsed a delicate flutter of the baby's chest. She glanced at Margery. Margery's vision was clouded with grief, and she had missed the ripples cast by a tiny beating heart. Margery wrapped the limp body in a clean blanket and held it to her chest as she struggled to her feet. A corner of the blanket fell away, exposing the baby's legs to an early spring draught cutting through the window shutters. The baby gave a tiny gasp, followed by a weak mewling sound.

'She's alive,' Margery said, wide-eyed with wonder.

Constance snatched the baby from Margery's arms, grasped her by the ankles and suspended her upside-down. She gave the child a sharp slap on the buttocks. The baby stopped her pathetic whimpering, paused, then gave a hearty cry.

'Lie down, Margery. The afterbirth will come soon.'

Margery lowered herself onto the bed. She kept her eyes fixed on her baby while Constance wiped vernix from the child's skin and then swaddled her in the blanket. Margery reached out to take her daughter in her arms and lay back against a pile of makeshift cushions. She ran her fingertips over the baby's rosebud mouth, button nose and plump little cheeks, and cooed soft sounds of reassurance.

'Look, Mamm, she's opened her eyes! It's as if she knows my voice.'

But as Constance opened her mouth to acknowledge her daughter's statement, the baby resumed her wailing.

'My beautiful little girl.' Margery stroked the baby's hot, angry face. She exposed an engorged breast from beneath her sweat-soaked shift and guided her nipple into the newborn's mouth. Constance saw her tense as the baby latched on, then relax when she sucked heartily.

Constance fussed at the foot of the bed, delivering the afterbirth and then replacing the blood-soaked bedlinen with a freshly laundered sheet.

3

A tentative call from her son-in-law came from somewhere near the foot of the stairs.

Constance clicked her tongue and furled the dirty linen into a tight bundle. 'Come on up, Simon,' she offered reluctantly.

Simon thundered up the staircase. He burst into the bedroom and hurried to his wife's side. 'I heard a baby's cry, but then it stopped. Is all well?'

Margery smiled. 'All is well, Simon. We have a daughter, and she has your eyes.'

Simon twisted his cap around his fingers and beamed at the baby suckling at Margery's breast. 'Mawde,' he said, grinning.

Constance backed out of the room, wrestling with the uneasy feeling she should not have allowed her grandchild to live. She dropped the soiled linens onto a fire blazing in the hearth. When the sheets succumbed to the flames, she shuffled outside into the courtyard and watched ribbons of blue-grey smoke unfurl and reach towards a cloudless sky.

'Dear God, I know not why you punish us with a child born during daytime darkness.' Constance raised her hands and tilted her chin towards the midday sun. 'But, in the name of our Lord, I declare the child's fate sealed. She entered the world with a rope around her neck, and so too shall she leave it!'

PART ONE
ST MAWES

CHAPTER ONE

MAY 1521

FROTHY WAVES LICKED the shore and dragged small stones towards the sea. Larger pebbles held their positions, rocking gently, resisting the pull of the ebbing tide. A patch of wet shingle lifted and dispersed, revealing a smooth oval of glistening russet and brown. A crab. From her vantage point on a cluster of rocks, Mawde kept her gaze fixed on the creature where it held its position between a line of seaweed and the receding water. Another movement, slow and subtle, as the crab rose on skinny legs and stretched out its chunky claws as if easing taut muscles after a heavy day's work.

Mawde grasped the coarse rope handle of her pail and jerked it through the air. Water sloshed over the rim, splashing her skirt and spraying her hand with cold salty drops. She checked the bounty she had gathered so far – a few prawns and several small handfuls of cockles. There was plenty of room for more. Returning her attention to the crab, she picked her way from one jagged peak to another, seeking gaps between green carpets of freshly exposed seaweed glistening in the late afternoon sun.

When she tried to quicken her pace, her wooden clogs slid across a patch of slippery fronds. Mawde tumbled forward and landed on all fours, dashing her head against a ring of jagged barnacles. She whimpered as she pushed herself on to her knees. Both hands sported multiple cuts, and there was a tear in the sleeve of her jacket. A gash on her left elbow had already soaked her shift with crimson and was invading the weave of her best woollen jacket. Mawde snivelled as she looked around. Fishermen's wives and daughters dotted a distant beach, digging for lugworms in a patch of cool grey sand. Across the water at Place Priory, monks tended to their herb beds. Not one person showed an interest in the antics of an unfortunate eight-year-old girl.

Blood trickled from Mawde's throbbing forehead. A large drop splashed onto her kirtle and spread through the tired fabric. Grandmother had cut down an old kirtle of Mamm's to make the dress and jacket, but both items were probably ruined now. Resigned to a tirade of angry words, Mawde scanned the rocks for her pail. Somehow, it had survived the fall unscathed and held on to most of its contents.

Mawde lowered herself on to the shingle and tiptoed towards a large cluster of bladderwrack, edging closer to her prey. The crab heaved itself onto its legs and moved with lumbering steps as if struggling to support its weight. It was large for a beach crab. Mawde muttered a few words of thanks for her unexpected good fortune. A taste of sweet crabmeat might put a smile on Grandmother's bitter face. Positioning her small hands on opposite sides of the shell and well clear of the pincers, she lifted the crab into the pail. She covered her precious hoard with a clump of damp seaweed and started the long walk home.

As Mawde reached the edge of the village, a glint in

the muddy road drew her to a stop. She bent forward to poke the shiny metal with her finger and gasped. It was the most beautiful button she had ever seen. She scratched off the dirt and studied the delicate craftsmanship. The button was twice as wide as her thumb and shaped like a little mushroom. It had a flower shape pressed into the domed metal, slender petals radiating from its centre, and a neat loop carved into the end of its tiny stalk. Mawde wrapped her fingers around it, wincing as the movement opened the cuts on her knuckles. The button would make a wonderful gift for her mother.

'Mamm?' Mawde's voice sounded feebler than she intended.

'Dearest child, what happened?' Her mother furrowed her brow as she angled Mawde's face towards the light and studied the wound on Mawde's forehead.

Unable to stifle her tears, Mawde buried her face in her hands and sobbed. 'I caught a crab,' she hiccoughed, once her distress finally eased. She pressed her cheek against her mother's pregnant belly. 'I heard you tell Grandmother the baby was giving you a taste for crab, so I caught it for you.' Mawde heard the creak of a chair as her grandmother struggled to her feet. She forced a smile. 'And I brought seaweed to ease the pain in Grandmother's hands and knees.'

'Dearest Mawde, you're always thinking of other people. Let's get you cleaned up, then we'll enjoy this delicious supper you've provided for us.'

'I have something else.' Mawde uncurled her fingers to reveal the silver button.

Mamm took the button and turned it over in her hand.

'It's beautiful, Mawde. Looks like it came off a fine piece of lady's clothing. Where did you get it?'

'I found it.'

Grandmother shuffled towards them and squinted at the button. 'What woman would be so careless as to lose a button as fine as that!' She turned her mean eyes on Mawde. 'Are you sure you didn't pinch it?'

'No, of course, I didn't!' She pointed at the button. 'You could stitch it on to your Sunday jacket, Mamm. See here? It has a loop.'

Mamm stroked Mawde's tearstained cheeks. 'It's a lovely gift. Thank you. I'll do as you suggest and stitch it to my best jacket. Come now, let me see to your wounds.'

Her mother bathed the cuts on Mawde's hands and elbow, then tended to the wide gash on her forehead. 'It's a nasty one,' she said, easing out strands of Mawde's matted raven hair. 'It'll fade with time, but I doubt it'll disappear completely.'

'A cursed child,' her grandmother grumbled. She pointed a crooked finger at Mawde. 'Now she's branded for all to see.'

'Hush, Mamm.' Mawde's mother gave Grandmother a warning look. 'Enough of your dark superstitions. Mawde's a delightful child, and kind to everyone, as you well know.'

'She *is* cursed.' Grandmother shuffled back to her chair. 'Don't ever say I didn't warn you.'

'Say it often enough and the poor child will believe you. Please, Mamm, stop trying to find fault with her, or indeed, anyone. Your obsession with curses and ill omens is turning you sour.'

Grandmother fell silent and scowled at one of Da's shirts as she set about repairing a frayed cuff.

Mamm planted a kiss on the crown of Mawde's head. 'Take no notice of your grandmother and her funny ideas.

While supper's cooking, I'll show you how to turn your seaweed into a balm for Grandmother's painful joints – it might even soothe her sharp tongue. But first, you need a dressing for your wound.'

Dusk fell, casting a chill as the sun dropped below the horizon. Mawde rushed to finish her chores. She chivvied the chickens into their coops and double-checked she had secured the latches to protect the birds from hungry foxes. She bade them a good night and hurried indoors.

Mawde ate her supper of bread, ham and cheese, then perched on a cushion at her father's feet. Da told stories about his adventures as a boy, and then they played Nine Men's Morris.

'That will do for tonight,' Da said, after Mawde won the third game. 'It's time for you to sleep.'

'Da,' she said, pressing her pale cheek against the coarse dark hair of her father's beard, 'do you love me?'

'You know I do. Why do you ask?' He took Mawde's hand and squeezed it, forgetting about the cuts and bruises from her fall earlier in the day.

Mawde tried to ignore the stinging and jerked her head in her grandmother's direction. 'She doesn't love me.'

'Your grandmother? Of course she does.' He smiled and hugged Mawde to him. 'She has a harsh tongue at times, but uses it to lash out at everyone.'

Mawde shook her head. 'She's different with me.' She lowered her voice. 'She never smiles at me, not even when I've been nice to her.' She pointed to the bandage on her forehead. 'She said I'm marked because I'm cursed.' Her bottom lip quivered. 'I'm scared, Da. If I am cursed, what will happen to me?'

A flash of anger darkened Da's face. He glared at his dozing mother-in-law. 'Grandmother can be foolish at times. Pay no heed. You're a good girl, Mawde, with a gentle manner and kind heart. Never forget how much Mamm and I love you. Whatever happens, that will never change. Now, off to bed with you. You can say your prayers by yourself tonight. I trust you to say them properly.'

Mawde threw her arms around Da's neck and kissed him on the cheek before heading upstairs to the bedchamber she shared with her grandmother. Kneeling on the floor, her sore palms pressed together, she prayed for a healthy baby brother or sister and for her mother to survive the birthing. As an afterthought, she asked God to forgive her grandmother's spiteful tongue and ease the burning in her joints.

Weary from events of the day, Mawde snuggled onto her plump straw mattress and drifted off to sleep.

CHAPTER TWO

MAY 1521, WHITSUN

BEFORE MAWDE COULD KNOCK a second time, the door to the farmhouse flew open.

'At last, you're here!' Tamsin's eyes widened. 'Mawde! Why do you have a strip of linen tied around your head?'

'Fell on the rocks and cut my forehead.' Mawde pressed on the bandage and grimaced. 'Mamm changed the poultice before church this morning. She said the wound looks deep and it'll leave a scar.'

'It'll fade in time,' Tamsin said. 'And anyway, what does it matter if you have a scar? It doesn't change who you are.'

Mawde met Tamsin's reassuring gaze. 'I suppose you're right.'

Tamsin peered over Mawde's shoulder. 'Did your mamm not come with you? Or Grandmother?'

'Mamm had a sudden urge for Da to rearrange the furniture in their bedchamber to make room for when the babe arrives. They'll only be a few minutes behind me.'

A loud thud struck the ceiling above their heads. Next came a volley of shouts from overexcited boys, and the rumble of heavy footfall as they chased each other towards the staircase. Tamsin rolled her eyes. 'We'll go on ahead without them. Could be ages before my brothers are ready to leave, and we don't want to miss anything, especially not the dancing.'

Tamsin scratched her head along the edge of her hair-line. Tiny white flakes of skin scattered like snowflakes across the shoulders of her green woollen jacket. Bending her fingers caused the skin of her knuckles to split into small fissures. Two of them started to bleed.

'That looks really sore,' Mawde said.

'It's uncomfortable, but I'm used to it.' Tamsin gestured for them to walk towards the kitchen. 'Summer's not far away, and my skin will improve when it sees a little sunshine. Did I tell you I'm banned from the dairy? Mamm said I'll spoil the butter and cheese.'

Mawde knew how much Tamsin loved working in the dairy. The cool air eased her itching, and the women employed by her aunt and uncle were always eager to share an entertaining tale or two. 'I didn't know. I'm sorry, Tamsin. What does she have you doing instead?'

Tamsin sighed. 'Cleaning and tidying after my broth-ers. It's not all bad though. She said now I'm almost eleven, I'm old enough to learn about running the home, and she'll even teach me how to manage the accounts.'

'What are they?'

Tamsin shrugged. 'Not sure. Something to do with the money we earn from selling butter and cheese, and counting how much we spend on running the house and farm. I think she's hoping that if I'm good at managing money, she'll be able to marry me off to a farmer's son. It's the only way I'll ever find a husband. No one will want me otherwise because of my skin.'

Mawde adored Tamsin. Despite the age gap of three

years, they were the best of friends. Mawde loved the way her cousin accepted her condition and made no complaint, even when it flared as badly as it had during the last winter, leaving patches of Tamsin's face taut and shiny. Grandmother made liniments and salves to keep the condition at bay, but too often Tamsin endured weeks of weeping sores and persistent flaking. Even the Truro physicians had failed to find a cure.

Aunt Mary, Tamsin's mother, was scrubbing the top of their large kitchen table. The girls announced their plans to set off for the village, and Aunt Mary nodded her approval. She drew a coin from her pocket. 'A ha'penny,' she said, pressing the coin into Tamsin's palm. 'Treat yourselves to something nice.'

'Thank you,' the girls said in unison.

Mawde hopped from one foot to the other, excited by the gift. 'I hope the monks bring honey biscuits. They're my favourites!'

Aunt Mary smiled. 'Away with you now. Be sure to come home well before dusk.'

'Won't you be coming to the village later?' Mawde asked.

'No,' Aunt Mary said. 'Your mother's babe is due any time now and I'd hate for her to be caught out on that steep hill. Anyway, Grandmother's knees are swollen again, so it makes sense for the three of us to spend the afternoon here. Go and have a wonderful time. You can tell us all about it over supper.'

Mawde and Tamsin paused on the brow of the hill. The village was a seething mass of bright colours, and the hubbub of chatter floated through the air. The tide was in, and boats of varying shapes and sizes jostled together in the harbour while a large crowd of people ebbed and flowed by the water's edge. Hot meat pies scented the air, teasing the girls' nostrils and making their mouths water. After a brief exchange of glances, they broke into a run and careered down the steep hill towards the heart of the village.

A large procession advanced towards the church house – grown men and gangly youths keen to make an early start on feasting and ale. Mawde and Tamsin tagged along behind until Mawde came to an abrupt stop.

'What's wrong?' Tamsin asked.

Mawde leaned towards her and lowered her voice. 'See that woman sitting against the wall of Widow Hitchin's cottage? I think it's Goodwife Mitchell with baby James.'

Tamsin wrinkled her nose. 'There's a resemblance, but that woman's filthy. I don't think I've seen her before.'

'Let's move closer and get a better look.'

Mawde tugged Tamsin's sleeve, pulling her along beside her.

'Goodwife Mitchell?'

'Widow Mitchell now,' came the sharp reply.

Mawde sank to her knees. 'I'm so sorry. I didn't know.'

The woman raised her gaunt face to stare at Mawde. Her eyes were bloodshot and sunken, rimmed by grey shadows. 'Didn't expect you to,' she rasped. 'Wouldn't expect you to care neither, living at the top of the hill like you do, lording it over the rest of us.'

Mawde frowned at the woman's bitter tone. 'We're hardly lording it. And we can't even see the village from our homes,' she said.

Tamsin pulled Mawde to her feet. 'I don't think she meant it,' she whispered. 'Come away. We should leave her be.'

'I can't, Tamsin.' Mawde softened her voice. 'What happened to your husband, Widow Mitchell?'

The young woman's eyes filled with tears. 'Left early to fish, same as every other morning. Then one day, 'e didn't come 'ome. Been missing several weeks now. No sign of 'im or the boat. Drowned, most likely. Now 'tis just me and the child. Left us with nothing, 'e did. Can't even pay me rent.' She drew the toddler to her, holding him tight and ignoring his protests. 'Ain't nothin' you can do about it, anyways.'

'We'll pray for you,' Tamsin assured her. 'We'll pray for your husband, too.'

Widow Mitchell gave a dismissive flick of her hand. 'Don't s'pose God can do much about it now.'

Mawde allowed Tamsin to lead her away, her high spirits replaced by sadness. 'We have to help her.'

'What can we do?'

Mawde chewed her lip. 'Maybe your mamm will take her on in the dairy? She'll be needing help now you're not allowed in there.'

'Maybe. I'll ask.' Tamsin broke into a smile. 'Look. The monks are here. I'll wager they're selling your honey biscuits.'

Cheered by the thought of her favourite edible treats, Mawde grinned at Tamsin and raced her to the stall. Tamsin handed over her halfpenny and eagerly accepted a package of biscuits in return.

One monk beckoned Mawde towards him. He rested his palm on her shoulder and gave her a warm smile. 'You have an aura of kindness about you, child. Your good deeds sometimes go unnoticed, but the Lord sees the goodness in your heart. Please, accept this gift.' He reached across the stall and selected a small earthenware pot, then pressed it into Mawde's hand, wrapping his cool fingers around hers. 'God bless you, child.'

Mawde had never seen such a beautiful pot. The smooth stone stopper was in the shape of a bee and held in place by a seal of shimmering golden wax.

'Honey?' Mawde asked.

The monk dipped his head in reply.

'Mamm says the monks make the best honey you can eat, and that it tastes like heather basking in sunshine.' She paused, then added, 'Aren't you supposed to sell it?'

The monk touched his fingertips to the binding that pressed a salve to Mawde's forehead. 'I witnessed your misfortune, child, and I know it occurred while you performed a deed intended to benefit someone other than yourself. You've already paid for this gift with your kindness.'

Puzzled, Mawde stuffed the pot into the pocket tied at her waist. 'Thank you, sir.'

The monk moved his hand to the top of Mawde's head and rested his fingers on her clean white cap. He closed his eyes and blessed her, then diverted his attention to another customer.

Tamsin nudged Mawde and pointed to a small patch of beach exposed by the turning tide. 'Let's sit there and eat our biscuits,' she said.

Perched on a rock, the girls peered inside the neatly wrapped package.

'How many do we have?' Mawde asked.

'Six.'

'May I have two?'

'You can have three,' Tamsin said, handing them to her. 'It's only fair we share them equally.'

Mawde thanked her and scrambled to her feet. 'Won't be long,' she said, striding away before Tamsin could reply.

She made straight for Widow Mitchell and held out her hand. 'These are for you. They're delicious, and James will like them too.'

Widow Mitchell reached up a skinny arm to take the biscuits from Mawde. Her lips twitched and her grateful eyes glistened. Mawde hurried away, not wanting to embarrass her.

'You are the loveliest person I know.' Tamsin enveloped Mawde in a tight embrace. 'I'm so proud to be your cousin.' She gave Mawde a biscuit and snapped another in half. 'We'll share the rest of these between us.'

The joyful sound of a fiddle cut through the noise of the crowd, temporarily silencing the revellers. A tinkling of countless tiny bells followed, and then the crowd cheered. Giggling and squealing, the girls merged with a throng gathered around a large group of Morris Men, shouldering their way towards the front to get a better view. They tapped their feet and bobbed to the rhythm of the music, delighting in the smiles and antics of the jolly dancers with jingling ankle bells and clattering sticks.

When the music stopped and the ruddy-cheeked men paused to catch their breath, the girls squeezed through the crowd until they reached a tall maypole. To their delight, they were beckoned to join the ring of dancers. While waiting for the dance to begin, Mawde gazed at the magnificent yellow pole and admired the green foliage winding its way from top to bottom. It looked elegant and regal.

'Dancers, prepare!'

Each dancer turned to their left. Mawde tapped her right foot to the beat of a tabor, eager to take a step forward with the first note from the pipe. Grinning, Mawde followed Tamsin, moving round the circle, keeping the maypole at its centre. She felt the heat rise in her cheeks and her breath catch in quick gasps as the pace increased and demanded more energy. Flushed and happy, she changed direction, keeping up with the fast pace until the dance slowed to a halt. She turned and beamed at Tamsin as they joined an inner circle, ready for the next dance to begin. The tabor took up the beat again and soon they were weaving in and out between other women and girls as two rings of dancers moved in opposite directions.

Happy but exhausted after a few more dances, Mawde and Tamsin staggered to a grassy bank and flopped to the ground. They lay on the grass with their kirtles billowing out around them, their faces turned towards the warm afternoon sunshine.

A small group of youths drew near, voices loud and cheeks florid from consuming too much ale. Mawde sat up and tapped Tamsin on the arm, encouraging her to do likewise. The tallest youth stepped towards them and raised his hand, instructing his companions to stay where they were. Something about his demeanour put Mawde on edge.

'Dunno why you look so pleased with yerself. Yer sitting there with an old cloth wrapped round yer 'ead, and a dried fish for a companion.' He sneered as he towered above them, casting them into shadow. 'It was a trail of 'er scales what led us 'ere, but it's disappointing to see the trail ends with you two. I was 'oping for a mermaid, and she ain't one of they.' He snorted and spat a large gobbet of mucus that landed on the grass next to Mawde's hand.

The other youths snickered and drew nearer.

Mawde shuffled closer to Tamsin and glared up at the

youth's arrogant pimply face. 'God curse you for your wicked tongue,' she said.

The youth picked at something between his teeth, then pointed his finger at Tamsin. 'Frightful, ain't she?'

Mawde squeezed Tamsin's arm. 'We should go.' She pulled Tamsin up and the girls moved towards the bottom of the bank. The youths closed in around them, leaving no room for escape.

'Please move aside,' Mawde said, forcing politeness. 'We'll be on our way and not bother you a moment longer.'

A younger boy reached out to touch a large scaly patch on Tamsin's wrist, then snatched his finger away as if scalded. ''Ow can you bear to touch 'er?' he asked Mawde, nodding at the girls' interlinked arms. 'You could catch what she's got and end up looking just like 'er.'

'I'd rather be like her than you!'

The tallest youth grabbed Mawde's free arm and yanked her away from Tamsin. 'You're a spirited little filly.' He put his face so close to hers that their noses were almost touching. His breath reeked of ale. 'I reckon I'd 'ave fun with you.'

'Bring her with us.' A fair-haired, stocky lad leered and rubbed his crotch. 'Bet no one's deflowered her yet so there's a treat in store for at least one of us.'

The other boys exchanged lewd comments and tightened their circle.

'Oi, you lot! Step away!'

The boys froze.

'Julian Viker, I told you to step away.'

Mawde was relieved to see Henry Salt striding towards them. His jerkin was slung over one shoulder and his taut muscles strained against the fabric of his best Sunday shirt. He elbowed the youths aside and squared up to Julian.

'Leave my sister and cousin alone or I swear I'll break every bone in your body.'

The tone of the young ploughman's voice was enough to scatter the boys, leaving their ringleader cowering beneath Henry's glare.

Henry jerked his head. 'Off you go. There's nothing more for you to see here.' Henry waited for Julian to slink away before giving the girls a cheerful smile. 'Those boys won't trouble you no more, especially not now they know you're related to me.' Henry was highly regarded in the village of St Mawes. He never started a fight, but was often the man to end one. 'Your da did well in the archery today, Mawde. We're hoping his good fortune continues with the cocks. You coming to watch?'

Mawde hated cockfighting and was relieved to see Tamsin wrinkle her nose in disgust. Both girls shook their heads.

'I'd rather go home,' Mawde said.

'Me too.' Tamsin reached for Mawde's hand. 'While we climb the hill, we'll remind ourselves of the good things that happened today.'

Henry asked Tamsin to tell their mother that the male members of the family would not be home until after dark. There would be plenty of merrymaking long after the cockfighting ended.

Mawde used a chunk of bread to mop up the last of the roasted mutton on her trencher. She licked her greasy fingers before wiping her hands on her skirt. Her fingertips brushed against the bulge from the jar of honey stowed in the pocket tied at her waist. She eased it out, keeping it concealed by the overhang of the table.

'Mamm?'

'Yes, Mawde?'

'I have a gift for you.' She produced the pot of honey with a flourish and passed it across the table.

Mamm marvelled over the detail of the bee stopper and tapped it with her fingertip. 'That'll be Brother Matthew's signature carving. It's beautiful, Mawde. How did you come by it?'

Mawde relayed her conversation with the monk.

'I'm sure the Abbott will have a thing or two to say about Brother Matthew giving away pots of honey like this. It's delightful, Mawde. Thank you. I'll use the honey to bake a cake after the babe is born.'

Grandmother clicked her tongue. 'How can you be sure she didn't swipe it from the stall?'

'Why would she? Mawde's not a thief, Grandmother.' Tamsin's face dropped. 'Oh, Mawde, we forgot about Widow Mitchell. Mamm, did you know her husband was lost at sea?'

Aunt Mary crossed herself.

'The poor woman.' Mamm shook her head. 'She's too young to be a widow.'

'Can you take her on in the dairy?' Mawde asked. 'You must need someone now Tamsin can't go in there anymore.'

Aunt Mary hesitated. 'I don't know. We won't be making extra money to pay wages, and any food we give her will have to come from our own supplies.'

Mawde recalled the stricken woman's gaunt appearance. 'She looked so pale and thin. Her little boy, too. I think they're starving.'

'I suppose we could use a little help,' Aunt Mary said. 'I'll speak to William, but I don't see why we can't put food in their bellies and give them somewhere comfortable to sleep.'

Mawde and Tamsin exchanged hopeful looks.

'Do you think Da will agree?' Tamsin asked, her brow creasing with concern.

'I'm sure we can persuade him.'

Mawde clambered up from the bench seat and rushed to embrace her aunt. 'Thank you,' she said. 'Widow Mitchell will be so grateful.'

Aunt Mary stroked Mawde's cheek and was about to say something when Mamm made a loud groan.

'Is the baby coming?' Mawde asked, alarmed by her mother's discomfort and watching her press her palms against her taut belly.

'Not yet, Mawde, but it won't be long now. We should go home.' Mamm eased herself up from the bench and gathered used wooden trenchers from the table.

'You can stop that,' Aunt Mary said with a fond smile for her sister. 'Save your strength, because something tells me you're going to need it soon. Send Mawde the moment you need me.'

Grandmother tutted. 'We won't need you. I've delivered every child in this family and I've no intention of stopping now.'

Aunt Mary shook her head. 'I know, Mamm, but your knees—'

'Never mind my knees. I'll manage, and Mawde will help me if needs be.'

Mawde gaped at Tamsin. For the first time in her life, her grandmother had referred to her by name.

CHAPTER THREE

MAY 1521

MAWDE LINGERED in the doorway of the small bedchamber, unaccustomed to the tension that was building between her parents.

'Why today, of all days?' Her mother massaged the tightening bump of her belly while glaring at Da. 'What were you thinking, Simon?'

'How was I to know you'd start labouring this morning! What was I supposed to do, refuse to negotiate in case my wife delivered a baby? We shook hands on a deal so I can't go back on it now.'

Mawde pressed her palms against the cool wood of the partition wall. 'Ma? Da? What's happened?'

'Da took on an apprentice, and he arrives today.' Mamm balled her fists and clenched her jaw, waiting for a contraction to fade. She glared at Da. 'Why couldn't you wait a few days? Did you flood your senses with ale?' She beckoned to Mawde. 'Make up a mattress for the lad because I can't do it in this state.' Her mother's face contorted as another contraction took hold.

'Leave us,' Grandmother said, flicking her wrist and shooing Mawde and her father from the room.

Da hesitated. 'I'm sorry, Margery, truly I am. You're right, I did let ale get the better of me. But when the black-smith suggested I take on his son as an apprentice instead of paying my debt, it made good business sense. Still does, if I'm honest.'

'Why did you owe the blacksmith money, anyway?' Mamm asked. 'I thought you settled the account when he came to shoe the horses.'

Grandmother tutted and rolled her eyes. 'Gambling at cocking again, no doubt.'

Da hung his head. 'I confess to losing a small wager, but that wasn't the sum of it. When the blacksmith came at the end of the winter, I couldn't settle the bill. But business is improving now, and I predict a busy summer, so I'll need an apprentice to keep up with demand.' Da gave a rueful smile. 'Also, the blacksmith said he'll shoe the horses any time I ask, at no charge, and provide any other ironwork we need for the business or home – within reason, of course. I think it's a fine arrangement. I'll have tools, locks and hinges whenever I need them, and I'll even have extras for spares.'

Mamm made a deep, bellowing sound. Mawde grasped her father by the hand and led him away, closing the bedchamber door behind them. They retreated down the stairs and Mawde served her father with bread and ale.

A loud rap sounded at the door.

Da wiped his mouth on his sleeve and rose to his feet. 'That'll be the apprentice.'

Eager to meet the newcomer, Mawde rushed across the room and flung the door wide open. 'Good day and welcome,' she said in a cheerful voice.

But her smile vanished, and bile burned at the back of her throat.

The apprentice was Julian Viker.

Da took Julian across the courtyard to his workshop, eager to set his new apprentice to work. Mawde stared after them, wondering if Julian would be kinder to her without his friends around. Cousin Henry must have neglected to tell her father about the incident the previous day, no doubt distracted by cockfighting and ale. Mawde reached for the broom propped beside the door and swept the rush matting while trying to ignore her mother's piercing screams. When, at last, the screaming stopped, she paused her sweeping and listened for the sound of a newborn's cry. Silence. She bit down hard on her bottom lip, fearing the worst, tasting the metallic tang of blood. Footsteps pounded back and forth above her head, but still no baby's cry. Mawde thrust the broom aside and pressed her palms together. She closed her eyes and pleaded with God, begging him to spare her mother's life.

'Mawde!' The shout was shrill with panic.

Mawde hurried to the bottom of the stairs. 'Yes, Grandmother?'

'Gather all the clean linen you can find. And hurry! 'Tis a difficult birthing. Too much blood.'

Mawde rushed to do her grandmother's bidding, praying her grandmother had the skills to save Mamm's life. She scooped up a pile of Da's shirts from the basket of linens awaiting repairs. Next, she snatched two aprons from a hook near the hearth, then ran upstairs to gather spare sheets from a trunk beside Grandmother's bed. She hurried into her mother's bedchamber and placed the linen pile on top of a large chest.

Grandmother registered Mawde's arrival with a brief nod. 'I need a small sheet for the babe and a larger one for your mamm. Quick as you can.' Grandmother pulled a crimson-soaked sheet from beneath Mamm and replaced it with a clean one. Mawde had never seen so much blood. Her vision greyed, and she feared she would pass out.

'Come closer, child. Stand next to me and be ready with the small sheet. You must take the baby so I may attend to your mother.'

Mawde snuck a peek at Mamm's face. Her cheeks were pink but slack with exhaustion. 'Grandmother, will Mamm die?'

Her grandmother shook her head; her lips set in a grim line of determination.

Mawde followed Grandmother's gaze and gasped in horror. There on the mattress lay a tiny body with arms and legs, but the head was still inside her mother.

'When I say so, press here,' she said, pointing to the lowest region of Mamm's distended belly.

Grandmother positioned the baby's body on her forearm and placed her other hand across its back, hooking her fingers over its shoulders.

Mamm stirred. A low-pitched groan rumbled in her throat and grew in volume.

'Now,' Grandmother said.

Mawde pressed hard against her mother's skin, keeping her eyelids tightly closed and jiggling up and down on her toes, willing herself to wake from what had to be a nightmare. She heard a rushing sound inside her head, and her heart thundered against her ribs. Her breaths came in quick, brief gasps. She heard the distant voice of her grandmother yelling but could not make sense of the words. A sudden sharp kick to her shin brought her to her senses.

'Foolish girl! Come here! Take your brother from me.'

Mawde snapped her eyes open. 'A brother. Is all well? Is he… is he…?' Then she heard it. A newborn's high-pitched wail. Mawde smiled at the squirming bundle of limbs in her grandmother's hands. She held out her arms in wonder as Grandmother passed her brother to her. She carried him to a little chair in a corner of the room where she wrapped him in the small clean sheet. She stroked his wrinkled, bruised face, and he paused his wailing. Mawde felt a rush of love for her tiny brother, a surge of emotion, the like of which she had never experienced before. The baby thrashed his legs within the sheet, forcing Mawde to tighten her grip for fear she might drop him.

'The danger has passed,' Grandmother said, dropping something dark red and shiny into a pail. She studied the pail's contents by the light of a candle and grunted her satisfaction. Next, she reached into another pail filled with clean water, drew out a cloth, squeezed it, then bathed Mamm's face, neck and hands. She threw the cloth back into the water and then shuffled across to the corner of the room to take the baby from Mawde's lap.

Mawde seized the opportunity to dash to Mamm's side and grasped her mother's limp hand.

Mamm lifted her weary eyelids. 'No need to fret, Mawde, I'm still here.'

Mawde beamed. 'Mamm, we have a little boy. I have a brother.'

Grandmother passed the baby back to Mawde and started fussing over Mamm. 'Your son will need feeding soon,' she said with a rare smile. 'Let's prop you up and get you comfortable.' She stripped off Mamm's sweat-soaked shift and replaced it with a dry one, then rearranged the cushions to give Mamm more support.

Mamm reached out to take the baby from Mawde and held him to her breast. At first, the baby fussed and struggled to feed. Mawde looked on with fascinated concern as his wailing escalated. He worked an arm free from his wrapping and struck Mamm's breast with his fist. Mamm laughed and stroked his forehead. The baby settled and latched his lips on to her nipple, contorted his face, then sucked greedily. When the milk flowed, his face relaxed. Overcome with emotion, Mawde cried.

'There, there,' Mamm said, taking Mawde's hand in hers. 'It's such a relief to have come safely through labour that I'm close to crying myself, and I suspect even Grandmother could shed a tear or two.'

Mawde looked up.

Her grandmother's eyes were dry, but a thin smile played on her lips. 'There's no greater pleasure than bringing a baby boy into the world. Today, the Lord has blessed us.'

'Mawde, fetch Da so he may admire his son. He'll want to see him before he's swaddled.'

Mawde scuttled out of the bedchamber, thrilled to be the messenger sent to give her father the good news. When she entered his workshop, he rushed over to her. 'Your mamm?' he said, his brow puckered. 'Is all well?'

'Yes, Da! Mamm's tired, but well.' Mawde gave him a beaming smile. 'Da, you have a baby boy!'

'A son.' Da grinned. He swept Mawde off her feet and spun her round in a circle. ''Tis wonderful news, indeed.' He released her and knelt in front of her. 'Listen to what I'm about to say, Mawde, and remember every word. There will be a lot of excitement about our baby son, but you are still, and always will be, my precious daughter.

Now, before we go inside, tell me what you think of this.' Da grasped Mawde's hand and guided her towards a long workbench. He hoisted her onto a stool and watched for her reaction. There, on the bench, stood a magnificent cradle.

'It's perfect.' Mawde traced the contours of rabbits and birds carved into the woodwork.

Da lifted her down from the stool. 'Now, if you would be so kind, I'd like to meet your brother.'

Mawde slipped her hand into her father's as they walked towards the door. Her gaze drifted towards Julian, where he was sweeping up wood shavings and gathering them into a pile. He leant on the broom handle and fixed her with a menacing stare.

CHAPTER FOUR
MAY 1521, CORPUS CHRISTI DAY

Mamm freed strands of hair from the crusty scab on Mawde's forehead. 'Keep your fingernails away, Mawde. The more you pick, the worse it will become.'

'I'll try, Mamm, but it itches.'

'I'm sure it does but have a care. You'll have a permanent scar as it is, but if you leave the scab alone, it will be a faint one. Keep picking and it will fester and leave an unsightly blemish. You may not care much for your appearance now, but you will when you're a young woman. I don't want you walking around the village with your head bowed towards the dirt. Let the wound heal and wear the scar with pride.'

''Tis the mark of Satan's curse.' Grandmother made an ugly scowl. 'The child's right to do all she can to hide it.'

A gentle rapping at the door stopped Mawde from speaking out of turn. 'They're here!' she cried, dashing towards the door and flinging it open so hard that it bashed against the wall.

John wailed.

Grandmother clicked her tongue. 'Now look what she's done! He'd just gone off to sleep.'

'Tamsin!'

Tamsin greeted Mawde with a beaming smile and stepped indoors. 'Good day, Grandmother. Good day, Aunt Margery.'

Mawde lifted her thin summer shawl from a peg by the door.

'Are you alone, Tamsin?' Mamm asked.

'Yes, Aunt Margery. Henry said he'd meet us at the ferry.'

'And Peter and John?'

Tamsin grinned. 'Not coming this year.'

Mawde sensed Mamm's escalating anxiety and threw her arms around her mother's neck. 'Goodbye, Mamm. We promise we'll be careful.' She stroked her baby brother's furrowed brow, then planted a feathery kiss on her grandmother's cool withered cheek.

'Don't forget to call for Julian,' Mamm said. 'He's in the workshop with Da. He promised to chaperone you and see you come to no harm.'

Mawde's excitement evaporated. 'Must he come with us? Cousin Henry will be there, so we don't need Julian.'

The thought of having Julian with them for the afternoon was almost too much to bear. He put her on edge, even though he behaved affably towards her. He was courteous to every member of the family and was proving especially popular with her grandmother.

'Julian has impressed your father, Mawde. He's only been here a short while, but he's worked hard. He deserves a day off as much as anyone else. As fond as I am of Cousin Henry, you and I both know that after a few ales he'll forget what day of the week it is, never mind the fact he has two young girls in his charge.'

Mawde turned dejectedly towards Tamsin. Tamsin shrugged. 'Of course Julian should come with us, Mawde. He won't spoil our fun like he did at Whitsun.' In a whisper, she added, 'We'll give him the slip when we get there.'

Mawde suppressed a chuckle and ran into the courtyard, yelling for Julian to make haste and join them.

Penryn was a seething mass of joyful revelry. As the ferry edged closer to the harbour, Mawde grew restless with excitement, willing the wind to strengthen and carry them towards the hubbub on the harbourside. After the ferry docked, Henry hoisted Tamsin ashore. Seconds later, he deposited Mawde next to her. Obstructing Julian, he flicked his right hand back and forth to send the girls on their way, giving them the freedom to roam at will. Julian's face contorted and his nostrils flared. Mawde giggled before turning her back on him and chasing Tamsin towards the town's centre.

Penryn was almost unrecognisable. A noisy crowd filled the narrow streets while the rise and fall of a fiddler's jig competed with tabors and drums from another corner of the town. Pageant wagons crowded the edges of the square, the performers fiddling with props and costumes, preparing for their turn to take to the stage.

'We missed the parade,' Tamsin said, frowning.

'It doesn't matter, Tamsin. We're in time to watch the plays.' Mawde pointed to a large gathering on one side of the square. 'Let's see what's happening over there.'

The girls edged their way forward, squeezing through the crowd, until they reached the front. They stood before a shrine carved in silver and covered by a rich blue damask canopy embroidered with shimmering golden thread. Two clergymen stood guard, one on either side, each man clasping a large silver cross.

Mawde's fascination soon waned. 'Let's look at the stalls,' she said, gripping Tamsin's hand and steering her back through the crowd.

The girls stopped at a stall displaying an extensive collection of religious trinkets. They admired smooth wooden rosary beads, plain crosses and small carved statues of the crucifixion. Mawde selected a miniature carving of the Madonna and Child. She traced the delicate features of the mother and baby with her fingertip, then replaced the carving on the table.

'I think you want to buy this.' A narrow-faced pedlar with large front teeth picked up the Madonna and Child and offered it to Mawde. He fixed his beady eyes on her, urging her to take it. She thought he resembled a giant squirrel daring her to seize an acorn.

Mawde felt the colour rise in her cheeks. 'It's lovely, but I don't have enough money to buy it.'

'Two pennies is all I'm asking. Not a lot for the exquisite craftsmanship, and I guarantee you'll not find a prettier one.'

Mawde clamped her top lip between her teeth and shook her head.

Tamsin tugged Mawde's sleeve. 'Let's go back to the square and watch the mystery plays. They'll be starting soon.'

The girls turned and moved away from the stall. Moments later, Mawde felt something catch on her shoe and a hefty shove from behind as someone fell against her. 'Forgive me,' she said, turning to apologise, thinking she might have caused them to stumble. Her face fell. It was Julian.

'Forgive me,' he echoed, in a high-pitched wheedling tone.

'Don't be mean,' Tamsin said. 'Come on, Mawde. We need to find a good place to sit.'

Mawde glanced up at the cloudless sky. 'It's almost midday. We should find a spot in the shade.'

The girls eventually settled on a small patch of grass beneath an oak tree, with a clear view of the main stage.

'What was Julian doing at a stall selling religious trinkets?' Mawde said, plucking silky fronds from a dandelion.

'Perhaps he's planning to make some. Your father thinks Julian's a skilled carver. You'd easily sell a few trinkets like that on market day.'

Captivated by the mystery plays, the girls soon forgot about Julian. Tamsin withdrew a cloth bundle from her pocket and unwrapped it to reveal two crusty bread rolls and a hunk of sweating cheese. The girls devoured the food, absorbed by the performances on stage. When the plays gave way to music and dancing, the girls joined in with the roundels and jigs.

Exhausted but content, the girls agreed it was time to head for home. Tamsin recognised a fisherman from St Mawes offering his vessel as a ferry. They hurried towards him and joined other villagers crowding aboard his boat. They handed over a penny for their fares, then made themselves comfortable on a pile of nets that stank of the morning's catch.

Julian burst through the door and staggered across the room. He steadied himself before perching on the bench, then rested his elbows on the smooth oak surface of the table.

'You look like you've had a good day,' Da said affably.

Julian hiccoughed. 'Very good day, thank you.' His speech was slurring and his eyelids drooping, heavy with overindulgence. He nodded at Mawde. 'That one gave me the slip, though. Looked for 'er to bring 'er home, like you asked, but couldn't find 'er or the other girl anywhere. Looked everywhere, I did.'

Mawde snorted, drawing a hostile glare from her grandmother. 'You couldn't have tried that hard to find me. I was in the square with Tamsin watching mystery plays, then dancing for the rest of the afternoon.'

Da raised an eyebrow at Julian. 'Did you let the ale cloud your vision? I know a young man likes to indulge in all the pleasures of a festival, but you shouldn't have let the girls get the better of you.'

Mawde jumped to her feet. 'We didn't, Da!'

Da fixed Mawde with a hard stare. 'Are you sure about that?'

Mawde sat down again and stared at her lap.

'I thought as much.' Da's expression was stern. 'Penryn's a raucous place at times, and especially on feast days. But, seeing as the girls had the sense to return home before dark, Julian, I'll let the matter drop. Next time I entrust my daughter to your care, you'll not let her out of your sight.'

Julian belched and mumbled an apology. 'I tried to keep me eyes on 'em, honest I did. I knew exactly what they were up to until the incident at the pedlar's stall. After that, they fled into the crowd.'

'What incident?' Grandmother's face tightened with hostile curiosity.

'It was nothing,' Mawde replied. 'Julian fell against me, that was all. And we didn't flee!'

'Liar!' Julian sniggered and pointed an accusing finger

at Mawde. '*She* even tripped me over on purpose, to give themselves a head start.'

Mawde rolled her eyes. 'Did not.'

'Yes, you did, and you know it.'

Grandmother made a disapproving grunting sound.

Julian massaged his temples, then turned to Mawde's father and said, 'Did she show you what she bought?'

'No.' Da's face softened. 'It must have slipped your mind, Mawde. Why don't you show us now?'

Mawde frowned at Julian. 'What are you talking about? I didn't buy anything. Between us, Tamsin and I only had enough money for our boat fares.'

Julian rubbed his eyes. 'My mistake. Could've sworn she took a trinket from a stall and slipped it in 'er pocket.'

Mawde slapped the tabletop. 'Now you're accusing me of stealing!'

'Well, did you?' Julian looked at Grandmother. 'I know 'tis none of my business, but I'd get 'er to empty 'er pocket, just to be sure.'

Grandmother sat forward in her chair. 'He's right. We should know for certain. Do as he suggests, girl, and empty your pocket.'

'I'm not a thief!' Mawde looked at her mother for reassurance. Her mother gave a sympathetic smile.

Mawde could see that her grandmother was enjoying her discomfort.

'If you've nothing to hide, you've nothing to fear.' Grandmother waggled a gnarled finger. 'Show us what you've got.'

Mamm shrugged her shoulders. 'You might as well, Mawde. Prove Julian wrong and empty your pocket, and then we can forget about it.'

Mawde untied her pocket from her waist and placed it on the table in front of her. She thrust her fingers inside and reached for the bottom to turn it inside out. A breath caught in her throat. Her fingers froze, her skin burning against a small object. She lowered her head and fought back tears.

'Well?' Grandmother demanded.

'What's wrong, Mawde?' Mamm asked.

'I shouldn't have this.' Mawde's vision clouded as she looked towards her mother. 'I picked it up to look at it, but I put it back on the stall and told the pedlar I didn't have enough money. Ask Tamsin. She saw me put it back. The last time I saw this, the pedlar had it in his hand. How did it get into my pocket?'

Grandmother shuffled forward on her chair until she was perched on the edge. 'What is it? What's the girl talking about?'

'Probably best if she shows you,' Julian said, widening his eyes at Mawde.

Mawde drew out the miniature carving and caressed the smooth folds of the Madonna's robe. 'I swear *on my life*, I didn't steal this.'

'How could you!' Grandmother crossed herself. 'Dear Lord, we beg your forgiveness for this child's sinful ways.'

Mawde buried her face in her hands. She could not explain how the carving found its way into her pocket, but she was certain it had something to do with Julian. She recalled the incident when he fell against her, reliving it over and over in her mind. She glared at him through hot tears. 'It was you, wasn't it?'

Julian pressed his hands to his chest. 'Me?'

'You were there at the stall where the pedlar was selling these.'

'That's right. That's where you were when I caught up with you. It was a relief to find you was safe. Got to say though, 'tis a pretty object you took.'

Da reached for the carving and turned it over in his hand. His face drained of colour. 'I must tell you, Mawde, I'm sickened by this. I didn't raise you to steal. Explain yourself.'

Mawde looked at her father, horrified. 'Da, please, you know I wouldn't steal from anyone. I promise I didn't take the carving! I don't know how it ended up in my pocket.'

'You leave me no choice but to punish you.' He stood and beckoned Mawde to do the same. 'Come to the workshop. I'll spare you the humiliation of a whipping in front of your mother and grandmother.'

Mawde's hands flew to her mouth. She looked towards her mother, but Mamm averted her gaze.

Da paused in the doorway. Looking first at Mamm and then at Grandmother, he said, 'No one is to mention this matter again. Mawde will take her punishment and repent.' He glared at Julian and added, 'If anyone breathes a word of this incident, they'll receive the same punishment as Mawde. We must protect our good name.'

Trembling, Mawde followed her father out of the house. As she passed Julian, he raised his eyebrows and gave her a smug smile.

Inside the workshop, Mawde's father pulled a stool from beneath a workbench. 'Sit.'

As she clambered on to it, he pulled out another and sat facing her. He placed the carving on the worktop. 'This is your opportunity to persuade me you're not a thief.'

Mawde swallowed and took a moment to compose herself. She described her first meeting with Julian and how he had bullied her and Tamsin until Cousin Henry shooed him away. Her father furrowed his brow and indicated that she should continue. Mawde relayed the events that occurred at Penryn. Deciding honesty was best, she included the ploy for her and Tamsin to give Julian the slip while Henry barred his way.

Her father remained silent after she finished her explanation, switching his gaze between Mawde and the carving.

'Da?' Mawde asked quietly. 'Do you believe me?'

Her father picked up the carving and wrapped his fingers around it. 'I do, Mawde. I didn't know Julian threatened you and Tamsin at Whitsun. Had I known, I wouldn't have taken him on as my apprentice.' He reached for her hand and uncurled her fingers. Pressing the carving against her palm, he added, 'The pedlar will have moved on by now. We'll give extra alms to someone needy in the village to make recompense for this.' He folded Mawde's fingers over the Madonna and Child. 'Keep it, Mawde, and let it serve as a reminder to live a good and generous life. Off you go now and tell Julian I wish to speak to him.'

CHAPTER FIVE

AUGUST 1521

THE HEAT WAS STIFLING. Doors and windows gaped open, but there was not even a hint of draught.

Mawde mopped her brow with a corner of her apron. Beads of sweat congregated on the back of her neck and trickled between her shoulder blades, her damp shift failing to wick the moisture away. It had been this way for several days, and they were all listless. John lay flushed in his cradle with his eyelids closed and a damp sheen glistening on his puckered forehead. His chest rose and fell in small undulations that suddenly quickened as if he were chasing something in a dream. Mawde touched his brow. His skin was hot and sticky.

'Mamm, shall I loosen John's bands?'

Mamm was stripping leaves from a large handful of herbs, adding them to a pottage simmering over a low fire. She turned away from the heat and met Mawde's worried gaze. 'I can't remember the last time we had a summer as hot as this. I agree, it's a good idea to loosen his bindings. It won't hurt to have the air on his skin for a short while.'

Grandmother leaned forward in her chair. Her face

was pinched, and she grimaced as she struggled to draw breath. She managed a feeble cough, then closed her eyes and flopped back in her chair. A drop of spittle lingered at the corner of her mouth, wobbling back and forth with her gasps. 'I need to lie down,' she said, 'but I've no energy to climb the stairs.'

Mamm hurried across to her mother and helped rearrange her in the chair, propping a cushion behind her back. 'Mawde, fetch down a mattress for your grandmother. I'll go out for some horehound. She needs something to loosen the congestion in her chest.'

'I'll go,' Mawde said, eager to enjoy a few minutes of cooling shade in the nearby woodland.

''Tis good of you to offer, Mawde, but I saw a clump in a hedgerow yesterday, and I know exactly where to find it.'

Mawde felt her spirits deflate. She watched her mother pick up a trug and bustle outside, creating a fleeting warm draught in her wake.

'Mattress?' prompted her grandmother with a rasping voice.

Mawde mounted the stairs, pulling herself up one step at a time, grasping the banister carved by her father a year before she was born. It gleamed from countless layers of wax, and despite the heat of the summer, the smooth oak felt cool and reassuring.

Upstairs was even more stifling with warm air trapped in a thick suffocating band beneath the rafters. Mawde pulled the mattress from her grandmother's bed and dragged it to the top of the staircase. She nudged it forward with her foot until it tipped forward and slithered to the bottom. It landed with a thud on the rush matting, buckling at its centre and driving up a thick cloud of dust. When the air cleared, Mawde did her best to plump the straw and checked for sharp ends protruding through the cover. She dragged the mattress across the hall, well away from the heat of the cooking fire that burned in the hearth, but close enough to an open window to catch any gentle breeze that might pass through. She smiled at her grand-mother, helping her stand and supporting her under her left elbow to steady her as she hobbled the short distance from chair to mattress. Grandmother waited for Mawde to ease her down, then flicked her wrist as a gesture of dismissal. After a spasm of hacking coughs, Grandmother settled for a nap.

Mawde struggled with her chores, taking longer than usual to finish her tasks. She wiped crumbs from the table, then stacked cups and plates on shelves. She scrubbed a cooking pot until it shone, ready for her mother to prepare the tisane of horehound to soothe Grandmother's chest.

Overwhelmed by fatigue, Mawde sat at the table. She rested her arms on the warm scratched oak and lowered her weary head. John mewled. Remembering she had not yet loosened his swaddling bands, Mawde dragged herself to her feet and tended to her baby brother.

'There, there, little one.' She was certain the florid pink of his cheeks would soon fade once his limbs were exposed to the air. Mawde rolled the bands into tight coils and took care to secure the ends by tucking them in. She stacked them in a corner of the cradle near John's feet and caressed his hot face. 'We're all struggling today, John,' she said. 'I'll fetch a pail of clean water so it's ready for Mamm when she comes home, and I'll use some to cool your face and neck.' She looked at her sleeping grandmother and listened to her quick breaths. 'I'll use some to cool her, too.'

Satisfied John and Grandmother would not need her for a while, Mawde fetched an empty pail from the kitchen area and stepped outside into the fierce sunlight. Her father and Julian were sitting in the shade of the overhanging roof of her father's workshop, fanning themselves with thin strips of wood. They had rolled up their sleeves and loosened the laces of their shirts to expose their necks and chests.

Mawde called to her father. 'Do you have more wood strips so we might cool ourselves in the house?'

'I have something better,' Da said, lumbering to his feet. 'Come with me. See what we've been doing this morning. It's too hot for heavy work, but we didn't sit idle.' He tapped Julian on the shoulder. 'Fetch some ale, Julian. We need refreshment.'

Mawde followed Da into the workshop. It was stuffy inside, but not as hot as the house thanks to its construction of thick stone walls and a single large window facing north. It had large double doors built into the east wall and the lack of direct sunlight meant it was usually as cool as any dairy. Da said it was easy to be efficient with manual work in a poorly heated building. The workshop usually had a comfortable working temperature in the warmer months, but it was often ice-cold during winter. Mawde approached the workbench that ran the length of the south wall. In the middle, there were three thin wooden paddles, each with a carved handle. She selected one and studied it intently.

'This is pretty.' Mawde traced the path of an ivy trail that wound its way along both sides of the handle, slipping in and out between intricately carved mayflowers. She waved the paddle back and forth in front of her face, grinning and relishing the draught created by the movement.

'I'm glad you picked that one first,' Da said, clearly pleased with her reaction. 'I made it especially for you. This one's for Mamm. See the snowdrops and bluebells she loves so much? And this one is for your grandmother.' He leaned in closer to whisper, 'It will suit her perfectly, don't you think?'

Mawde giggled. The handle on Grandmother's fan was decorated with five-petalled dog roses. Thorns peeked between flowers, looking sharp and threatening, but they were perfectly smooth to the touch.

Da smiled and shooed her away. 'I should get back to work.'

With the fans in one hand and the coarse rope handle of the pail in the other, Mawde scuttled out of the workshop in time to see Julian emerge from the house. He appeared flushed and agitated. Reluctant to walk anywhere near him, she turned and headed straight for the well on the far side of the yard.

By the time Mawde staggered through the door with the pail full to the brim, she was relieved to find all was quiet indoors, aside from soft rumbling snores from Grandmother and the gentle ticking of the cooking fire. Mawde set the pail on the rushes, slopping water over the rim, then carefully placed the fans on the kitchen table. She ladled water into the pot she had scrubbed earlier and set it on a trivet over the fire to boil.

Mamm stumbled through the door and slumped into a chair. 'The heat…' she said, fanning herself with her hands.

'Rest, Mamm. I'll make the tisane.' Mawde riffled through the herbs and wildflowers wilting in the trug. She selected a sprig of horehound, picked off the flower heads and dropped them into the pot of boiling water. Next, she chose a bunch of sweet cicelies, flicked the dried soil from the roots, and added it to the pot. A fragrant aroma soon sweetened the air.

Grandmother fidgeted on her mattress, coughing with the effort of rolling onto her side.

Mamm loosened the laces of her kirtle and adjusted the neckline of her shift. 'It's time John woke for a feed.'

She leaned forward to reach into the cradle but withdrew abruptly. Mawde watched her face contort, and then Mamm roared with grief.

Mawde hurried to her mother's side. John lay perfectly still, his face ashen, his lips mauve. Mawde scooped him into her arms and blew across his face, hoping her breath would encourage him to take one of his own. Mamm snatched John from her and ran into the courtyard. 'Simon, help me! John's not breathing!'

'What's going on?' Grandmother demanded, struggling to ease herself into a sitting position. 'What's all the noise?' Her chest seemed to rattle as she fought to catch her breath.

'It's the baby,' Mawde murmured. 'There's something wrong with John.'

She joined her mother in the courtyard. Already stripped of his swaddling bands, the baby lay naked and lifeless in Mamm's arms. The first cloud for several days passed across the edge of the searing sun and cast them into shadow. Mawde shivered.

Da and Julian emerged from the workshop.

'What's happened?' said Da, hurrying towards Mamm with long strides.

Da slid his large, callused hands beneath the baby's body and prised him from Mamm's arms. He sank to his knees and lay John across his thighs, turning him face down and slapping him hard on the back. Mamm shrieked. Da cradled the baby in his left arm, then blew several times into his mouth and nose. Mawde held her breath, hoping John would make a sound, but his lips stayed blue, and his limbs limp and lifeless.

'Simon?' Mamm's voice was pleading and desperate.

Da shook his head. 'He's gone.'

Mawde stood fixed to the spot, her legs trembling but

her feet unwilling to move. She felt a pain in her chest and tasted bile in her mouth. Her father prised John's lips apart and put his little finger between the baby's lips. Frowning, he probed deeper and opened John's tiny mouth as wide as it would go. He reached inside with finger and thumb. After a few attempts, Simon pulled out a short length of linen. It was ragged at one end, as if ripped from a longer strip. Mawde turned aside and vomited on to the stony ground. Light-headed and distraught, she staggered away from her keening mother and emptied her stomach onto the sun-baked earth. With nothing left to bring up, she looked forlornly towards the workshop. Julian was by the wall, pulling on a clean shirt. He glanced briefly at Mawde and then retreated into the workshop.

Da carried the baby into the house and lay him out on the table. Mamm paced back and forth, pummelling her head with the heels of her hands, her eyes as dark as widow's weeds.

Grandmother crossed herself, muttering one prayer after another. At last, she turned towards Mawde and pointed a bony finger. 'I predicted something like this would happen. No good ever comes from a child born during the daytime darkness!'

Mamm strode across to Mawde and grasped her by the shoulders, her nails digging in like sharp talons. 'That cloth looked like swaddling band. What did you do?'

'Nothing!' Mawde's chest tightened, and her knees shook violently beneath her kirtle. The walls seemed to wobble and press in towards her. 'Mamm, I swear it wasn't me.' She grasped the edge of the table to steady herself and forced more volume into her voice. 'I removed the bindings one at a time and rolled each one tightly, taking care to tuck in the loose ends. I placed them at the end of the cradle.' Mawde closed her eyes and relived her earlier actions. Not a single band had been ripped or frayed. 'Someone tore off that piece of cloth and pushed it into John's mouth!' She peered inside the cradle, searching for a band with a frayed end. They were as she had left them, tightly rolled and stowed in a line along the foot of the cradle. But might one be missing? Mawde pointed an accusing finger at her grandmother. 'You were alone in the house with John when I went out to the well. You did this!'

'How dare you accuse me!' Grandmother's thin lips twitched as she turned to look at Da. 'I wouldn't harm a precious little boy.' She glared at Mawde; her lips puckered in a nasty grimace. 'I knew I should have followed my instinct and let you die the moment you were born. I should have known from tales of what passed before – no darkling child should be allowed to live. I made a poor decision that day. Now history repeats itself. Now the troubles begin.'

CHAPTER SIX
JANUARY 1522

Mawde's stitches were uneven. She jabbed the needle through the thin linen of her father's shirt and barely felt the prick of the needle when it penetrated the pad of her index finger. She stared at the pale skin and waited for the inevitable small bead of crimson. It did not come. Her fingers were so cold that her blood had retreated from the surface. She returned the shirt to her mending pile in a basket and sat on her hands to warm them. Her father deserved neater stitches.

Mamm shuffled across the hall to check the window-shutters were closed against an icy wind raging outdoors. She shivered and drew her coarse woollen shawl tighter around her before returning to her chair and staring at a meagre fire burning in the grate. It had been the harshest winter for many years. Businesses were failing. The villagers were starving.

The last of the reed candles burnt out, leaving the pale light of feeble flames to illuminate the room. It was the middle of the morning, but with the door and shutters closed, it might as well have been the middle of the night. Mawde sat furthest from the hearth and fidgeted on a rickety old milking stool. Her back ached from hunching forward to keep warm, and her feet were numb with cold. She picked a frayed thread on her worn-out shift, wondering when the seams would break down altogether.

Grandmother snored and woke with a start. She clicked her tongue and licked her dry lips, adjusting her blankets as she struggled to keep warm. Moments later, her head tipped forward and her breathing resumed the slow cadence of deep sleep. Mawde's attention drifted to Da. John's death had aged him. His black hair lacked lustre and glistened with thick bands of silver and grey. He tapped the floor with a makeshift walking stick, the rhythm fast and desperate. His lips were pursed, his brow furrowed, and his eyes were locked in a faraway gaze – an expression Mawde had grown used to since his terrible fall on the ice at the start of the bitter winter.

Julian sat next to Da, smoothing the rough surfaces of a crude comb. Mawde wondered why he bothered. No one was buying trinkets these days. She watched his nimble fingers tame the splintered wood. How she'd love to break off the biggest shard and stab it in his eye! His bullying was relentless, his mean streak discrete and preserved only for her. Tripping her up was his favourite pastime, followed by poking her in the back with one of her father's sharp tools. He had even swiped a small hunk of stale bread from her trencher and denied it when Mawde dared to complain. Mawde's heart had lifted when her mother questioned his presence late one evening, then sank just as fast when Da pointed to his injured ankle and said, 'We can't do without him, and anyway, a deal's a deal.'

Julian emptied his palm of wood dust into the fire. A

tiny flare flickered with small orange flames, but the brief burst of heat disappeared as quickly as it came. Mawde stared into the grate, dreaming of warm sunny days, full bellies and laughter at the table. Hunger pangs gnawed deep inside her stomach. She felt lethargic and weak. She longed for an embrace from her beloved father, but his spirit and energy were draining away. Several days had passed since he last trapped a rabbit. Even the village's fishermen were struggling for decent catches, and most of their hauls went to the fortunate few whose pockets still jingled with the sweet sound of silver. For the sake of her family, Mawde needed to act. She dragged two of her father's shirts from her mending basket and layered them over her bodice. Then she wrapped herself in a threadbare blanket before enveloping herself in her cape. She snatched up a pail and made for the door. With her hand on the latch, she paused and turned.

'Julian, will you help me?'

Julian raised his eyebrows. 'With what?'

'You've set traps before with my father. Go and set a few now.' Bristling at the tone of her voice, she added, 'Please.'

She caught a glimmer of hope in her father's eyes as he raised his head to look at Julian. Julian caught it, too.

'Right away,' he said, rising to his feet. He pointed at Mawde's pail. 'You comin' too?'

Mawde shook her head. 'I'm going to the beach to find winkles. I'm hoping the tide's on its way out and the women from the village haven't stripped the rocks bare. We need wood for the fire, too, if you can carry it.'

'Wood'll be wet, most likely, but I'll see what I can find.'

'Thank you,' Mawde said, taking more care with her tone. She was angry that Julian needed instructions, but grateful for his help.

Delicate snowflakes fluttered in the wind, coating the icy courtyard with a layer of white dust. Mawde took small apprehensive steps, nervous of a fall. Julian barged past, knocking her sideways. She glared at his back as he strode towards the fields, carrying traps in his arms and a sack slung across his shoulders. Turning in the opposite direction, she headed towards the nearest beach.

The ebbing tide was taking its time to reveal fresh clusters of winkles glistening on rocks. A group of women were plucking shells and tossing them into pails, moving in a line across the rocks and beach. Spurred into action, Mawde scrambled on all fours over craggy outcrops, slipping and sliding on wet seaweed. Struggling with numb fingers, she filled her pail with winkles and mussels, then heaved it towards a patch of shingle higher up the beach. Her arm muscles burned, but her spirits were high. She dried her hands on her cape, then blew across her fingers to warm them. She gathered up the pail and eased the rope handle onto her forearm, using a couple of folds of blanket to prevent the coarse fibres ripping into her flesh.

By the time Mawde reached home, snow was falling thick and fast. She checked on the chickens that were roaming in the stable, safe from the mouths of hungry foxes. She contemplated sacrificing a chicken for the pot but decided against it. Come spring, the hens would start laying again and they would need every egg. Meanwhile, the beach and woodland would provide food, albeit hard to find.

Julian returned with two small rabbits and the sack was two-thirds filled with wood. The wood was mossy but dry enough to coax a flaming fire with fragrant curls of smoke. Mawde threw two sprigs of rosemary into a pot of boiling water. The rosemary was woody and brittle, long past its best, but good enough to add a little fragrance and flavour to their supper. She considered the pail filled with shellfish but decided meat would be more wholesome than fish. They would eat the winkles and mussels for supper.

Julian gutted and skinned the rabbits. Mawde ripped meat from the carcasses and added it to the pot. It was the first time she had prepared a meal completely by herself, and it was harder than she expected. The rabbits were tiny, the meagre pickings difficult to shred. Determined to create something as delicious as her mother's cooking, Mawde persevered. At last, the pottage was ready. Mawde tried to lift the cauldron from its hook, but the pot was too heavy, and she was too weak. Julian smirked but did nothing to help. Unbeaten, Mawde left the pot suspended and started ladling the contents into bowls.

'Da, please eat.'

Her father acknowledged her with bloodshot eyes. He cupped the bowl in his hands and blew across the watery pottage. Then he took a small sip and winced when the steaming liquid touched his lips.

'Tastes good,' he said. His voice was as brittle as the rosemary.

Grandmother accepted her bowl from Mawde and took a noisy slurp. Next, Mawde prepared a bowl for her mother, taking care to include a few meaty chunks. Mamm had taken to her bed complaining of headache and fatigue, and Mawde was sure it was because her mother was starving. The bowl was almost full to the brim and Mawde had to hold it with two hands to keep it steady. She hesitated at the bottom of the stairs, fretting about tripping over her skirts and spilling the valuable contents.

Julian appeared at her side. 'I'll carry it for you,' he offered.

Mawde looked at him, surprised.

'I want to 'elp,' he said. ''Specially while there's not

much to do in the workshop. I don't want to be a burden to your family. I enjoy living 'ere.'

Mawde muttered her thanks, wondering if she might have misjudged him. After all, he was only a few years older than her and had been sent to live with them with no say in the matter. She waited for the exchange of voices as he delivered the meal to her mother before returning to the hearth.

Da had placed his bowl on the cold earthen floor where the rush matting had worn away. He had touched very little of the contents. Mawde passed it back to him, desperate for him to eat and regain his strength.

'Things will get better, Da.' She guided the bowl towards his lips. 'The snow will melt, spring will come, and food will be plentiful again.'

Da took a small sip, then waved the bowl away. 'Things will never be as they were. My ankle's taking an age to heal, and I fear we've seen the last of your mamm's smiles. I can't bear to see her broken-hearted like this.'

'John may be gone, but you still have me,' she said, trying to sound reassuring. 'Grandmother blames me for every bad thing that happens, but I'm not a bad person, Da. I swear I'm not. I try to do the right things, like helping Grandmother with the chores, and I've been tending to the chickens all by myself. I go to the farm most days to help Aunt Mary and always bring home any food she can spare.' Mawde broke into a sob. 'I don't know what else to do. Mamm's hardly said a word to me since John died. I wish she could see how hard I'm trying.'

'I can see, Mawde.'

Mawde whirled around. Her mother was pale and gaunt, but her arms were extended and beckoning Mawde to approach.

'My dear child, you could not have tried harder, and it's

taken too long for me to notice. I'm sorry. I've mourned and wallowed in self-pity for long enough. It's time I resumed my role of caring for this family.'

Mawde wrapped her arms around her mother's thin waist, fearing she might break if Mawde squeezed too hard.

Mamm prised Mawde's arms away. 'Look at you! You're nothing but a bag of bones. Serve yourself some of that delicious pottage.'

Mawde helped her mother settle on a chair and spread a blanket over her lap. She smiled at her father as he drained his bowl and served him another half a ladleful. Then she served Julian a generous portion containing several chunks of rabbit meat – a gesture of gratitude for rousing her mother from her bed.

'Thank you,' Julian said, his eyes wide at the bounty in his bowl and his sincerity catching Mawde unawares.

The cauldron was almost empty and easier to lift. Mawde used a cloth to remove it from the hook and placed it on the side of the hearth before spooning the dregs into her bowl. She was relieved to find a small chunk of rabbit meat lingering at the bottom. It wasn't much, but it was something. Her stomach growled as she cupped her bowl in both hands and shuffled towards her stool.

Julian shifted and moved his legs to make space for her to pass, leaning to one side as if steadying himself on a swaying boat. Suddenly, Mawde's foot slid forwards. Her upper body jerked backwards, and she landed on her bottom. A sharp pain seared at the base of her spine. Her bowl rolled away, leaving a wet trail across the rush mats speckled with wet rosemary leaves and the precious chunk of meat. Mawde salvaged the meat and dropped it into her bowl, clenching her teeth so hard that her jaw ached. She was determined not to cry.

Grandmother snickered. 'Careless wench. Good job it was only your bowl you dropped.'

Julian slithered from his seat and made a show of helping her onto her stool. While supporting her with one hand, he reached towards the floor with the other. Twice he ran his fingers across the partially exposed earth, and twice he plunged his fingers through the opening of his jerkin. Something caught Mawde's eye on the floor beside her stool. It was small and round. She discretely reached for it and nestled it between two fingers. She picked the rabbit meat from her bowl and chewed, keeping her gaze fixed on Julian. He was staring at the floor, frowning.

Mawde swallowed. 'You look worried, Julian. Is all well?'

His nose seemed to twitch as he met Mawde's gaze. 'I was looking for chunks of rabbit, making sure you'd found 'em all. You've had so little to eat.'

Da leaned forward and insisted Mawde finish what was left in his bowl. 'I've had plenty,' he said, before she could protest.

Mawde rolled her thumb across the surface of the hard object concealed within her hand. It was a tiny wooden ball, identical to the ones children played with when they threw them up in the air and tried to catch them in a small cup. Her father used to make such toys to fill gaps between big orders. He must have resumed making them again.

Julian grew increasingly restless. Mawde stifled a smile. She knew Julian was fretting that one of her parents would find the little wooden ball. Worse still, it might cause someone else to fall. If her father found the ball, he would know someone had taken it from the workshop – and that it could only have been Julian. If he discovered that, what other suspicions might he have about his sly bully of an apprentice?

Mawde secreted the ball into the bodice of her kirtle. She would relish every delicious moment of Julian's discomfort.

CHAPTER SEVEN
23 APRIL 1522

Mamm waited for Mawde to tie her apron strings before passing her a basket. 'We've a busy day ahead of us,' she said. 'Be quick about collecting the eggs, then help me put fresh straw on the beds. After that, you can start refreshing the rush matting in the hall while I wash the linens. It's a perfect drying day.'

'Where's Grandmother?' Mawde asked. It was unusual for Grandmother to be absent on a washday.

'She's staying at Aunt Mary's until the baby arrives, so it'll be just the two of us for a few days.'

Mawde liked the sound of that. She stepped outside into the courtyard and tilted her face towards the sun, revelling in its warmth. Spring was the season of new beginnings. The chickens were laying eggs and her uncle's cows were producing rich creamy milk. The Lord had even seen fit to bless her mother with the promise of another child. Setting eggs on a layer of straw in her basket, Mawde listened for the familiar sounds of banging and scraping in the workshop.

Silence.

Peering through the open door, Mawde found neither her father nor Julian standing at the workbench. Next, she looked inside the stables. They were empty. Both horses were missing. Curious, she ran back to the house.

'Mamm, where's Da?'

'Left for Gerrans before dawn.' Mamm hoisted a cauldron of hot water from the hook above the fire and heaved it outside. Huffing and puffing, she tipped the water in to a large vat half-filled with soiled shirts and shifts. 'The church needs a new door. They'll be gone until late tonight, so we've plenty of time to freshen the house before they get home.'

Mawde could not remember a day when it had been only the two of them at home. It would be a treat to have her mother all to herself, without her grandmother scowling from beneath mean wrinkled eyelids. Mawde stowed the basket of eggs beneath a low table in the corner of the hall and then set about clearing tired sections of rush matting. Next, she hauled the mattresses off the bed frames and dragged them out of the bedchambers. The sleeping areas weren't proper chambers, but a narrow loft space split in two by a thin wooden partition crafted by her father. She'd heard her aunt talk about fine bedchambers in the grand houses on the edge of the village. Aunt Mary had served as a maid before she married, and loved to reminisce about large stone hearths, glass windows and tapestries lining walls. Mawde dreamed of living in such a fine house herself one day, but the Lord only knew how that would ever happen. She pushed the mattresses down the stairs and hauled each one into the courtyard, well away from where her mother was pounding laundry with a large stick. Mawde pulled out the old straw, beat the dust from the sacking covers, then stuffed them with fresh filling. By the time she had lugged each one back up the stairs, her arm and back muscles burned and her throat itched from the dust clouds she had created.

'It's time we had refreshment.' Mamm stood with her palms resting on the soft swell of her belly. A flicker of angst twitched on her brow.

'I miss John, too,' Mawde said softly.

A wistful smile settled on Mamm's lips. 'I pray the good Lord will permit me to keep this one. I'll never understand why John's life was taken, but it must have been God's will.' She clapped her hands together. 'Enough maudlin for one day. Pour us each a glass of ale.'

They sat in the shade cast by the workshop, their backs resting against the stone wall. They lifted their cups in unison, their soft slurps the only sounds in the yard apart from the soft chuck-chucks of chickens as they strutted across the sun-baked ground.

Mawde waited for her mother to drain her cup before breaking their comfortable silence. 'Mamm, do you ever wish I'd not been born?'

Her mother looked horrified. 'Goodness, Mawde, no. Whatever made you ask that?'

'It's the things Grandmother says sometimes. She's never liked me, and she blames me for... you know... John not being with us.'

Mamm shifted position until she was facing Mawde. 'Whatever happened that day, someone put a piece of linen in John's mouth, knowing it would choke him, and I will never forgive myself for not being there to protect him.'

Mawde felt as if a large rock had hit her hard in the stomach. 'You're still wondering if it was me!? Mamm, it wasn't, I swear!' Her cheeks flamed and tears dripped on to the ground, staining the dried earth with dark splotches.

DIONNE HAYNES

'Mawde, I left John with you and your grandmother that day. There was no one else in the house.'

'Then it must have been her!'

Mamm turned and slapped Mawde hard across her face. Mawde started, her cheek stinging, and her mouth rounded into a perfect "o".

Mamm's lips were taut and pale. 'Your grandmother is an upstanding, God-fearing woman. She would never do such a thing!'

'Oh yes, she would! She said she should have ended my life as soon as I was born, just because the sun went dark for a while.'

'She says she wonders if she should have saved you! That's not the same thing at all! The cord was around your neck, and you weren't breathing, but thanks to your grandmother, you lived.'

'But she considered letting me die. That's as good as killing a baby!'

Mamm clenched her fist and pressed it to her lips. 'Someone from this household murdered my little John.'

'It wasn't me!' Mawde bunched her apron in her hands. 'I'd prove it if I could.'

Mamm shook her head. 'I don't know what to believe. Am I supposed to think a stranger tiptoed into the house, killed my child, then ran away without being seen?'

'A stranger?' Mawde was struck by a memory. 'No! Julian went inside the house.' Mawde grasped her mother's arm. 'Mamm, it must have been Julian!'

Mamm gave an exasperated sigh. 'For goodness' sake, Mawde, who will you accuse next? Julian was working with your father.'

'Not all the time. Father sent him indoors to fetch something.'

'In which case, you or your grandmother would have seen what he did.'

Mawde's thoughts were in turmoil. Her head hurt. 'Grandmother was unwell, remember? It was so hot that day. I went outside to fetch water to cool John and Grandmother. I remember now. She was asleep when I left them.'

'Oh, Mawde, I know you don't like Julian, and I confess I'm not fond of him either, but you can't pass the blame from one person to another.'

'Julian's a bully.' Raising her voice and releasing her grasp, Mawde said, 'Do you remember the day I fell and spilt my rabbit pottage? It was Julian's fault. He put little wooden balls on the floor to make me fall over.' Mawde could tell Mamm didn't believe her, but she pressed on. 'He tried to gather them up, but I got to one of them first. I've still got it if you want to see it. Then there was that time at Whitsun when he made it look as if I'd taken...' Her voice faded away. Even to her, it was starting to sound ridiculous. 'I just know it was Julian.'

Mawde scrambled to her feet and went to walk away, but Mamm grabbed the back of her kirtle, giving her no choice but to turn and meet her mother's stern gaze.

'John's left us for good, Mawde, and nothing we do or say will ever change that. Let us agree to never speak of his passing again.'

Mawde felt desolate, her heart aching with the knowledge that her mother still harboured a suspicion she might be responsible for John's death. They finished the laundry in silence, spreading sheets and shirts over a low stone wall to dry. Next, they fetched armfuls of rushes from a store in the stable and set about weaving them together, making mats to cover the earth floor indoors.

At last, Mamm broke the silence. 'We should sweep the hall and fill the divots before we lay the mats. There's a pile of mended shirts to go back to the farm, and I don't want to cover them in dust. Will you take them for me?'

Grateful for an excuse to get away, Mawde collected the shirts from the settle and set off towards the farm without uttering a word.

❁

Aunt Mary welcomed Mawde with a tight embrace despite the bulk of her unborn child becoming wedged between them.

Mawde placed her hand over the bulge of Aunt Mary's apron. 'I thought the baby would have come by now.'

'He or she will come when they're ready and not a moment before.' She reached for a small basket covered with a linen cloth. 'Take these for your mamm.' Peeling back the cloth, she added, 'Your grandmother made honey cakes this morning and I know how much my sister adores them. Be sure to have one yourself.'

'I will. Thank you, Aunt Mary.' Mawde's gaze drifted across the room. 'Is Tamsin here?'

'No, I'm sorry, Mawde, she went to the mill with Uncle William.'

Mawde was crestfallen. 'I'd better be going then.'

Aunt Mary stroked Mawde's cheek. 'Do I sense all is not well?'

Mawde shook her head. 'Mamm and I are having a bit of a tidy up. It's tiring work.'

'I know what you mean,' her aunt said with an understanding smile. 'Off you trot, and I'll see you on Sunday.' Aunt Mary planted a kiss on Mawde's coif and ushered her towards the door.

Her aunt's good humour had improved Mawde's mood. As she skipped along the lane, she swung the basket back and forth, but not so high as to spill the contents. The sun was warm across her back and birds sang in the hedgerows. As Mawde turned onto the track that led towards home, pounding hoofbeats approached from behind. Someone was riding towards her, and fast. As she turned to see who was galloping with such urgency, a large bay horse loomed towards her. She jumped out of the way just in time. The rider pulled hard on the reins, circled back towards her, then slid down from the saddle.

'I'm looking for Simon Hygons. Do you know him?' His voice was deep and commanding. 'I was told this track leads to his workshop. Was I correctly informed?'

Mawde nodded, captivated by the deep furrows on the man's weatherworn face. 'He's my father, but he's not home. He's at Gerrans.'

The stranger squinted towards the sun. It was low in the sky and less than two hours from sinking below the horizon. 'I don't have time to go to Gerrans. It's important I speak to him. Do you expect him home soon?'

'Mamm said he'll be gone until after dark, but she won't mind if you wait. Especially if it's important.'

The rider wrinkled his brow, making the furrows even deeper. 'Can't stay. I must get back to Lanihorne Castle by nightfall.'

Mawde's eyes widened. She'd never met someone from the castle before. 'You could talk to my mamm, if you like. She'll pass a message to my da when he gets home.'

'You're his daughter, you say?'

Mawde straightened her posture. 'Yes, sir.'

'It's a simple enough message. Will you pass it on to him?'

A visitor from Lanihorne Castle was trusting *her* with an important message. 'I will.'

'Tell your father Henry Penhale called by. He knows

who I am. Tell him the Master Carpenter at Lanihorne spoke about a job coming up at Glasney College, in Penryn. A renovation job that will change the fortunes of the man who takes it on. Glasney's carpenter died last week, so they're offering for local craftsmen to bid for the work. Anyone interested must attend the college mid-morning tomorrow. It will mean your father staying in Penryn for a few weeks if he gets the job, but it's too good an opportunity for him to miss. Tell him to take samples of carvings and a bagful of tools. A boat leaves St Mawes early every day for Penryn, so he can make it to Glasney in time. Will you tell him all that?'

Mawde smiled. 'Yes, sir. Da needs to be at Glasney College in Penryn tomorrow morning with samples and tools.'

'Good girl.' The man placed one foot in a stirrup, lifted himself off the ground and flung his other leg over the saddle. 'Don't forget, will you? If Simon makes a good impression, his reputation will spread across Cornwall, and he'll have an endless supply of work.' He turned the horse and dug his heels in, setting off at a gallop towards the highway and leaving Mawde staring after him from the midst of a cloud of dirt.

Mawde checked her basket and was relieved to see the honey cakes were still covered, albeit by a cloth coated with a film of brown dust. She resumed her walk home, quickening her pace, eager to share the news with her mother. If her father went to work at Glasney College, he would take Julian with him. She would miss having her father around at home, but the thought of a few weeks without Julian was pleasurable indeed.

A rustling in the bushes brought Mawde to an abrupt halt. Moments later, there was another rustling, followed by a forlorn yelp. Mawde placed the basket on a smooth part of the track and crept towards the foliage on the verge. There, cowering among the undergrowth, was a spaniel. Mawde screwed up her nose. Flies were congregating on a large festering wound on one of his hind legs.

'Oh, you poor thing!' Mawde crept closer, careful to avoid frightening the injured animal. She extended her arm and gently rested her fingers on his head. Sad eyes looked up at her. She crouched down and shooed away the flies. The spaniel plopped his head onto her lap and whined.

'I can't leave you here,' she said, stroking his head. 'I'll take you home. My grandmother will know how to heal your leg. She's not very nice, but she is good at healing.' Mawde attempted to scoop the dog into her arms, but he growled, forcing her to back away.

'Don't be afraid,' she said, her heart racing. She knew injured animals could turn aggressive when they felt threatened. 'I'm your friend. I won't hurt you.'

Calmed by the gentle tone of her voice, the spaniel allowed Mawde to lift him from the ground. Mawde took care to support the injured leg without putting pressure near the wound. As she stepped back on to the track, she spotted the basket of honey cakes. Grimacing under the weight of the dog, she bent her knees and grasped the handle with one hand, then she staggered towards home, puffing and panting.

Mamm was sweeping the yard. She cast her broom aside and hurried towards Mawde. 'What have you got here?' she said, taking the dog from Mawde's arms.

'Careful, Mamm, he's injured.'

'So I see. Poor little thing. Abandoned too, from the looks of his scrawny body. Injured in the hunt, I suspect. An injured dog's no good to a pack, so they probably abandoned him and left him for dead.'

'So, they won't want him back?' Mawde's heartbeat quickened. 'Mamm? Can we keep him?'

Mamm hesitated. 'For the time being, yes. But if someone comes to claim him, you'll have to let him go.'

Mawde beamed at her mother, but then her expression turned serious. 'Can you treat his wound? Make a salve or something?'

Her mother studied the dog's damaged leg. 'Grandmother will know what's best. We ought to do something soon or the poor creature might die. You'll have to run back to the farm and ask Grandmother's advice.'

'Now?' Mawde hopped from foot to foot, her heart filled with love and concern for the dog.

'Go on then, but quick as you can, mind, because we still have much to do here. I'll make up a bed for him in the stables. He'll be warm and dry in there. And Mawde, it'll be up to you to look after him.'

'I will, Mamm, I promise.' Mawde remembered the basket slung over her arm. 'Oh, I forgot! Aunt Mary sent honey cakes for you. The baby hasn't come yet, but she said it will be here soon.'

Mamm smiled. 'Mawde, I had a good think while you were gone. What with that and seeing your concern for this dog, I want you to know that I don't believe it was you who harmed our baby.'

Tears pricked at Mawde's eyes. She embraced her mother, then set off back towards the farm as fast as her legs would carry her.

With new rush mats covering the floor and the evening chores finished, Mawde went outside to chivvy the chickens into their coop. She secured the latch and then tiptoed into the stable. The spaniel pricked his ears and lifted his head. Seeing Mawde, he wagged his tail, beating it over and over against his straw bed. His injured leg was cocooned in an old square of blanket, a salve of lavender and hypericum having already been applied and covered with a protective bandage.

Mawde nestled on the straw beside him. 'You need a name,' she said, running her fingers over his silky coat. 'You're far too gentle for a hunting dog, but you're so brave.' Mawde closed her eyes, considering and dismissing one name after another. 'I've got it,' she said at last, cupping the spaniel's head in her hands. 'Hero. My Hero.'

Darkness fell, and the temperature dropped inside the stable. Mawde bade goodnight to Hero and prepared herself for bed. She said her prayers, taking longer than usual because much had happened that day for which she was thankful. She ticked them off one at a time. Her mother's trust. Her aunt's kindness. The chance encounter with Hero. Food in her belly. And a comfortable bed.

She clambered onto her plump mattress, curled onto her side and closed her eyes. Within moments, she drifted into a deep sleep.

CHAPTER EIGHT
APRIL 1522

'Oh no!' Mawde scrambled to her feet, knocking over a cup of ale and sending it spinning across the table towards Grandmother. 'Da, you have to leave now or you'll miss the boat!'

'My dear child, whatever are you talking about?' Mamm asked.

Mawde's heartbeat thrummed in her ears. She dashed to Da's side and grasped his chair, trying to drag it away from the table.

Da chuckled. 'Mawde, calm down! Anyone would think the world is about to end.'

'Please, Da, gather your things and hurry to the harbour. You have to go to Penryn.'

Da grasped Mawde's arms and met her frantic gaze. 'Take a deep breath and explain the urgency. Why must I hurry away to Penryn? Can't it wait until tomorrow?'

'No!' Hot tears spilled on Mawde's cheeks. She wiped them away with her palms. 'How could I have forgotten? Oh, Da, I'm so sorry. I met a gentleman in the lane yesterday. He said he was from Lanihorne Castle and asked me to pass on a message to you. I forgot about it because of Hero, and by the time you arrived home, I was already asleep. Hurry, Da, get your tools and some samples. I'll help you. You must not miss that boat!'

'What were you supposed to tell me?' Da said, rising from his chair.

'They need a carpenter at Glassy College for a renna... ren...'

'Renovation?'

'Yes, that was it! The man said he knew you from before and wanted you to have a chance of getting the job.'

'She means Glasney College,' clarified Grandmother unhelpfully.

'Of course she does!' Mamm raised her hand to apologise for her exasperated tone. 'Mawde, go with your da and explain everything while he gathers his things. Julian, ready one of the horses.'

Da strode across the courtyard. Mawde trotted along behind him, struggling to keep pace. 'The college carpenter died, Da, so they're giving other men a chance to do the work. You're to take your tools and samples to show how good you are. Trouble is, you'd have to stay for several weeks if they give you the work.'

'That wouldn't go down well with your mamm, but Lord knows, we need the money.' Da threw a small selection of tools and wooden offcuts into a bag. 'I'll knock up a couple of joinery samples while we're under sail.' He opened a box and selected a carved baby's rattle and a small statue of a rabbit. The detail on the rabbit was so fine, Mawde almost believed it had real fur. 'I made these for John,' Da said. 'Perhaps, if I show them as examples of my carving skills, they'll bring us the good fortune we need.' He pulled a drawstring tight to close his bag and marched out into the courtyard.

'The man said his name is Henry. Who is he, Da, and how does he know you?'

'Henry from Lanihorne.' Da grinned. 'It can only be Henry Penhale. So, he's been as good as his word. I saved his life once. Drunk, he was. Fell into the river and couldn't swim, so I dived in after him and dragged him out.' Da waited for Julian to adjust the girth, then eased himself up onto the saddle. Taking the reins from Julian, he added, 'He said he'd find a way to make it up to me, and he'll have more than settled his debt if they choose me today. Wish me luck, Mawde. I have a good feeling about this.' Da urged the horse to move forward. 'Julian, make your way to the harbour to collect the horse. I don't want to leave him tied up there all day.' Da flicked his reins to make the horse quicken, kicking up clouds of dirt as heavy hoofbeats pounded the dusty track.

Grandmother and Mamm stitched neat little cloth bags. Mawde stuffed each one with dried lavender before closing with a length of thin grey ribbon. She held a bag to her nose and inhaled through her nostrils, relishing the sweet aromatic fragrance, then placed it in a basket with other bags ready to be sold at the market.

''Tis a fine day today,' remarked Grandmother, straining her eyes by the light of the window and struggling to thread a needle. 'Let us pray for a bountiful spring and summer.'

Mawde plucked the thin shard of bone from between her grandmother's fingertips, deftly passed the thread through the eye at one end, then passed the needle back to her, giving her a warm smile. Grandmother responded with a haughty sniff.

Mawde cocked her head to one side. 'Do you hear that?' Soft beating sounds. Da dum, da dum, da dum. Gradually growing louder. Mawde placed her palm over her chest, thinking it was her heartbeat, but the timing was different, and the sound was more urgent. She turned her head towards the door. 'Hoofbeats?'

The colour drained from Mamm's face. 'A horse coming at a fast gallop. That can only mean bad news.' She rose from her chair and waited by the open door.

'Who is it?' Grandmother demanded, frowning with irritation.

'I can't see yet, Mamm. Oh! It's George Wyn, the vintner. Why does he come at such a pace?'

Vintner Wyn was a popular villager, favoured by the landowners and merchants for his ability to procure the best French wines. He was well-liked by the locals, who enjoyed small tipples at his expense on every wedding and feast day. Wiry and with pinched facial features, he had a warm personality and was a welcome visitor to any home.

'Vintner Wyn, it's a pleasure to welcome you across our threshold today.'

George Wyn mopped his brow with a square of white linen, then eased himself down from his saddle.

Mamm gestured for him to step inside the house. 'Can I tempt you to a cup of cool ale? 'Tis very warm for April.'

The vintner shook his head. 'A kind offer, Goodwife Hygons, but I must refuse.' As he approached the house, he removed his cap and lowered his gaze towards the ground. 'I regret that my call is not a social one today.' He twisted his cap in his hands. 'I come as the bearer of distressing news.'

Sensing a shift in atmosphere, Mawde sidled up to her mother.

Vintner Wynn lifted his head and peered at Mamm

with miserable eyes. 'You should sit before I share my news. All three of you, if you please.'

'Enough with the suspense, Vintner,' Grandmother said in a clipped tone. 'Out with it!'

A distant movement caught Mawde's attention. It was Julian emerging from the workshop, shielding his eyes to see who had ridden into the courtyard with such urgency.

Mawde shifted her gaze to Vintner Wyn. His eyes were dark, like bottomless rock pools devoid of reflections. She shivered.

''Tis about your husband,' the vintner said to Mamm.

Grandmother shoved Mawde aside. 'Did something happen on the boat? Is Simon injured?'

'He wasn't on a boat. Carpenter Hygons wasn't even at the harbour.' The vintner's Adam's apple jiggled up and down as he swallowed. 'Please, I beg you, sit before I say more.'

'Whatever it is, Vintner Wyn, tell us without delay,' Mamm said.

Mawde grasped her mother's trembling hand.

'There's no easy way to say this.' The vintner's mouth turned down at the corners. 'I regret to inform you that your husband has passed.'

A piercing scream filled the air, circling around Mawde and threatening to squeeze the life out of her. She covered her ears, but no matter how hard she pressed her hands to her head, she could not block the sound. A clawed hand gripped her shoulder, causing Mawde to realise that the noise was of her own making. She fell silent.

'How?' Grandmother sank her talons deeper into Mawde's shoulder.

'There were no witnesses, but from what we could surmise, the horse lost its footing going down the hill. Carpenter Hygons fell from the saddle somehow. We think the horse panicked and… um… well…' He pursed his lips and made a peculiar puffing sound. 'A carthorse is a heavy creature, no matter how delicate its temperament. I regret to inform you, the horse trampled on his chest.' A long pause. 'I was near the bottom of the hill making a delivery when I heard the commotion. I hurried to him as fast as I could, but by the time I reached him…'

Mamm dried her face on her apron and stared up at the vintner with the saddest expression Mawde had ever seen. 'Did he suffer?'

The vintner shook his head. 'I don't believe so. He sustained a heavy blow to the head when he struck the ground. After that, I doubt he was aware of anything.'

'Where is he now?' Mamm asked.

'Laid out in the church. I'll take you to see him.'

Mawde stepped aside to allow Grandmother to throw a shawl across Mamm's shoulders. Her legs shaking violently, Mawde fetched her own shawl and pulled it tight around her. She felt as cold as if it were mid-winter.

The vintner linked arms with Mamm to support her. Mawde went to hold her mother on the other side, but Grandmother brushed her away.

'Not you, girl.' She jabbed Mawde in the chest. 'This is your doing.'

'How is it my fault?'

'If you'd given your father the message first thing this morning, he wouldn't have been rushing down the hill to catch the boat.'

'Mamm?'

Mamm turned towards Mawde, but her eyes seemed to look straight through her. She gave a slight shrug of the shoulders before turning back and taking unsteady steps towards the vintner's horse.

Mawde sank to the ground, her kirtle rippling around

75

her like a giant puddle of tears. The sun beat down from a clear blue sky and birds chattered in the branches of nearby trees. Chickens clucked and strutted in the yard, and the tinkling chime of a distant goat bell carried on a gentle breeze. The perfect spring day was at odds with the fact that she wouldn't see her father again. She watched the sad group progress towards the lane. Julian followed along behind at a slow and steady walk, keeping a respectable distance.

As soon as they were out of sight, Mawde ran into the stables. She snuggled up to Hero and wept until her tears ran dry.

CHAPTER NINE

JULY 1522

'THOUGHT I'D FIND YOU HERE.' Tamsin settled herself beside Mawde and reached for her hand.

Mawde gratefully squeezed Tamsin's fingers, keeping her eyes on the frothy surf. The tide was on the rise. Waves fractured over limpet-covered rocks, coating the girls' skirts with a fine mist of salty spray.

'I can't imagine what it's like for you, Mawde. I understand why you blame yourself, but you really shouldn't. Anyone could have been asked to pass the message on to your da. It just so happened it was you. 'Twas bad luck he was late home, and you were already abed.' Tamsin stroked the back of Mawde's hand, the dry scaly tips of her fingers strangely soothing, like fingernails easing an itch. 'We're all worried about you. Your mamm said you're refusing to eat and that you've not said a word since your da's burial. I miss you. Why don't you come to the farm anymore?'

Mawde shrugged and switched her attention to a hole in her sleeve.

'Please, Mawde, say something.'

'There's nothing to say.'

Tamsin rested her head on Mawde's shoulder. 'No, I don't suppose there is. Nothing that's going to make you feel better anyway.'

'Mamm dismissed Julian yesterday, and Da's tools were sold at auction this morning. Now his workshop's all but empty and it's like he was never there.' Mawde stared at the fissures and ridges on Tamsin's hands. The skin was tight in some areas, cracked and weeping in others. She loosened her grip. 'That looks painful.'

'It is,' Tamsin said. 'But you're hurting inside more than I am on the outside.'

Mawde swallowed a sob and turned her face towards her cousin.

Tamsin gasped. 'Mawde, you really are a pitiful sight. Your face is pale and thin, and your eyes…'

Mawde had stared at her reflection in her mother's hand mirror earlier that morning, and barely recognised herself. Her vibrant cornflower eyes had lost their lustre and looked sunken in their sockets ringed by violet shadows. The rosy bloom on her cheeks had faded to grey, and her glossy raven hair hung in straggly dull tangles beneath her coif.

Tamsin withdrew a biscuit from her pocket and broke it in two. 'Have a piece of this.'

Mawde shook her head.

'You must,' Tamsin insisted. 'You look like you haven't eaten for weeks. You'll starve to death if you're not careful.'

'Wouldn't be a bad thing. Then I'd be with Da.'

'Don't say that. There's been enough sadness in your family to last a lifetime. Imagine how distressed your ma would be if she lost you too.'

'Some people would be happier if I wasn't around.'

Tamsin sighed. 'You mean our grandmother? I doubt

she really feels that way, and anyway, she won't be around forever. I've seen her catching her breath with everything she does. She's a cranky old woman, Mawde, and sharp with all of us. Take no notice of her.'

Mawde's heart ached with grief as images of her father flashed through her mind. 'I didn't mean for it to happen, Tamsin.'

'Of course you didn't. Your ma knows it, too. It's not as if you were hiding on the hill waiting to startle the horse. Please, Mawde, I know you're sad, but drag yourself out of this despair.'

Mawde's head throbbed, a combination of dehydration, hunger and wretchedness. 'I've had one disaster after another,' she said. 'Julian convinced Grandmother I was a thief, John died, and now Da's gone.' She looked at Tamsin. 'None of it was my fault, you know. I can't help thinking Julian had something to do with each of those things.'

'I don't know, Mawde.' Tamsin sucked her knuckle where a bead of blood had bubbled on her skin. 'I'm sure he put the carving in your pocket that day at Penryn, but I don't think you can blame him for the deaths.'

Mawde lacked energy for an argument. There was no doubt in her mind that Julian had caused her brother to choke, and she suspected his involvement with her father's accident, too. Vintner Wyn had said something about her father falling from the saddle, and Mawde believed Julian had left the girth strap loose. She'd mentioned her suspicion on the morning of her father's funeral, but Grandmother had been quick to defend Julian and declared it unlikely he would hurt the man who provided his income and a future.

'I wish it was Grandmother who'd died,' Mawde said, taken aback by how much she meant it.

Tamsin's hand flew to her mouth. "'Tis a sin to wish someone dead, Mawde. Even if you think about it, you shouldn't say it aloud. What if someone heard?'

'You can't stop a suspicion once it settles in your mind. It grows and creeps like ivy on a tree until it's so entangled there's no way to remove it.' Mawde spied a fishing boat making its way back towards the harbour. Gulls screeched and circled the boat, looking for scraps from the catch. She wondered how sweeter life would be if her grandmother were not a part of it. Probably no better, if the truth be told. Da and John would still be missing. But even so.

A thin trail of blood trickled along the back of Tamsin's hand, leaving a pale stain in its wake. Tamsin wiped her hand on her kirtle. 'Some families get a run of bad luck, Mawde. None of us know why things happen. 'Tis probably the will of the Lord, although I struggle to see why He would want us to suffer. You have no choice but to get through it. Your mamm needs your help more than she's ever needed it before. Do what you can for her and take no notice of Grandmother. I know it's been hard for you, but life is hard for everyone. You're strong enough to get through this. I know you are.'

The tide crept higher towards them, threatening to lick the soles of their shoes. Water shimmered with flashes of silver as a school of fish reflected the warm rays of the sun. It was like a shiny parcel of promises of better days to come.

'You can be bossy when you want to be,' Mawde said, rising to her feet and reaching out her hand to help Tamsin do the same. 'I love the way nothing gets you down. Even the bullying about your skin. I want to be more like you. I know I did nothing wrong, and that should be enough, shouldn't it?'

'There she is,' Tamsin said. 'That's the Mawde I know and love.'

'You're right, though. I need to do more to help my mamm, especially as there's a baby on the way.'

'Grandmother can't do much these days, so you'll have to do all the things grandmother used to do. Now, eat that piece of biscuit and then I'll walk you home.' Tamsin yawned. 'Baby James had colic last night and fussed and yelled until dawn. I should get back to the farm and help my mamm, but I'll stop by your house first because Grandmother promised to make a fresh balm for my hands.'

Mawde chewed on her fragment of biscuit and forced herself to swallow even though her mouth was dry and she had no appetite. The time had come for her to stop feeling sorry for herself and to start behaving more like Tamsin.

Mawde's throat tightened, and she watched in sullen silence as Grandmother massaged balm into the cracked skin of Tamsin's hands and elbows. Tamsin didn't get the sour looks or barbed comments that Mawde endured daily. Instead, Grandmother's cold eyes warmed, and her mean lips softened as she murmured words of affectionate reassurance. Mawde yelped when her sewing needle penetrated deep into the pad of her finger. She withdrew it, sucked the blood away, then concentrated on making neat stitches along the seams of a lavender bag.

'All finished,' she said triumphantly, placing it on a pile of other bags in a basket. 'Mamm, may I walk Tamsin home? I've neglected Hero recently and he could do with a run.'

Her mother kept her eyes fixed on her spinning wheel. 'Very well. Don't be gone long, though, because I still have much to do here. You can prepare supper when you get home. Oh, ask Uncle William if he can spare one of the boys tomorrow. One of the windows won't shut properly, and I have a couple of other little jobs that need doing.'

Mawde collected Hero from the stable, then skipped along the lane, arm-in-arm with Tamsin. Hero zig-zagged from one side of the track to the other, sniffing at the undergrowth, wagging his tail.

'Grandmother cured his leg,' Mawde said. 'He doesn't even have a limp.'

'You see, she does do good things sometimes,' Tamsin teased. 'I wonder if she's using the same balm on me.' She turned her hands one way, then the other, her greasy skin shimmering in the light of the waning sun. 'It's already less sore than it was. She said if I use this every day, my skin might heal completely, apart from the scars I have already.' Tamsin turned her hands over. 'Imagine that, Mawde, me with skin as smooth as yours, and no reason for the village boys to tease me.'

'It shouldn't matter what you look like,' Mawde said. 'There's never an excuse for teasing.'

'That's easy for you to say when there's not a blemish on you.'

'I've got this,' Mawde pointed to the scar above her right eyebrow.

'It's faded a lot since you did it. Anyway, it's just a blemish and something that makes you different. Don't resent it. Treasure it.'

'If you say so.'

'Race you to the fork,' Tamsin shouted, dashing forward to get a head start.

Mawde chased after her, skirts flapping about her legs, strands of hair tumbling from beneath her coif. Hero barked and wagged his tail. He joined the race, scampering ahead, then trotting back towards them, eager for them to run faster. By the time the girls reached the fork, they were running side by side. They slowed their pace and drew to a halt, then collapsed against the verge, breathless and giggling.

'I was sure I'd win, seeing as you've been starving your-self,' Tamsin said between gasps.

'Wasn't easy to keep up.' Mawde wiped a sheen of sweat from her brow. 'You'd have beaten me if we'd gone any further.'

'Typical! We'll have a longer race next time,' Tamsin said. 'Come on. We'd better get moving. Mamm'll be wondering where I am. I was due home hours ago.'

Mawde cajoled Hero into the stable. With the stalls standing empty, it was as cold and quiet as a tomb. Without Da's income, they could not afford the horses, and had no need for them now the business no longer existed. Julian was back with his family, his apprenticeship abruptly curtailed. Mawde would have considered that a blessing if it had not cost her father's life.

With Hero settled, she secured the stable door and crossed the courtyard to the house. With her hand on the latch, she hesitated as raised voices carried from inside. Mawde pressed her ear against the cool oak.

'Give the girl a chance, Mamm! If you keep treating her like a villain, eventually she'll start behaving like one.'

'She's like a wormy apple,' Grandmother said, her voice rising into a shrill screech. 'Shiny and appealing from the outside, but inside she's rotten to the core. You should send her away! No good will come from letting her stay under this roof.'

'Mamm, that's my daughter you're talking about! I don't know why you've never taken to her. She's the sweetest girl, kind and helpful. She's a victim of circumstance, nothing more. I don't believe she murdered her brother, and I don't believe she's ever stolen anything either. That dreadful boy set her up, I'm sure of it.'

Mawde felt a tug of affection for her mother.

Grandmother was still intent on defending Julian. 'The blacksmith's mother was one of my dearest friends, God rest her soul. They're a good family and would have raised the boy well. He wouldn't do such a terrible thing.'

'We're a good family, Mamm!'

'We were until *she* was born. I've told you before, a darkling child taints a family. You know the story!'

'One ancestor, Mamm. One! A man who was likely to stray from righteousness no matter what the circumstances of his birth. This stubborn belief of yours, it's irrational!'

Mawde thrust open the door and hurtled into her mother's arms. 'Thank you, Mamm. Thank you for believing me.' She released herself from Mamm's tight embrace and stood in front of her grandmother. 'You're a mean old crone and I hate you with every bone in my body. I look forward to the day you die!'

'There it is,' Grandmother said with an ugly sneer. 'Yet again, the girl's evil is revealed.'

CHAPTER TEN

JULY 1524

THE SECOND ANNIVERSARY of Da's death passed. Every day, Mawde imagined his footsteps on the stairs and his voice calling from the yard, sometimes unintentionally, other times because she sorely missed him. The women had settled into a routine: Grandmother spinning and weaving, Mawde and Mamm baking and tending to the garden, then making all manner of items that would fetch a price at the village market. Little Agnes was growing fast and had already mastered walking. She was an eager little assistant who loved helping Mawde feed the chickens and see to the daily chores.

Two baskets were full to the brim with lavender bags, and a third was piled high with herbs plucked fresh from the garden that morning. Mamm lifted another basket onto the table and packed it with straw and eggs.

'Mawde, will you take Agnes to the farm? Grandmother's too ill to look after her today. Aunt Mary won't mind watching her. I'll make a linctus to soothe Grandmother's throat. It'll be ready by the time you get home and then we'll take all of this to the market.'

Mawde crouched to tickle Agnes under the chin. 'Lucky Agnes,' she cooed. 'You get to spend the day with Cousin Tamsin.'

'Tamdin,' Agnes echoed with a gummy smile. She raised her arms towards Mawde and waited to be lifted from the rush matting.

'I'm not carrying you all the way there. You're getting too heavy.' She scooped her little sister into her arms and nuzzled Agnes's neck, sending her into fits of giggles.

Agnes pressed her chubby hands against Mawde's cheeks. ''Ero coming?'

'Definitely. He won't want to miss the fun.'

Agnes twisted in Mawde's arms and opened and closed her fingers, waving goodbye to Grandmother.

'Dear, sweet Agnes,' Grandmother said, gazing at the toddler with adoring eyes. 'How your da would have adored you.' A breath seemed to catch in her throat, sending her into a spasm of coughing. Her face turned ashen, and her lips took on a lilac tinge as she struggled to catch her breath.

Mawde turned her back towards her grandmother and wondered why God had allowed the old woman to outlive Da.

'No dilly dallying, Mawde,' Mamm said. 'I want to get to the market early. We should do well today and make enough money for a length of linen. Lord knows we're all in desperate need of new shifts.'

Villagers and stalls packed the main street. Warm summer sunshine beat down on the village and the hubbub of conversations carried on a soft, warm breeze. The menfolk sought alehouses while women jostled for space to scrutinise the goods offered for sale. Children shrieked as they played on the beach, chasing each other across sand and shingle, or launching large pebbles into the shallows to see who could make the biggest splash. Musicians clustered at the far end of the street, smiling at their generous audience as silver coins clinked into an upturned hat.

Mawde and Mamm lowered their baskets to the dusty ground.

'It's not where I wanted to be, but it'll do,' Mamm said with a wistful gaze towards the crowd congregating by the stalls along the seafront. 'I hope the women have money to spare by the time they get to us.'

'I'm sure they will.' Mawde sounded more optimistic than she felt. 'At least with the crowd thinner here, they can see what we're selling and won't have to fight their way to us.'

George Wyn was walking behind a cart stacked high with crates of wine. He leaned towards his companion and made a comment before peeling away to greet Mamm.

'Good day to you, Widow Hygons.' He doffed his hat and leaned forward into an extravagant bow. He angled himself towards Mawde and bowed again. 'And to you, too, young lady.'

Mawde blushed. She had never been called a young lady before.

Mamm tutted. 'Vintner Wyn, you're making a spectacle of yourself. I trust you are well?'

The vintner's expression turned serious. 'I am well, but alas, my wife is not. She's confined to her bedchamber with dreadful pains in her chest.'

'I'm sorry to hear that,' Mamm said. 'Please pass on my good wishes for her recovery.'

'Indeed, I will. Now tell me, how are you bearing up since the tragic passing of your husband?'

Mawde sensed her mother tense beside her.

'We're managing well enough.'

The vintner nodded his understanding. 'It's never easy for a wife to lose her husband.'

'Plenty of widows have coped before me. I have no choice but to do the same.'

'I admire your spirit.' He pointed to the baskets. 'Lavender bags. My wife adores them. I'd like to purchase them from you.'

Mamm selected the plumpest bag and held it out to him. 'That'll be half a penny.'

'Forgive me,' the vintner said, 'but I didn't make myself clear. I'd like to purchase the entire contents of a basket. My wife hangs lavender at every window, stuffs it inside pillows, buries it among her clothes, and who knows where else she hides it!'

'A whole basket?' Mamm said. 'Are you sure?'

'Certain of it. No, in fact, make that two!'

Mawde gaped at her mother.

Mamm elbowed her. 'Close your mouth, Mawde. You look like a strangled pollock.' To the vintner she said, 'If you're sure you wish to have them all, there are forty bags in each basket, making eighty in total. It will cost you forty pennies.'

George Wyn smiled. 'I'd rather give you a crown.'

'That's too much.'

'But you'll suffer a temporary inconvenience, as I will need to carry them in your baskets.'

'A crown it is then,' Mawde said, cutting off her mother's attempt at another refusal.

George Wyn tipped a handful of coins from a leather pouch and handed a crown to Mamm. As Mamm reached down towards the basket handles, the vintner pressed a shiny new sixpence into Mawde's hand. She gazed up at him, and he touched his index finger to his lips. Mawde wrapped her fingers around the precious coin and thanked him with a discrete smile.

'A peculiar gentleman,' Mamm said, watching the vintner disappear into the crowd.

'I like him.' The warm sixpence was comforting against Mawde's palm.

Mamm stared at the coins in her own hand. 'Many a villager has remarked on his generosity. They weren't exaggerating.'

'He gave me this,' Mawde said, adding her sixpence to her mother's collection.

Mamm plucked it from the pile of coins. 'No, Mawde, it was his gift to you and is therefore yours to enjoy.'

Since Da's death, life had been a struggle. The money raised from the sale of his tools had very quickly dwindled. Mawde had tried her best to fill their bellies with shellfish and the occasional small rabbit caught in Julian's old trap. They had relied on her uncle and cousins to chop wood for the fire, but too often, the woodpile ran low, forcing them to be frugal and use the minimum needed to cook. Summer's arrival had been a relief, the warm air taking the chill from the house and ripening a good crop of vegetables in their garden.

Mawde gave the coin to her mother. 'You have it, Mamm. Buy something for Agnes if you don't want it.'

'You've a kind heart, Mawde. Thank you.'

'Got any combs?' An unfamiliar woman stood in front of them, her feet planted wide apart, and hands on her hips.

Mawde fought the urge to wrinkle her nose at the rancid smell emanating from her body. Folds of unwashed shift spilled out over her bodice, the linen tired and stained. Strands of matted red hair framed her pock-marked face, and she spoke with a lisp because her front teeth were missing.

The woman snorted and swallowed. 'No one else has combs today.'

'I haven't either,' Mamm said. 'I'm sorry.'

Mawde pitied the woman. As scruffy as she was, she must be keen to improve her appearance if she was desperate for a comb. 'Mamm, we have a few at home. Da and Julian made them when Julian first came to stay. They're still in the workshop.'

Mamm turned to her customer. 'Do you mind coming back later? My daughter's a fast runner. It won't take long for her to fetch them.'

The woman dug dirty fingernails into her hairline and scratched a patch of dried skin. ''Tis good of ye. Me old comb snapped. I need one with stronger teeth to get the knots and lice out. I'll come back later s'afternoon.'

Mamm waited for the woman to waddle out of earshot. 'She needs more than a comb, if you ask me. She could do with a hefty dose of soap and lye. Bring all the combs you can find, Mawde. If no one else is selling them, we could do well with ours today. And while you're home, check on your grandmother.'

'Of course,' Mawde replied, rolling her eyes as she turned away.

Mawde pushed through the thickening crowd until she emerged at the foot of the hill that led towards home. She climbed the steep incline, moving as fast as she was able, leaning forward and taking small steps to stop her leg muscles from burning. After pausing at the top to catch her breath, she ran along the dusty rutted highway and turned off into a lane that split in two – one track headed towards her uncle and aunt's farm, the other to her home. As she crested the brow of the hill and looked down towards the house and workshop, her blood ran cold in her veins. Orange and red flames licked two of the timber walls of the house, devouring the sides of the building, having already consumed a large section of thatched roof. Crackles and pops echoed across the valley. The air was thick with the smell of burning wood, and a cloud of thick grey smoke hung heavy in the air. A sidewall tilted and crashed to the ground, sending up a spray of bright orange sparks. A shrill scream came from somewhere within the inferno, high-pitched and frantic, then a small, hunched figure staggered from the burning wreckage. Grandmother. She stumbled into the yard and landed on all fours, then reached out with both arms and pleaded for Mawde's help.

Mawde ran to the courtyard and stopped by Da's old workshop. Even from that distance, she could feel the intense heat of the fire. Grandmother called out to her, but her words were a tangle of shrill panic. She tried to slither forward but seemed to have lost all strength, and she dropped her head onto her arm and lay prostrate on the ground. Mawde watched the old woman struggle. Why did her grandmother have to be such a mean old goat? Mawde's gaze drifted to the tall orange flames licking the timber-framed walls. Her father had often talked about rebuilding the house to increase its size and replace the wattle and daub with stone. But he only managed the chimney and hearth and the addition of two small bedchambers in the loft.

Grandmother waved her arm to catch Mawde's attention. Mawde could see her eyes were wide with terror as her pleas for help were stifled by smoke. A chunk of burning doorframe fell to the ground and caught the hem of Grandmother's skirt. The wool smouldered, slowly at first, but soon caught fire and burned.

Grandmother rolled onto her side and pressed her

hands to her chest. She coughed and gasped, then coughed again before shouting out to Mawde. 'Please… help…' Her words were almost lost against the noise of the raging inferno. Her face contorted with agony, then slackened as the fire devoured her flesh and clothes.

Mawde stood still, her heart thudding in her chest, as she watched her grandmother burn. The heat of the flames stole Mawde's breath. Sweat prickled on her skin.

Frantic barking sounded in the distance, gradually drawing nearer.

'Hero?' Stirred into action, Mawde hurried towards the lane, surprised to see her dog bounding towards her when he should have been with Aunt Mary.

'Stay there,' she shouted. 'Don't come any closer.' The spaniel darted towards her and knocked her aside as he continued onward. He skittered across the courtyard, then jumped through the billowing smoke and into the burning building.

Mawde screamed. 'No, Hero!' Her desperate cries went unheeded. She called and called, pleading for him to come back to her. His frenzied barking pierced the air, a blood-curdling howl, and then the barking stopped.

Mawde's whole body trembled as she dragged her gaze away from the fire. Blinded by tears, she ran along the dirt track, stumbling over stones and ruts in her desperation to find help. She heard voices in the distance and quickened her pace.

'Hurry!' she yelled, drying her eyes on her sleeves. 'The house is on fire!'

A small crowd advanced over the brow of the hill. Aunt Mary and Uncle William, Cousin Henry and two farmhands. Aunt Mary drew Mawde towards her, enveloping her in a tight embrace. 'We were in the top field with the cows and saw the smoke in the distance.' she said. 'What happened? Are you hurt?'

'No. Not me, but Grandmother…' Mawde's words gave way to sobs as a wretched guilt consumed her. She should have dragged the old woman to safety.

Aunt Mary released Mawde from her embrace. 'Where's your mamm?'

'At the market. She sent me home to get combs.'

'Find her!' Aunt Mary's voice was taut with panic. 'Hurry!'

Mawde ran back to the village, careering down the hill while thoughts tangled in her head. She threw herself at Mamm, shedding huge tears for Hero and trembling with regret.

'Mawde? What is it? What's wrong?' Mamm held Mawde at arm's length. 'I smell smoke on your coif!'

Mawde blurted the news about the fire. Abandoning the unsold eggs, mother and daughter hurried home to find her uncle and cousins staring at the ruin of their house, and the charred remains of Grandmother partially covered by a farmhand's jerkin.

Aunt Mary was on her knees, rocking back and forth with her face in her hands. Mamm knelt beside her, shedding tears of her own for their deceased mother. Mawde sat a little apart from them, eyes fixed on her grandmother's smouldering shoes, and grieved for Hero.

At last, Mawde staggered to her feet. As she shook dust from her skirt, she spotted Mamm struggling to support Aunt Mary's weight as they progressed along the lane, heading towards the farm. Mawde hurried to catch up with them. Mamm's whispered words of comfort did nothing to ease Aunt Mary's pain. Aunt Mary's moans grew louder, her sobbing more intense.

'Mamm, what can we do for her?'

'Nothing will take Aunt Mary's pain away.' She glanced back towards the house and lowered her voice to a whisper. 'She sent Tamsin to sit with Grandmother. Tamsin died in the fire.'

Mawde recalled the shrill scream and her grandmother's plea for help. No wonder Hero leapt into the fire – he went inside for Tamsin.

Mawde's stomach lurched, her legs buckled. And then she was falling.

CHAPTER ELEVEN

JULY 1524

THE BELL TOLLED for the last time and faded to silence. Mourners processed through the churchyard towards the lychgate, leaving Mawde alone by the graveside. She withdrew to the shade of an oak tree and stood with her back pressed against its gnarled trunk. A band of gravediggers eyed her uncertainly, then advanced towards the gaping hole in the ground, shovels at the ready.

Soil arced through the air, each shovelful landing with a "thwump" on the shrouded bodies of Tamsin and Grandmother. The diggers paused their work to exchange a few words. A quip triggered raucous laughter and a round or two of back-slapping. Mawde clenched her fists so hard a fingernail ripped the skin of her palm. She turned her back towards the diggers and followed a well-worn path to the nearby creek. She picked up a jagged fragment of rock and launched it into the water. Ripples radiated out in perfect rings and then diminished to nothing. Mawde dropped to her knees, grimacing as sharp stones pressed through her skirts and pricked her shins.

'Why did you have to take Tamsin?' she yelled at the vast and cloudless sky. 'Was it to punish me?'

She closed her eyes and pictured the charred ruin of her home. Everything had been destroyed by the fire – clothes, furniture and a few of her father's carvings that had been stowed inside a trunk. Even the cooking pots were blackened and warped beyond redemption. Fortunately, Aunt Mary and Uncle William had welcomed them to the farmhouse, where they all crammed together and shared each other's grief.

An urgent flapping of wings drew Mawde's attention. She stared towards a clump of trees that were hunched over, the tips of their branches teasing the surface of the creek water. A large crow flew out from the shadows, the beat of its wings stirring a draught.

Mawde shuddered. She scrambled to her feet and stomped along the beach, staring towards the church while shielding her eyes against the glare of the midday sun. She burst through the door and strode angrily towards the altar. 'YOU SHOULD NOT HAVE TAKEN TAMSIN!' She crumpled to the floor and curled into a ball, pressing her tear-stained cheek against the chill of a large flagstone.

'Don't cry, Mawde. What's done is done and can't be changed. It's time to lay your grief aside and live the best life you can.'

Mawde felt a gentle pressure on each arm as her companion helped her to stand. Mawde dried her eyes and took deep breaths, then turned to thank the person who had shown her such kindness.

The aisle and pews were empty.

Mawde was alone.

CHAPTER TWELVE

AUGUST 1524

As the weeks slipped by, Mawde settled into life on the farm. She loved rising early to help Uncle William and her cousins milk the cows, and then spending the rest of the day in the laundry or baking with her aunt. At first, it was difficult with every person grieving, but stifled sobs and tearful sniffs were gradually replaced with exchanges of happy anecdotes and sharing fond memories.

'Tamsin never did master the art of neat crimping,' said Aunt Mary, watching Mawde seal the pastry lid for a pork and apple pie. 'You have a knack for it. Your fingers work so quickly, it's as if they move of their own accord.' Aunt Mary broke off a chunk from a large ball of raw pastry and started rolling the lid for another pie.

Hoofbeats clattered in the yard.

'That'll be Thomas!' Aunt Mary wiped flour off her hands. 'Come, Margery. Our brother deserves a warm welcome.'

Mawde glimpsed a flicker of apprehension on Mamm's face.

'I had no idea you were expecting him, Mary. What a

wonderful surprise!' Mamm lifted a pot of simmering fruit away from the heat of the cooking fire and followed Aunt Mary into the bright August sunshine. She dashed forward to greet her brother as he slid down from his saddle.

Mawde lingered in the shadows of the doorway. She had a vague recollection of a visit from her uncle several years ago, but the man embracing her mother did not fit with the faded image of an arrogant young man who had been stifled by the lack of career opportunities in Roseland. Tall, immaculately dressed, and his dark beard neatly trimmed, this man radiated an aura of sophistication and calm.

Aunt Mary beckoned to Mawde. 'Come and greet your Uncle Thomas.'

Mawde hesitated. Something about her mother's demeanour suggested all was not well.

Uncle Thomas removed his hat and blotted his sweat-dampened brow with the frilled cuff of a white linen sleeve. 'Does she ever speak?' He sounded concerned.

Mamm nodded. 'Sometimes.'

Uncle Thomas approached Mawde and looked her in the eyes. 'You've been through a difficult time, child.' He glanced over his shoulder towards his sisters and then returned his gaze to Mawde. 'I've come here today with an offer of help.'

Mawde wanted to reply, but words failed her. Instead, she kept her eyes fixed on his kind face, praying he could lift the weight of misery that pressed down on her.

'Perhaps we should talk indoors?' Uncle Thomas said, straightening to his full height. ''Tis roasting in the sunshine. Is there somewhere with shade where Nicholas can wait with the horses?'

'Of course.' Aunt Mary smiled at Uncle Thomas's companion. 'There are a couple of empty stalls in the stables and clean water for the animals. I'll fetch a cup of chilled ale for you.'

A youth, perhaps four or five years older than Mawde, was holding the reins of two horses. He was tall, neatly dressed in breeches, shirt and leather jerkin, and had a confident demeanour. He clicked his tongue and led the horses towards the stable block, keeping his eyes politely averted from the emotional family reunion.

Mawde followed the adults into the kitchen and shuddered at the harsh scraping of stools across flagstones.

'Sit beside me, Mawde.' Uncle Thomas gestured to an empty stool between him and Mamm.

Mawde's sense of foreboding worsened. She looked at her mother. Mamm dipped her head.

Uncle Thomas waited for Mawde to sit. 'We have an important matter to discuss, and it concerns you, Mawde.'

Her heartbeat quickened. She placed her hands on her lap and grimaced at her red swollen fingers, damaged by lye from long hours of work in the farmhouse laundry. They reminded her of Tamsin. It was as if she was wearing her dead cousin's skin as well as her clothes. A plump teardrop spilt on to Mawde's kirtle, staining the woollen cloth with a dark spot.

Uncle William entered the kitchen reeking of toil and muck. 'Thomas! 'Tis good to see you. I hope you didn't mind me sending word of our misfortunes, but I didn't know where else to turn.'

Mawde furrowed her brow. So, her uncle had requested Uncle Thomas's help. But why?

Mamm rested her hand on Mawde's arm and gave a gentle squeeze of reassurance.

'I'm glad you thought to write to me,' Uncle Thomas said. 'Sir William was sorry to hear of your plight and asked me to pass on his condolences.'

Aunt Mary murmured her appreciation. Mamm remained silent and still.

'He's a benevolent gentleman and sent this purse with his compliments.' Uncle Thomas deposited a leather pouch on the table, the jingle of coins unmistakable. 'I added what I could, but alas, with high rents in Exeter...' He threw Aunt Mary and Uncle William a look of sympathy. 'Sir William knows money can't replace departed loved ones, but it will help feed the extra mouths and provide much needed clothing.'

Uncle William nodded sadly. 'Please pass on our sincere gratitude.'

Uncle Thomas dipped his head. 'Of course. And I come with good news. Sir William's fortune is changing for the better as he rises in status at court. The timing of your letter was fortuitous because he has decided to employ more staff and offered a position to Mawde.' He smiled at Mamm. 'I accepted on your behalf.'

'No!' The colour drained from Mamm's face.

Mawde threw a grateful sidelong glance at her mother.

'It's a remarkable offer, Margery,' Uncle Thomas said kindly. 'Mawde won't get another opportunity to work at a grand house like Powderham, and I couldn't decline, especially after learning about what happened here.'

'But there's no need for Mawde to leave us. She's settled here and doing well with whatever task you ask of her, isn't she, Mary?'

Aunt Mary pinched her lips together and looked towards her husband.

'I'm sorry, Margery, but she can't stay here.' Uncle William sounded brusque. 'We've too many mouths to feed.'

'But Will, you need her in the laundry!'

'Mary will take over some of Mawde's laundry duties.'

Uncle William retrieved the purse from the table and weighed it in his hand. 'Even with this generous gift from Thomas and Sir William, we don't have the means to support all three of you, especially with Mary expecting another child.'

'But Powderham is so far away.' Mamm pulled Mawde into a tight embrace.

'Dearest sister, you know we'd keep Mawde here if circumstances were different.' Aunt Mary blotted tears from her own cheeks. 'The farm's not as prosperous as it was, and one more poor harvest could see us destitute.'

Tightening her arms around Mawde, Mamm addressed Uncle Thomas. 'Sir William is most generous. We graciously accept his kind offer.'

'No!' Mawde thrust Mamm's arms aside and jumped to her feet, sending her stool skimming across the flagstones.

Uncle Thomas grabbed her arm, stopping her from fleeing the room. ''Tis for the best, Mawde. It doesn't feel like it now, but one day you'll understand.' Loosening his grip, he added, 'Gather your things. We leave this afternoon.'

Mawde thundered up the stairs and threw herself onto the pallet that had been Tamsin's. She buried her face in the crook of her elbow and sobbed. A hand rested on her back, the pressure gentle and kind. Mawde turned her head to the side and peered through bloodshot eyes to see who offered her comfort. When she saw her mother kneeling beside her, Mawde sat up and threw her arms around Mamm's neck, pressing her face against the soft skin of her mother's neck.

'Aunt Mary found an old pair of breeches you can wear. Put them on under your kirtle and bunch up your skirts while you're on horseback.' Mamm drew Mawde in closer and kissed her damp cheeks. 'I'm sorry it's come to this.' A sob caught in her throat. 'I can't bear the thought of you leaving, but there's nothing I can do. God willing, this move to Powderham will turn out well for you and give you opportunities that don't exist here in Roseland. I'll miss you, Mawde, but you'll always be in my thoughts and prayers.'

In silence, they gathered Mawde's meagre belongings and tied them in a bundle – one spare shift, a comb that had been Tamsin's and a thin, threadbare shawl. Mawde squeezed the pocket tied at her waist to check that the small carving of the Madonna and Child was still stowed inside.

'Mamm, will I ever see you again?' asked Mawde, her voice faltering.

'One day.' A sob caught in Mamm's throat. 'If we don't meet again in this life, we will in the next.'

'Do you have everything you need?'

'Yes.'

Uncle Thomas tilted Mawde's face towards him. Her eyes were sore, and her throat ached from crying, but she bravely met his gaze.

'You have my sympathy, Mawde. Your mother and Agnes too. But this is what we must do to secure a future for all of you.' He bent forward and cupped his hands in front of his knees. 'Put your foot here and grasp the saddle while I bump you up. You can ride with me.'

Nicholas gave Mawde a reassuring smile as she flopped over the saddle and struggled to heave herself upright. A cloying aroma of warm waxed leather filled her nostrils and made her retch. She lifted her head and drew slow deep breaths, willing the nausea to pass. Cows lowed in a nearby field. Chickens fussed and clucked between pecking at the ground in the yard. From the corner of her eye, Mawde saw her mother appear at the farmhouse door and raise her hand in a sad gesture of farewell.

Uncle Thomas clicked his tongue and flicked the reins, urging his horse to move forward. Mawde straightened in the saddle and stared straight ahead.

It was time to look to the future. Time to leave her troubled past behind.

PART TWO
POWDERHAM

CHAPTER THIRTEEN
AUGUST 1524

FINGERS OF MIST beckoned the ship through the water and engulfed it in a damp pall of grey. Mawde was familiar with the sea fog that often cloaked the Roseland peninsula, but this was different. Sinister. Her jaw muscles tensed. Her hands trembled. The soft swish of the hull cutting through the smooth estuary did little to calm her nerves. Land was close, she could sense it. Soon, she would start a new life in an unfamiliar environment, and she did not know what to expect. If only they could drop the anchors and linger on the river for a while.

'Almost there,' Nicholas said. 'Powderham's different to anything you've seen before.' His eyes seemed to dance as he watched Mawde for a reaction. 'Don't look scared. You'll settle soon enough.'

A gloomy shadow morphed into a small fishing boat. The skipper raised his hand to acknowledge the ship's master, then passed by without a second glance, his attention focused on reaching safer waters. Something was heading towards Mawde, the air shifting around it and creating a waft of dank river water. Her knees buckled, causing her to sink behind the gunwale. She was almost too afraid to look up. The shape expanded, then shot up skyward. A gull, shrieking as it faded into the gloom. Nicholas chuckled. He offered his hand to help Mawde back to her feet. His fingers felt warm despite the unseasonal chill of the morning.

Feeble rays of light split the mist, then wide fractures appeared and stretched into passageways through a maze of low clouds. August sunlight burned off the last of the haze and revealed a magnificent manor house. Tall towers stood sentinel to the main body of the building, their granite bricks glowing golden in the soft light of the dawn. A breath caught in Mawde's chest – there was glass at every window.

'Has the same effect on me every time I see it.' Uncle Thomas placed a reassuring hand on her shoulder. 'I think you'll be happy here, Mawde. It'll be strange at first, but you'll get used to it.'

A wherry drew alongside the ship. Mawde's stomach twisted. 'Will I see you again, Uncle Thomas?'

Her uncle's smile faded. 'I rarely come to Powderham. My home is in Exeter and my work for Sir William takes me far and wide.' His expression brightened. 'But if I do have cause to come here, I promise to seek you out.'

Crows cawed in the distance. The bark of a dog carried in the wind. Mawde had never felt so alone.

Sails were furled, and anchors dropped. Mawde climbed down into the wherry and settled nervously on a bench. Oars dipped in and out of the water, and all too soon, they reached land. Nicholas jumped ashore, then helped Mawde step up onto a small landing platform. She followed him up a set of steep stone steps and paused at a gateway to a magnificent rose garden. Bees hovered above fragrant pink blooms. Butterflies lingered on leaves, their wings spread open, basking in the sunlight. Mawde breathed through her nose, revelling in the sweet perfume of glorious summer blooms.

'Time for you to meet the people you'll be working with,' Uncle Thomas said, striding towards the guardroom.

Mawde followed her uncle through the main entrance to the house. When she entered the great hall, she came to an abrupt stop. Her eyes widened at the sight of servants scurrying about, some arranging trestles and boards and covering them with cloths, while others carried benches and lowered them into position. At one end of the hall, there was a table raised on a dais centred beneath a large coat of arms – three red spots on a gleaming golden background. Huge tapestries adorned the walls, the neat colourful stitches depicting hunting scenes and religious tableaux. A door opened at the far side of the hall. The aroma of meat juices wafted into the room. Mawde's stomach gurgled – she had not eaten since early the previous day when nerves destroyed her appetite.

A group of gentlemen were deep in conversation. The tallest participant smiled at Uncle Thomas and raised his hand to silence his companions. 'Thomas, you're back! An uneventful journey, I trust?'

Uncle Thomas bowed. 'It was, Sir William, thank you.' He placed his hand on the small of Mawde's back, urging her to step forward. 'This is Mawde, my niece. My family and I appreciate you for taking her into your household.' He gave Mawde a discrete prod, prompting her to lower herself to a curtsey. She peered up at Sir William, admiring the quality and elegance of his clothes. His russet breeches had vertical slashes to reveal wide streaks of shimmering copper beneath. His cream doublet was edged with russet cord and embroidered with leaves of green and auburn.

'The timing of her arrival is fortuitous.' Sir William's

booming voice echoed through the hall. He gestured for Mawde to rise. 'We lost a kitchen-hand to a fever last night so Cook can find a use for her.'

Mawde sensed several servants turn their heads to look at her. She lowered her gaze and scrutinised the rushes strewn across the flagstones. She wondered why they were loose and not woven like the matting she had grown accustomed to at home.

'In that case, I shall take my niece to the master cook right away.' Uncle Thomas bowed and backed away from Sir William.

Mawde bobbed another curtsey and followed her uncle across the hall. They passed a gentleman urinating in a corner, and the reason for the loose rushes became clear. Mawde smirked. Her mother would be appalled. At home and on the farm, they had used a pot and emptied it at the back of the house by the wall with no windows.

They passed through an arched doorway and into a large and noisy kitchen. Flames danced in a large open fire and the aroma of bread wafted from the open door of a brick oven. Sacks and barrels huddled against one wall, and shelves almost buckled under the weight of pots and jars. The intense aroma of roasted meat, baked fish and vegetables made Mawde's mouth water. There was a momentary hush as flustered members of the kitchen staff looked at the newcomer, then the hubbub returned as they continued about their business.

Mawde's optimism faded, and her tongue seemed to grow too large for her mouth. She struggled to swallow, and she feared she might faint. The kitchen was humid, and a thick blanket of air robbed her of breath. She felt small and vulnerable in a domain dominated by men who all reeked of sweat. She cast a nervous glance at her uncle, but he was watching a boy butcher a side of pig.

A short, stout man approached, his cheeks flushed, his apron speckled with a multitude of stains. 'Good day to you, Master Hygons. We haven't seen you here for a long while.'

'Sir William keeps me busy, Cook.'

Cook appraised Mawde as if sizing up an animal for slaughter. 'Who's this?'

Uncle Thomas looked at Mawde and smiled. 'My niece. Sir William thought she might be of use to you.'

'Did he, now? Well, I'll not turn down an extra pair of hands so make yourself useful.' Cook pointed to the far end of the main kitchen table where a young man was working a large ball of pastry. 'Start by helping Ambrose. I presume your mother taught you how to roll a decent pie lid?'

Mawde nodded, grateful that her first task at Powderham would be something familiar. Something she was good at.

Uncle Thomas stooped and whispered in her ear. 'Have courage, Mawde. Things will seem difficult at first, but they'll improve.' He gave her an encouraging smile before turning on his heels and marching out of the kitchen.

'Put this on.' Cook threw Mawde a tatty apron. 'It's seen better days, but it's all I can spare for now.' He eyed Mawde's small bundle of possessions. 'I expect the mistress will provide you with a set of clothes before long, and a new apron. Put your belongings in the scullery until you're shown to your sleeping quarters later.'

Mawde did as she was told and then stood beside Ambrose at the table. Too nervous to speak, she picked up a wooden roller and flattened the pastry, shaping it into a large disc. Her stomach growled. Ambrose chuckled.

'What's your name?' Cook asked.

'Mawde.'

'Speak up, girl.' Cook lifted a cauldron off its hook above the fire, puffing and wheezing as he struggled with its weight.

'Mawde,' she repeated, struggling to raise her voice above the clatter and din of the kitchen.

'Tell me, Mawde, how exactly did you end up here, in my kitchen?'

Mawde's chest ached with longing for the home she had lost and the family she had left behind. 'Our house burned down, and we had to move in with my aunt. My uncle told Sir William, and he offered for me to come and work here.'

A pimple-faced youth looked up from scraping scales from a fish. 'What did she say? I didn't understand a word of that.'

Ambrose looked at Mawde and smirked. 'Couldn't say for sure. Didn't sound like English.'

'I recognise the accent,' Cook said. 'Cornish, if I'm not mistaken?'

Mawde clamped her lips together and nodded.

'Well, let me give you some advice. The Cornish ain't been popular since the '97 uprising, so, if I were you, I'd lose all traces of that accent.'

'Yes, Cook.'

A young female servant breezed into the kitchen clutching an earthenware pitcher. Mawde smiled at her, relieved to see another female in the kitchen, but her relief was short-lived. Cook took the pitcher from the servant and sent her to gather herbs from the kitchen garden, depriving Mawde of an opportunity to make a friend. Mawde doubted she would ever settle in the male-domi-nated environment and wondered why Sir William had a kitchen full of men when at home the cooking was the responsibility of women.

The hours passed slowly. Six smartly dressed men appeared and lined up just inside the doorway. Cook clapped his hands to get everyone's attention. 'Time to get the food out. Mawde, help Ambrose load the platters and pass them to the servers. We'll eat in the kitchen a little later. With so many guests this afternoon, our place in the lower hall's been taken.'

Light-headed with hunger, Mawde marvelled at the quantity of food leaving the kitchen. Fragrant steam rose from bowls of pottage, and the aroma of herbs emanated from several varieties of fish. Her mouth watered as she imagined Sir William devouring slices of tart, followed by stewed fruits and lashings of custard. She wondered how much longer she would have to wait before the servants would take their turn to eat.

At last, it was time to clear the tables. Trenchers, plates and platters arrived back at the kitchen, and those bearing food were placed in the middle of the main table. Benches scraped as they were dragged out from beneath the table and the kitchen staff took their places, squashing together with grooms and housemaids.

Cook ladled pottage into wooden bowls and handed them out to be passed along the table. Perched at the end of a bench, Mawde was the last to receive her share. Expecting the contents to be cold and bland, she took a large sip. Flavours exploded in her mouth, catching her unawares. Her mother had used mint and rosemary to flavour watery offerings, but this pottage was different. It was thick and exotic, with a mysterious ingredient that gave it a tingly warmth. After sating her appetite with a large slice of fish, Mawde considered the food. It had more flavour than anything she had eaten before. Her thoughts drifted to her mother and Agnes, and she wondered what simple fare they would eat later that day.

Dishes were rapidly cleared away. Grooms and house-maids returned to their posts. Mawde kneaded one batch of dough after another, placing the worked dough close to the fire to prove. Ambrose baked the loaves, checking they were of even size before placing them in the bread oven. Mawde worked in silence, listening to the hum of chatter around her and repeating phrases in her mind. Desperate to be accepted, she was already working on losing her Cornish accent.

By the end of the day, Mawde's arms felt heavy and stiff, and her back ached. Exhausted, she followed a house-maid to the sleeping quarters on the top floor of the manor. The maid pointed to a battered truckle bed located beneath a small window. Mawde stowed her bundle of possessions under the mattress and stared through mottled glass at a dark sky speckled with stars.

CHAPTER FOURTEEN
AUGUST 1524

'ADAM! Put your shirt and jerkin on!' Cook struck the spit boy with a wooden spoon, leaving a vivid red welt across his shoulder.

Adam cowered beneath Cook's glare. 'S... sorry, Cook, but I'm melting! It's so hot.'

'You'll melt for real if pig fat spits on your skin.'

Alice, the only other female working in the kitchen, handed a shirt to Adam. He thrust his arm into a sleeve and scowled at Cook's back.

Mawde sympathised. Rivulets of sweat trickled down her neck and back. Her damp shift clung to her body and her scalp felt hot beneath her coif. She envied the kitchen cat stretched out on the windowsill. It was more interested in catching a thin whisper of draught to ruffle its fur than catching a small rat feasting on food debris on the kitchen floor. A hound wandered in from the stable yard, drooling over the aroma of roasting meat, but chose not to linger, preferring the sun-baked cobbles outdoors to the suffocating heat of the kitchen.

'Tell us about where you're from,' Ambrose said, touching Mawde's forearm.

Mawde pushed his hand away and resumed kneading.

'Is Cornwall as different to Devon as they say?'

Mawde held her silence.

'Come on, Mawde, you can't keep this up forever,' persisted Ambrose. 'You've barely uttered a word since you arrived.'

Mawde kept her eyes lowered. She had been paying close attention to the way the other servants spoke, trying to pick out their favourite words and phrases and practising them silently in her head. She wasn't ready to try them aloud. She needed to be confident that when she did speak, they would have no reason to mock her accent.

Alice pressed her hands to the tabletop and leaned over towards Mawde. 'We don't mean no harm, Mawde. It's rare to meet someone from Cornwall and we can't help ourselves. Go on, tell us about yourself and where you're from.'

Mawde concentrated on shaping a ball of dough.

'Wasting your breath talking to that one,' John said. He was the pimple-faced youth who had been the first to tease Mawde the day she arrived. 'Don't know what Sir William was thinking by letting her come here. With any luck, she'll be on her way back to Cornwall before the month's out, taking her awful stench with her.'

Mawde tensed. She knew her clothes were stinking. She had changed her shift the day after she arrived, but the linen was already soiled and in need of changing. The woollen fabric of her kirtle gave off a pungent scent, a mix of stale cooking odours, wood smoke and sweat. It desperately needed airing and sweetening with herbs. Mawde's reluctance to speak had prevented her from enquiring about laundry arrangements. The maids who shared her sleeping quarters had no linens airing in the room, and she wondered where they took their clothes to wash them and lay them out to dry. Mawde longed for her mother and the sweet scents of Roseland – gorse, sea breezes, meadow flowers and the fresh aroma of shirts and shifts blown dry in the courtyard. She could almost smell the sawn oak that had fragranced her father's workshop, and his musky, woody scent after a long day's work. She took a deep breath and swallowed hard, trying to dismiss memories of home.

Alice signalled something to John. He looked at Mawde, then snorted with laughter.

'Enough! Get back to work, all of you. Sir William's guests will soon be here.'

Mawde met Cook's gaze and gave him a grateful smile. He scowled at her in return, shaking his head, forcing her to retreat into a lonely silence.

Mawde devoured a bowlful of flavoursome stew and soaked up the remaining drops with a hunk of bread, leaving no trace of the gravy that Cook had infused with spices and wine.

'Poor little wench,' a groom said. 'Has Cook not been feeding you?'

Laughter rippled along the benches.

'She's from Cornwall,' John said. 'Lost her tongue when she crossed into Devon.'

'Probably swallowed it with the rest of her dinner.' Alice pretended to gobble her food and choke, much to the delight of the grooms and maids huddled at one end of the table. 'Have you seen the way she eats? Stuffs food in her mouth like she thinks someone's going to steal it from her.'

Mawde looked along the table, seeking a friendly face. Not one. She was a stranger lost in a crowd. She struggled out from her position on the bench and passed through the kitchen and into the stable yard. The sun had passed its zenith, leaving a corner of shade between the house and a wall. Mawde leaned against the relative cool of the stones. A horse whinnied in a stable, as if sympathising with her plight. Mawde's tension eased a little.

'The longer you stay out here, the harder it'll be to come back inside, and I don't mean because of the heat from the kitchen fires.' Cook loomed in front of her. He stood with his feet apart and hands on hips. 'I know you're barely more than a child, but you're old enough to stand up to the other servants. Take my advice and don't let them get to you, or they'll make your life hell.' Cook cocked his head to one side and waited for Mawde to respond. 'Well?'

A sudden sharp pain gripped Mawde across her chest. She bent forward and pressed her hands against her breastbone, trying to massage the pain away. She felt nauseous and light-headed.

'Indigestion, I'll wager,' Cook said. 'You devoured that food like you hadn't eaten for weeks. I'll give you a couple of mint leaves to chew on. They'll soon set you right. Come on, back to work.'

Cook's tone was sharp, but his words hinted at kindness. He turned and strode back into the kitchen with Mawde following in his wake. Conscious of the other servants watching her, she lifted her head and absorbed every stare with a boldness she did not feel. She piled platters and plates ready for cleaning, then stood to one side to await Cook's orders.

By dusk, Mawde and Ambrose had baked more than enough bread for the following day. Ambrose started pickling vegetables but had no need of Mawde's help. Everyone but Mawde had something to do. She found a broom and started sweeping the kitchen floor.

'Don't do that while we're preparing food. You'll get muck in the pastry.' Cook snatched the broom from Mawde's hands. 'Go to the pantry. Wipe the shelves, check for spoiled food and scrub the floor. That should keep you busy for a while.'

The pantry was a welcome respite from the kitchen. The air was cool, the solitude a relief. With the shelves soon cleaned and tidied, Mawde scrubbed hard at the flagstones, watching them change colour as she erased footprints that had accumulated over several months. Reluctantly, she rinsed her scrubbing brush and pail and set them outside to dry in the warm night air before she returned to the heat of the kitchen.

Mawde was kneading bread dough when Lady Courtenay entered the kitchen.

'Sir William has one of his headaches and won't let me send for the apothecary. He's growing more irritable by the hour, and I fear he'll say something to upset a guest.'

Lady Courtenay sounded distraught.

'I'll have Alice prepare a poultice, my lady,' Cook said, in a soothing voice.

'No, Hugh, that won't do at all! Sir William will not want his guests to see him press a cloth to his head.'

'A small bunch of lavender then, placed on his lap to allow the fragrance to rise to his nostrils.'

'He won't countenance that, either.'

Mawde wiped her hands on her apron and approached Lady Courtenay. 'My grandmother used to make tisanes of feverfew and rosemary for maladies of the head,' she said, eager to help her mistress.

Lady Courtenay raised her eyebrows. 'Did she?' She scrutinised Mawde's face. 'I don't recall seeing you before.'

Mawde averted her eyes, knowing she had spoken out of turn. Her grandmother would have ordered a beating for such insolence.

Cook waddled across the kitchen, semi-bowing as he approached Lady Courtenay. 'Forgive her rudeness, my lady, but she's new and hasn't yet learnt her place.'

Mawde's bottom lip quivered. She knew a tisane of feverfew would ease Sir William's discomfort. It would be wrong to keep such information to herself, especially as Lady Courtenay had not had a specific remedy in mind.

'Sorry, my lady.' She articulated her words carefully, fearful that Lady Courtenay might not understand her accent. 'I was trying to be helpful, and I didn't mean any harm.'

Lady Courtenay placed an elegant finger under Mawde's chin, forcing her to look up and meet her gaze. 'I'm sure you didn't.' Her green eyes twinkled with merriment. 'Tell me more about your grandmother. Is she very knowledgeable about remedies for ailments?'

When Lady Courtenay removed her finger, Mawde's gaze drifted downward. She studied the exquisite detailing of Lady Courtenay's over-gown. Flowers worked in yellow thread framed the opening of a moss green robe where it revealed a sage coloured jacquard kirtle beneath. It was the most decadent dress Mawde had ever seen.

'My grandmother died, my lady. But she always knew which herbs were best for a wound poultice, or to put in a tisane to ease a pain. Everyone in the village trusted her advice, and many said she was better than any apothecary.'

Lady Courtenay looked surprised. 'And which village would that be?'

'St Mawes, my lady. It's in Roseland.'

'I'm not familiar with that village, nor an area named Roseland.'

'It's in Cornwall, my lady. I'm not from this area.'

'I suspected as much from your accent.'

Mawde clenched her fingers. 'I know my words can be difficult to understand, but I'm trying to lose my accent.'

'Oh no! You mustn't do that.' Lady Courtenay shook her head. 'We should never be ashamed of where we come from, no matter who we are.'

'But the rebellion, my lady, and then supporting the usurper! People hate the Cornish because of those things.'

'Nonsense! Those events happened nigh on thirty years ago and few people here are old enough to remember them. Shame on anyone who holds a grudge against you for that.'

Mawde sensed a shift of atmosphere in the kitchen. She caught Ambrose and Alice exchange odd glances, both looking unhappy at the attention Mawde was attracting from Lady Courtenay.

'I'm not from this area either,' Lady Courtenay continued. 'So, you and I have something in common. Tell me, what is your name?'

'Mawde, my lady.'

'Well then, Mawde of Roseland, it's my pleasure to welcome you to Powderham.' She looked at Mawde's tatty clothing and frowned. 'I'll have a kirtle sent down to you and order new aprons. Tell me, do you know your grandmother's recipe for the tisane you mentioned?'

Mawde nodded eagerly. 'Yes, my lady. I used to help her make it.'

'Excellent. Prepare a cup for my husband and send it up to the solar as soon as it's ready. I'll send word to my husband that I need a private word and encourage him to drink it before he returns to his guests.'

Mawde bobbed a curtsey and set about finding a small pan to boil water. When Lady Courtenay left the kitchen, Cook marched over to Mawde and cuffed her across the ear.

'How dare you embarrass me in front of the mistress! Do not speak to her again unless she speaks to you first.'

Mawde cupped her palm over her stinging ear and stared wide-eyed at Cook. His face was puce, and his nose was twitching. 'But I knew I could help, and she seemed pleased with what I said!'

Cook struck her again. Mawde shrank away from him, afraid he might lash out a third time.

'You say nothing for days and when you do open your mouth, it's humiliating. Mistress will think me incapable of controlling my staff. Get out of here! Fetch the herbs you need for Sir William's cure and be quick about it.'

Mawde snatched up a trug and hurried outside, eager to leave the hostile atmosphere of the kitchen. She stood in the courtyard and took a moment to appraise her surroundings. On the opposite side of the courtyard there was a gated archway between two stables, and another set in the wall to her right. Choosing the one on the right, she was relieved to find a path leading to a kitchen garden. She slowed her pace when the herb beds came into view and inhaled the perfumes rising from sun-kissed plants and flowers. The atmosphere in the garden was calming and peaceful. Birds sang out from hidden branches, and a garden maid was singing while doubled over weeding, her voice rising and falling in a melancholic song.

With sufficient herbs laid out in the trug, Mawde steeled herself to return to the kitchen. With each step towards the house, she grew more determined to feel at ease at Powderham and to thrive as a valued member of staff. She would become a favourite of Lady Courtenay's, and the envy of every servant in the house.

CHAPTER FIFTEEN

AUGUST 1524

'Sir William feels better, Mawde, but I'd like him to have more tisane to be sure the headache won't worsen again.'

'Yes, my lady.' Mawde curtseyed. 'I'll see to it as soon as I've finished working this batch of dough.'

'You'll see to it right away, girl!' Cook softened his tone. 'Apologies, my lady. Mawde should know better than to keep you waiting. I'll see she learns the error of her ways.'

Mawde removed her apron and folded it neatly.

Lady Courtenay smiled at Mawde. 'You'll have two kirtles and two new shifts within the next few days. And I've ordered new aprons for everyone. Be sure to stitch your initials so you know which shifts are yours when Goodwife Doddes returns the clean clothes. I expect the girls have already told you about our laundress's twice-weekly visits?'

They had not.

'Yes, my lady,' Mawde replied, relieved she would soon enjoy a set of fresh clean clothes.

Lady Courtenay turned towards Cook. 'Don't be hard on her, Hugh. It takes time to adjust to new surroundings.

The poor girl is so far from her family that she won't even be able to visit during a half-day holiday.'

Mawde gave her a grateful smile and excused herself to collect fresh rosemary for the tisane.

The kitchen garden was a hive of activity. Maids were cutting back herbs to encourage new growth while men pulled carrots and onions from the ground. In an adjacent orchard, a fruit harvest was underway, the pickers gathering an abundance of plums and cherries for pies, sauces and jams. The maids shared snippets of gossip, while the gardeners exchanged news and opinions. Mawde envied their camaraderie – it was a contrast to the daily sniping that took place in the heat of the kitchen. She considered asking for a transfer to the gardening team but dismissed the idea when she realised it would distance her from Lady Courtenay. After helping herself to sprigs of rosemary, lavender and feverfew, she cast her eyes along the herb beds. A clump of taller, unfamiliar plants caught her attention. Small white flowers nestled in loose clusters and the leaves had neatly scalloped edges. Mawde rubbed a leaf between her finger and thumb, then inhaled the scent on her skin. It was light, fresh and fragrant. Sweet balm. They had not grown it at home, but Grandmother had used it now and again to make a brew to ease a fever. Mawde was certain her grandmother had used it to treat headaches, too. Deciding the sweet balm would make the tisane more palatable, Mawde added a couple of sprigs to her collection.

The sun was high in the sky, warning Mawde not to linger among the herb beds. The kitchen was approaching its busiest time of day, with all members of the kitchen staff finishing the dinner preparations. Mawde ran back to the courtyard, lifting her skirt to prevent it from tangling around her legs. As she passed through the archway and into the courtyard, she slowed to a brisk walk.

A high-pitched screech came from behind, the sound wretched and desperate. Mawde froze. She had heard the sound before, a few times at dawn and once late in the evening, but had been too shy to ask what it was. Another screech echoed through the courtyard, its source sounding closer this time. Mawde whirled around and dropped the trug, scattering herbs over the dusty cobbles. A strange looking bird strutted towards her, its neck and chest feathers glowing iridescent blue, and dragging a long tail across the dirt. The bird stretched its neck forward and bowed its head, then raised its tail from the ground and opened it into a large fan. As the creature drew closer, the blue-green circles on the tail feathers evolved into a quivering wall of eyes. Mawde's hands turned clammy, her mouth dry. Backing away, she reached for the trug and scrabbled around in the dirt to retrieve the spilt herbs. The bird continued its menacing advance, jabbing its head forward as if eager to peck her with its pointed beak. Mawde turned to run into the house, colliding with Ambrose as she burst through the kitchen door.

Alice had everyone's attention. 'You should've seen her.' She snorted with amusement, tears streaming down her cheeks. 'Her arms flew up like this as if she might try to fly away.'

Raucous laughter echoed through the kitchen while Alice imitated Mawde's shock at seeing the bird. Encouraged by John's tears of amusement, Alice continued. 'White as snow, she was. Anyone would think she'd never seen a peacock before.'

A portly woman from the village, who had recently taken over as the brewer after her husband died, raised a hand to her mouth and stifled a giggle. Cook rolled his eyes.

'I hadn't seen one before.' Mawde kept her tone even, determined to keep an air of dignity. 'There aren't any peacocks where I'm from.'

'Better get used to them,' Ambrose said. 'Sir William likes them served up at banquets. Unusual to get one in the courtyard, though. Rose garden's more their scene.'

Cook slapped his hand on the table. 'Enough chatter. Mawde, prepare that tisane as fast as you can.'

Mawde carried a small cauldron of water to the fire. As she lifted it towards a hook, Alice snuck up behind her and screeched in her ear. Mawde stumbled sideways, dropping the cauldron and striking her head against the edge of the table. Everyone laughed. Cook helped Mawde back onto her feet and retrieved the cauldron. Ambrose spared her a brief glance of sympathy before rushing out of the kitchen with a silver salver loaded with vegetables. Everyone else filed out after him, ready to take their seats at the lower end of the hall.

Mawde refilled the cauldron and set it over the fire. Alone in the kitchen, she sat at the table, her hot angry tears landing in divots and scratches on the oak tabletop. She reached for a pitcher filled with ale intended for the staff to drink with their dinner and allowed droplets of her misery to fall inside.

'If you insist on upsetting me, you can share my distress,' she muttered to herself. She pushed the ewer towards the end of the table favoured by those meanest to her. Annoyed with herself for crying, she dried her eyes and went into the courtyard to find the peacock. By the time she found him, her fear of his plumage had given way to admiration. 'I want to be like you,' she said. 'Proud to be here and worthy of my place. I need to impress the people who matter most, and with something more accomplished than boiling herbs for a tisane. I'll think of something. You just watch me.'

By the time the servants returned from the hall with empty trays and platters, Mawde was pouring the herbal drink into a pewter cup. She walked out of the kitchen, and with confident steps, she carried the tisane to the top table and curtseyed. Encouraged by a nod from Lady Courtenay, she stepped forward and offered the cup to a grateful Sir William.

CHAPTER SIXTEEN

MAY 1526

'Oh, Hugh, the subtleties at court were breathtaking.'
Lady Courtenay's voice fizzed with excitement. 'Marchpane castles, garlands of flowers, woodland scenes. They
even had a palace crafted from sugar. Sugar! Imagine that!
No wonder Sir William was reluctant for me to attend. He
knew I'd come home and insist we recreate them here, at
Powderham.'

Cook blanched. 'Forgive me, my lady, but that's
impossible.'

'Nonsense. Nothing's impossible. You're the best cook
in the county.'

'But I'm no confectioner. His Majesty will have people
in his kitchens who do nothing other than make such
things. And we have very little sugar. Certainly not enough
for making palaces and castles.'

'Oh yes, we do!' Lady Courtenay's sing-song voice
sounded triumphant. 'I don't expect you to make grand
sculptures, but please, Hugh, have a go at something small
for our table.'

Mawde could see Cook squirming and revelled in his unease. The teasing had continued unabated since her arrival, and he had done little to quash it. He had even encouraged it at times.

'My lady, forgive me, but I don't know how to go about such a thing. Marchpane turned into castles and forests?' Cook lowered his head in a gesture of defeat.

'I made a few notes and sketches of the confections produced at court. Imagine our guests' reactions if we have table decorations as grand as those created at a royal palace! You'll make excellent work of it using my notes as a guide.'

Cook's Adam's apple bobbed up and down. 'You forget, my lady, that I'm unable to read.'

Mawde added chopped sorrel to a pot and stirred the simmering green sauce that would accompany the main fish course. Ideas tumbled through her mind. This was an opportunity too good to waste. She looked over her shoulder towards Cook and Lady Courtenay. 'Forgive me if I'm speaking out of turn, my lady, but I'm willing to make the decorations you've described.'

Lady Courtenay beamed.

Cook was in a fluster. 'You can't read either!' A moment's hesitation. 'Can you?'

Mawde shook her head. 'Alas, I cannot, although it is my ambition to learn one day.' She approached Lady Courtenay, keeping her gaze lowered as a sign of respect. 'Perhaps my lady would read the instructions to me? I believe we'd be able to create something remarkable if we work it out together.'

Cook spluttered. Ambrose dropped his knife.

'How dare you suggest Lady Courtenay should work in this kitchen with a servant! And anyway, I can't spare you to waste time playing with sugar.'

Lady Courtenay was unperturbed. 'Nonsense, Hugh.' With a glint in her eye, she added, 'We have no guests due for a day or two, and I rather fancy seeing what Mawde can do.'

'As you wish, my lady.' Cook returned to his worktable with heavy shuffling steps.

Mawde wanted to embrace her mistress. With Lady Courtenay in the kitchen, there would be no hostility from the other servants for at least two days. 'Thank you, my lady. You won't regret it.'

'I believe I shall enjoy it! I'll sketch a few more designs, then we'll choose which to try first. Meanwhile, I'll have a groom find the sugar and almonds that we brought home with us.'

With a swish of her skirts, Lady Courtenay left the kitchen. Mawde stared after her and smiled.

'You needn't look so smug,' Cook said. 'Make a batch of pastry for mutton pies.'

'Yes, Cook,' Mawde replied sweetly, gliding towards the larder and ignoring hostile glares from Ambrose, John and Alice.

'Don't just stand there gawping.' Cook wore an unpleasant smile. 'Now you see why I wanted nothing to do with it. It's not the easy option you thought it would be, is it?'

Mawde lifted a heavy cone of sugar and turned it over in her hands. 'What do I do with it?'

'Break it into pieces and grind it. There are three more when you're done with that one.'

Mawde tried to slice off the tip of the cone with a knife, but the cone was too hard and the blade slipped, sending the cone skidding across the table. Embarrassed, she retrieved it and tried slicing slivers from the sides instead. Small fragments broke away, but progress was slow. Mawde's hands grew hot and sweaty. Fragments of sugar stuck to her fingers and turned sticky. It was a struggle to grip the knife handle. Soon, Mawde's skin was sore and blistered. She wiped her hands on her apron and blew on her inflamed fingertips to cool them, but the skin burned with searing pain as soon as she applied pressure to the knife.

By late afternoon, Mawde had a meagre pile of sugary slivers. Her fingers were clawed from gripping tightly and protested at any attempt to straighten them. Blisters oozed on her palms.

'Should have used this to break up the cone.' John pulled a small iron pickaxe from a pocket concealed beneath his apron. 'Would've been easier than scraping with a knife. Quicker, too. It's what we've always used in the past when we've had to prepare sugar. Surprised you didn't ask for it.'

'Wouldn't have been as fun to watch, though,' Alice said.

Mawde stared through the mullioned window. She couldn't recall ever seeing a sugar cone before. In fact, they'd rarely used sugar at Powderham all the time she had been there. 'I'll bear it in mind for next time,' she said, keeping her voice calm. Months ago, John's actions would have upset her. Not anymore.

'You'll be needing this now,' said Cook, sliding a large pestle and mortar across the table.

Mawde scooped shards of sugar into the bowl, then grasped the handle of the pestle and started grinding. The handle agitated the blisters on her hands. Blood seeped into the woodgrain.

'Stop!' A flash of remorse passed across Cook's face.

His tone softened. 'Let me see to your hands before you do any more damage.' He bound linen strips around Mawde's hands with a tenderness he had never shown before. 'It'll seem awkward at first, but you'll get used to it.'

The work was laborious and painful. Tiny stones and pieces of grit hampered progress, chafing against the grinding surface of the pestle. Mawde persevered. She pounded and scraped at the sugar, picking out pieces of dirt and debris. By suppertime, her hands and wrists were throbbing. She still could not straighten her fingers, and the bindings had stiffened with sugar and blood. Mawde winced and yelped when Cook peeled them away and applied clean linen strips.

Darkness fell. All kitchen tasks for the day had been completed, but Mawde continued grinding sugar. Cook, Ambrose, John and Alice perched on stools and watched, unable to conceal their respect for Mawde's determination.

'You've done well,' said Cook. 'Now, the sugar needs cleaning, but you won't be doing that. First thing tomorrow morning, John will boil all of this in water for you.'

'Why me?' asked John, looking indignant.

Cook's raised eyebrow prevented John from protesting further.

Mawde stared at the ground sugar. 'I didn't know it would be as difficult as that.'

'The more you do it, the faster you'll get. And you will do more of it. I've worked for Lady Courtenay for several years now and I can tell you now, this won't be a one-off. You can go now, Mawde. The rest of us will clean up for you.'

Mawde removed her apron and took slow steps towards the door. Her legs were heavy with fatigue after so many hours standing at the kitchen table.

'Mawde?'

She turned. 'Yes, Cook?'

'You're a hard worker. Don't think I haven't noticed.'

Mawde dragged herself up the stairs and stretched out on her truckle bed. A few minutes later, she was enjoying the sweetest of sleeps.

CHAPTER SEVENTEEN

MAY 1526

IT WAS A BALMY EVENING.

Mawde sat on a stone bench in the shade of a pear tree, watching gardeners tidy away their tools. A blackbird called from the boundary wall, his sweet chirrups accompanying the rustle of leaves in a gentle breeze. Mawde closed her eyes, relishing her solitude in a tranquil corner of the orchard. For the first time since leaving Roseland, she felt contented. Cook had shown his sympathetic side by tending to her wounds and applying a salve, then wrapped her hands in a fresh batch of bandages. John spent the morning boiling and cleaning the sugar, and Cook persuaded Lady Courtenay to postpone her confectionery plans for one more day to allow Mawde's skin to heal.

Tolerating unkind stares from Ambrose, John and Alice, Mawde had completed the less arduous tasks of tidying shelves and gathering herbs for dinner. When all the dishes and platters were cleared away, Cook had banished Mawde from the kitchen and sent her to the steward in the great hall to offer her services there. She then spent a pleasant afternoon checking table linens, picking out those that needed replacing from those that might be repaired with a few discrete stitches.

Her work finished for the day, Mawde allowed her thoughts to drift to happier times – memories of helping her mother, Sunday afternoons with Tamsin, and watching her father turning wood in his workshop. She smiled at memories of scrambling across cornfields, chasing after Tamsin when they were supposed to be foraging for food. A bolt of sadness struck her in the chest and knocked her breath away. If Grandmother had not been such a bully, Mawde might have felt compelled to rescue the old woman, and then she would have known that Tamsin was trapped inside. God curse the old woman's soul! Mawde might have saved them both. Somehow, she would return to Roseland and make amends for that one poor decision. But first, she had to get there.

A sudden movement caught her eye. She squinted against the rays of the late evening sun, trying to see what had dashed from one tree to another. A girl emerged, moving backwards with small steps. She stepped into a pool of sunlight and sat on the grass, one arm outstretched and fingertips grazing the ground. A squirrel approached, hesitant at first, then boldly nibbled at something balanced on the girl's palm. Mawde was captivated. Tendrils of orange-red hair escaped from beneath the girl's cap and gleamed like polished copper in the sunlight. Her stature suggested she was similar in age to herself, perhaps a little younger, and Mawde wondered why she had never seen her before.

Twigs snapped in the distance. The squirrel raised his head, then scampered away and scaled the trunk of a tree to the safety of a hiding place beneath a canopy of leaves. Mawde rose from the bench, eager to introduce herself.

The young girl turned as Mawde approached and scrambled to her feet.

'Don't go!' Mawde said, quickening her pace.

But it was too late. A flash of orange-red left through a small side gate.

Mawde rushed after her, emerging on to a narrow lane. She shielded her eyes and peered in both directions, straining her ears for the sound of retreating footsteps. Branches creaked. Crows cawed. But otherwise, the lane was quiet and Mawde was alone.

CHAPTER EIGHTEEN

MAY 1526

'CAN'T YOU WORK FASTER?' Lady Courtenay paced the length of the kitchen.

'I'm sorry, my lady, but we're doing our best.' Cook was flushed and wheezing as he pounded blanched almonds into a fine powder.

Mawde was vigorously whisking a sugar solution with egg whites. She carried the bowl across to Cook. He glanced inside and shook his head. Suppressing an urge to roll her eyes, Mawde resumed whisking.

'What's taking so long?' Lady Courtenay asked, peering over Cook's shoulder.

''Tis a lengthy process, my lady. We must get it right or it won't work. The sugar needs to be pure. The egg whites will set and draw out any remaining dirt. This afternoon, Mawde will skim the top and pass the sugar through a cloth. Then it will be clean enough to use. We'll pour it into shallow dishes to dry, then I'll grind it again and prepare a batch of marchpane. You'll create your first subtlety before the day is out, my lady.'

'We should start with something simple, Mawde. A

posy of flowers, perhaps?' Lady Courtenay's face dropped. 'But Mawde, your hands! Are they very sore?'

Mawde checked the dressings. They were clean. ''Tis just a few blisters, my lady, that's all. They've stopped weeping, so there's no reason why I shouldn't help you this afternoon.'

Lady Courtenay clapped her hands. 'Excellent! I'll fetch my sketches from the solar.'

Mawde frowned at the sketches. They were far more detailed than she had anticipated.

'Forgive me, my lady, but I fear these designs are complicated and too difficult for our first attempt at subtleties.'

Lady Courtenay pouted. 'Do you think so?' She spread the sheets of paper across a bench and peered at each one. 'We have to start with something.' She reached for a sheet covered with roses in different stages of bloom and tied with a trailing ribbon. 'I'm sure we can achieve something like this between us. We've nothing to lose by trying.'

The afternoon slipped by with Mawde and Lady Courtenay moulding marchpane. At first, Mawde was in awe of her mistress, almost overwhelmed by having Lady Courtenay so close that their skirts brushed against each other. But Lady Courtenay had a gentle disposition and was complimentary towards Mawde's first foray into marchpane sculpture. Mawde sensed the truculent glares of the kitchen men and revelled in their discomfort. They had to swallow their scorn while Lady Courtenay ruled their domain. A contented smile danced across Mawde's lips as she scored veins into leaves with the tip of a knife while Lady Courtenay twisted and pinched petals, assembling them into delicate flowers.

'I'd say that looks rather fine,' Lady Courtenay said, admiring a marchpane rosebud. She furrowed her brow. 'How will we bind them together to resemble the posy in my sketch?'

Mawde looked at the items spread across the workbench. There were three wooden bowls of varying size, a ball of unused marchpane and a pile of discarded cut-offs that could be re-rolled and used again. 'What if we drape a layer of marchpane over a bowl and secure the flowers in place with dress pins? We can cut a strip off marchpane and shape it into a ribbon as if it's flowing out from underneath. It would be as if we're looking down on a posy.' She met Lady Courtenay's gaze. 'I think it would look rather pretty.'

Lady Courtenay patted Mawde's arm. 'I like your creativity, Mawde. Yes, that will do nicely, but we should use a clean bowl.' She spun around and called to Cook. 'Hugh, find us something suitable, will you?' To Alice, she said, 'Fetch the box of dress pins from my chamber.'

Cook muttered something under his breath. Mawde stifled a chuckle. Cook reached up to lift a pewter dish from a shelf and handed it to Lady Courtenay. She passed it straight to Mawde.

'I'll give you the honour of assembling our creation. I'm sure you'll do a far better job than I ever could.'

Mawde turned the dish upside down and sprinkled it with ground sugar. Lady Courtenay rolled a layer of marchpane and placed it over the dish. Mawde pressed it into a dome shape and used the blunt edge of a knife to trim the excess from the rim.

When Alice returned with the pins, Mawde selected an open bloom and attempted to pin it to the centre of the upturned bowl. 'The pin doesn't go deep enough. We'll have to find something else to stop the marchpane collapsing under the weight of the flowers. Even a wooden bowl is no good. The pins won't pass through it.'

Mawde's gaze drifted to Cook. He was rolling a ball of pastry into a disc. 'Raw pastry would support the weight of the flowers and take the pins.'

Cook tutted. 'Waste of good pastry, if you ask me.'

Lady Courtenay seemed oblivious to Cook's irritation. 'You have plenty, Hugh. Spare us some, if you please.'

At last, the posy was finished, with each bloom carefully pinned in place.

'It's good,' Lady Courtenay said. 'But it's a little dull. From now on, we'll colour the marchpane and decorate the petals with gold leaf.'

'From now on?' Cook said, rolling his eyes.

Lady Courtenay ignored him. 'Tomorrow, Mawde, your subtlety will sit on a silver salver and lead in the dinner. It'll be a wonderful Whitsun surprise for Sir William. He'll love it, I know he will. And he'll want to see many more, especially when we entertain important guests. We'll be the talk of the county!' She clapped her hands to attract the attention of all members of the kitchen staff. 'After dinner tomorrow, you may all spend the afternoon as you please. Enjoy yourselves. I believe there will be dancing and cockfighting in Kenton.'

The atmosphere in the kitchen lifted and soon conversations took place about the pleasures they would enjoy the following day. Mawde waited for Lady Courtenay to leave the kitchen, then removed a few flowers she considered haphazardly placed. Taking care to position them precisely, she secured them with pins and stepped back to admire her work. The subtlety was now far more pleasing to the eye. Her father had been skilled with his hands, creative with his carpentry and wood carvings. Mawde was certain she had inherited his artistic ability, and she had found the perfect opportunity to use it.

She also knew that if Da was still alive, he would be very proud of his daughter.

CHAPTER NINETEEN

JULY 1527

SUMMER SUNSHINE TOASTED the cobbles in the courtyard, and roses bloomed with a heady perfume.

The heat in the Powderham kitchen was unbearable, and Cook's temper flared. He snatched an earthenware pot from a pile awaiting scrubbing and hurled it towards Mawde. It caught on the edge of the table and fractured into several large pieces.

'The grange is overflowing with guests, we've another feast to prepare, and you're telling me you're too busy to make pastry!'

Mawde retrieved the larger fragments from the flagstone floor. 'I'm sorry, Cook, but Lady Courtenay insisted I make a subtlety for dinner. Something to impress, she said. I've started it, but it'll take an age to finish, and I can't rush it.'

Cook flicked his hand. 'Get on with it, then. And it had better be spectacular for all the time it's taking.' He shook his head. 'God's blood, the sooner that woman goes into confinement, the better. She invites an ever-increasing number of guests, but the kitchen gets no bigger and I've no extra staff. We've barely enough space to prepare one course for a banquet, let alone all of them.'

Two housemaids skulked at one corner of the large kitchen table, commandeered to help with basic preparations. While they peeled and sliced vegetables, pitted cherries and squeezed strawberries into a purée, Adam skulked by the spit, turning a large roasting boar. The brewer was instructing three grooms on the fastest way to pluck a small mountain of chickens, having been told they would help her in the brewery once their task was complete. Ambrose sweated beside the bread oven, removing a large batch of fragrant loaves before filling it with another. Alice was moaning in the scullery where she was cleaning up after the butchers in their cramped temporary location.

Mawde retreated to a small space in the corner of the kitchen, a protected area for her sugar work. Lady Courtenay had lost interest in working on the creations herself but had persuaded her husband – and by default, Cook – that the kitchen should have a section dedicated to making confectionery. Despite the cramped working conditions, Mawde was thankful for a role she enjoyed. While perfecting her artistry, her thoughts wandered at will. She imagined her father nodding and smiling at her artistic creations as she incorporated patterns from his old woodwork samples into marchpane wreaths and wheels. She dreamed of making a name for herself, perhaps even opening a small shop in Exeter, supplying local nobility, and making enough money to put some aside for her return to Roseland. How proud her mother would be if Mawde could make a success of her life and return to St Mawes as a woman of modest means.

A pewter plate clattered to the flagstones, jarring Mawde back to reality. What foolishness allowed her to believe a young girl like her would ever be anything but a servant! No woman could simply open a shop and build a business of her own. And where would she find a husband who would indulge her dreams and move to a small Cornish village? Mawde pushed her dreamy thoughts from her mind to concentrate on the task at hand. The design was intricate, and she was determined to impress Sir William's esteemed guests. She dipped the tip of a feather in water and moistened the edge of a delicate marchpane petal. Next, she applied a small strip of gold leaf, holding it lightly at one corner and smoothing it into place with a small dry coney tail brush given to her by Cook. After a few false starts with unsightly creases in the gold, Mawde achieved a perfectly smooth finish. With a smile of relief, she set about gilding the rest of the petals.

Hours passed. The light in the kitchen faded. Mawde stepped back to study her design. With nimble fingers, she had built a miniature rose garden with two tiny strutting peacocks and a fountain at the centre. Sir William's discovery of gum dragon powder had allowed Mawde to make pliable sugar pastes that were easier to work with than marchpane and dried to a hard texture that was easy to paint. Her latest design was therefore more intricate than anything she had made before, but it still needed a few finishing touches.

Mawde approached Cook, keeping her eyes lowered towards the flagstones. 'May I have your permission to leave the kitchen, Cook? I need real flowers to decorate my display – edible ones to add a finishing touch. I can fetch anything you need from the kitchen garden while I'm gone.'

'Off out to enjoy the summer sunshine, are you?' Ambrose sucked in his cheeks and looked like he might spit out a wasp. 'Can't have you suffering like the rest of us, can we, stuck in here, melting in the heat?'

'I'll pick flowers for you, Mawde.' Alice was stuffing an enormous bird with a thick paste of breadcrumbs and crushed herbs. 'You take over from me for a while. Remind yourself what it's like to do proper work in a kitchen.'

John sniggered. 'No, let me go.' His neck and arm muscles strained as he lifted a heavy cauldron from a hook above the fire. 'You need to be strong to pick flowers.'

Cook flicked his hand to dismiss Mawde from the kitchen. 'There's too much attention being paid towards your frivolous decorations, if you ask me. Go on, away with you, and pick your damned flowers!'

'I'll be quick, Cook, I promise.'

Alice sniffed. 'Course you will.' She snatched a knife from its resting place on a chopping board. Her fingers were greasy and the metal handle slipped, the sharp blade catching the tip of her finger as it fell. She stared at the deep gash, then pressed her apron against the bloodied end of her finger. Fat tears rolled onto her cheeks. 'It's not fair. Mistress rewards you for painting flowers, but what do I get for spilling blood? Nothing!'

Mawde grasped the clean linen of her new apron and twisted it in her hand. 'Once I have the flowers, I'll finish in no time, then I can help you, Alice.' She looked at Cook. 'Unless there's something else you had in mind for me?'

Cook shook his head and poured stewed fruit into a large pastry case. Grey wisps of hair clung to his sticky brow. 'Now I come to think of it, we could do with some rosemary and sage.' He jerked his head towards the door and instructed her to make haste.

Visitors wandered about the rose garden cooing over the colours and fragrances of the varieties on display. Mawde kept to the path running along the edge of the garden towards the jetty while maintaining a respectable distance from Sir William's guests. First, she selected unblemished flowers that would make an elegant sugar-coated treat for discerning palates. Next, she picked smaller blooms, barely out of bud, to decorate the border of her subtlety. She paused to look towards the river. A sailing boat was making slow progress towards the manor, bringing more guests. The water was calm, the breeze delicate but refreshing. Mawde's thoughts drifted to Roseland and the temperamental sea that fluctuated from serene and blue one moment to a grey seething surf the next. Dear God, how she missed it. Misty-eyed, she turned and hastened towards the kitchen garden where she busied herself with selecting unblemished sprigs of sage and rosemary for Cook. Head bowed so as not to draw any attention, she wept silent tears, creating dark wet spots on the sun-baked soil. She closed her eyes and breathed deeply, struggling to compose herself.

A cool finger slid across her cheek. Mawde snapped her eyes open. The flame-haired girl was kneeling beside her, and with a gentle stroke, she swept away another tear.

'Thank you.' Mawde used her skirt to dab her damp cheeks. 'We saw each other once before, do you remember? Last summer, in the orchard.' She gave a rueful smile. 'I wasn't weeping then.'

The girl's face remained impassive.

'You were feeding a squirrel.' Mawde glanced over her shoulder towards the house. 'I work in the kitchen. Are you one of the garden maids?'

No response.

'You're shy. I understand. My name's Mawde.'

The girl placed her palms on Mawde's cheeks and

looked into her eyes, then shifted her gaze towards the sky. She scrambled to her feet and hurried away.

Mawde plucked a sprig of sage from her trug and caressed the green furry leaves. She sniffed the crisp, earthy aroma and then returned to the kitchen with a lightness of spirit she had not felt in a very long time.

Mawde separated petals from roses. She painted them with syrup and dusted them with sugar that had been ground to a fine powder. Next, she dipped an entire bloom into the syrup, holding it still while the excess dripped off, then sprinkled sugar over the flower while turning the stem to ensure an even coating. As she lay it on a board to dry, she was aware of Cook standing behind her.

'Looks pretty,' Cook said, offering a rare compliment.

Tiny sugar crystals glistened like miniature diamonds.

'Thank you, Cook.' Mawde turned to face him. 'While I was in the kitchen garden, I came across a girl with fiery hair. I spoke to her, but she said nothing in return. Do you know who she is?'

Cook studied Mawde for a moment. 'Don't waste your time with that one. She's an idiot. Deaf and dumb.'

'Is she a garden maid?'

'No. She spends hours each day tinkering in the garden, but she's no maid.'

'What's her name?'

Cook waved his hand in a dismissive gesture. 'Her name doesn't matter. Every town and village has an idiot, and she's ours. Blacksmith's daughter. Creeps around, hiding behind walls and trees and never makes a sound.'

'She's the perfect companion for Mawde.' Alice

giggled. 'One doesn't speak at all, while the other's impossible to understand.'

'I speak as clearly as you.' Mawde glared at Alice. She knew her accent had softened during her three years at Powderham. 'In fact, I speak two languages: Cornish and English. My father encouraged me to speak English at home because he wanted me to have words to speak to anyone, including vile people like you.'

'Oooh, temper,' mocked John. 'Careful what you say, Alice, or Mawde'll start another Cornish rebellion.'

Cook rapped the tabletop with his knuckles. 'Enough! All of you, back to work.'

Mawde dipped the last of her roses and showered it in a fine mist of sugar. She pushed the complete ensemble towards the wall to dry and then wiped sticky sugar from her fingers. She approached the main table and picked up a knife, then sliced her way through a large bundle of leeks.

The hall was noisy, the chatter and laughter of finely dressed guests reverberating around the room. Mawde gazed with longing at the fine lace trim on gentlemen's shirt sleeves, and the decorative embroidery on ladies' dresses. Jewelled rings and fancy brooches glistened in the sunlight that streamed through the large windows. The hubbub died down as the gentleman usher processed towards the top table. How she wished she were the person carrying the subtlety and revelling in the admiring "oohs" and "aahs" as the guests admired her exquisite representation of Sir William's rose garden. By the time the subtlety reached Sir William, she was beaming with pride. She watched him lean forward and study the flowers glistening with gold leaf on their tips. He picked up a sweet shaped like a peacock and popped it into his mouth, grinning as he crunched on the bird, then nodded his appreciation for the small urn fountain spouting delicate thin strands of clear spun sugar.

It was the finest tableau she had created so far, and Mawde was proud of her achievement. She retreated into the corridor and made her way back to the kitchen to arrange the final confections that would mark the end of the meal. As she stepped through the door, Alice rushed up behind her and shoved her forward. Mawde fell to her hands and knees, scuffing her wrist against the edge of a stone step. She grasped the doorframe and pulled herself back on to her feet. Alice glowered.

Mawde held her angry gaze for a few long moments, then picked up a large platter of crystallised rose petals and smiled.

CHAPTER TWENTY

AUGUST 1527

'Stop being pathetic, Mawde. Open your eyes!' Alice was on her tiptoes, digging her fingers into Mawde's shoulder as she tried to peer beyond a sea of hats, caps and bonnets.

A murmur rippled through the crowd.

'They're climbing the steps to the cart!'

Mawde felt a pair of hands press against her back as those behind her surged forward in their eagerness to get a better view. She opened her eyes and wrinkled her nose at the sharp tang of sweat rising from so many men and women baking in the heat of the midday sun.

'There he is!' Alice tugged the sleeve of the woman in front of her. 'What did he do, do you know?'

The woman twisted around to answer. 'He set his neighbour's house on fire after a row about a debt. Neighbour's mother was trapped inside.'

'Murderer!' an onlooker shouted, brandishing his fist near the front of the crowd.

'Rot in Hell!' another yelled as he launched several pieces of decaying fruit towards the condemned man.

Alice gave Mawde a sharp nudge. 'They're putting his head through the noose!'

Mawde's eyes turned towards the man facing his death on a rickety old cart. A piece of sackcloth covered his head; his hands were tied behind his back and his ankles were bound together. A rope dangled from crude gallows and looped around his neck. The carthorse shook his head and whinnied, as if protesting against his involvement in the grim proceedings. A man grasped the reins and pulled to encourage the horse to move. The horse refused. Someone slapped the animal hard on the rump, startling it into taking a jolting step forward. People in the crowd roared. The horse reared. It took another step, and then another, before finding its stride. The cart slid out from beneath the condemned man's feet, leaving him twitching and jerking as the noose tightened around his neck.

Mawde turned and barged her way through the crowd, fighting the tide with her fists and elbows. At last, she broke free and fell to her knees. Struggling to draw air deep into her lungs, she rocked back and forth. No matter how hard she tried, she could not erase the image of flames devouring her home with her beloved cousin trapped inside. Her head throbbed. Her chest burned. She prayed for God's forgiveness and staggered towards the cool sanctuary of a shadowy alley. Clutching her chest with one hand and supporting herself against a battered wooden door with the other, she doubled over and vomited her regret.

With Sir William and his family in London, the servants of Powderham had the entire afternoon to spend as they pleased. Most of the servants had taken boats to Topsham.

Mawde wished she had joined them instead of letting Alice talk her into walking to Kenton to watch "a special performance". She hurried across the dusty cobbles of the courtyard and through the gate leading to the kitchen garden. To her delight, she saw the flame-haired girl standing with a butterfly perched on her finger. When the butterfly flew away, the girl stared solemnly after it.

Mawde drew alongside and touched her on the hand by way of a greeting. The girl turned her head and locked gazes with Mawde. Then she drew her hand away and took two steps backwards.

Mawde shifted her feet on the hard dry ground. 'Please don't go,' she mouthed carefully, hoping the girl could understand her. She looked towards the house and said under her breath, 'I know what it's like to be different.'

The girl cocked her head to one side, studied Mawde for a few long seconds, then walked away. She turned to glance over her shoulder. Her lips flickered at the corners and Mawde knew that next time they had an encounter, the girl would not rush away.

Bees and butterflies went about their business investigating flowers that bloomed in neat rows. Lavender scented the warm air while playful finches darted between trees and disappeared into thick green foliage. Mawde noted the position of the sun. There was still at least an hour to use as she pleased before she was due back in the kitchen.

A canopy of leaves shrouded the lane to the forge, creating a long, green tunnel. Undergrowth rustled as animals scurried about unseen, and wood pigeons cooed to each other high in the trees. Every footstep stirred up a fine cloud of dust and dried twigs snapped underfoot. Mawde had been hoping for another glimpse of the blacksmith's daughter, but now feared she might scare her away if she turned up to her home uninvited. She stopped in the lane and watched a squirrel jump between trees. No, she would not risk undoing the progress with their friendship – and she was certain that's what it was.

A loud crack echoed through the lane, like a brittle branch breaking away from a trunk. A flurry of wings followed as birds panicked, flapping and squawking above the trees. The calm of the woodland soon returned, and birds settled back in their nests and on branches. A new sound penetrated the air. Smothered giggles. Mawde peered deeper between the trees. With light footsteps, she crept to the wide base of an oak tree. Another giggle. Mawde peered out from behind the trunk and glimpsed a flash of light grey – the colour of the woollen kirtles worn by Powderham housemaids.

Holding her breath, Mawde concentrated on the sounds of the countryside. Birdsong and chirruping crickets. The hum of flies hovering over a half-eaten mouse. Mawde strained her ears and picked out a young woman's voice, her words soft and enticing. Then came the sighs of a young man and satisfied grunts like the noises her father used to make when settling into his chair after a long day in his workshop – or after dark when her parents were in bed. Mawde moved closer, slipping from the cover of one tree to another, and treading lightly on soft tufts of grass. She spotted a large clump of bracken and crouched behind it. Peeking through a gap, Mawde spied a couple locked in a passionate embrace. The woman's back was against a tree while the young man, a stable groom, pressed his hips hard against hers. The woman tilted her head back and closed her eyes while the groom nuzzled her neck and whispered something that made her chuckle. He kissed her earlobe and plunged his hand inside her shift, groaning with delight. The maid whispered something in his ear and then untied his breeches.

Mawde shrank lower behind the bracken, desperate to stay out of sight. The young woman was Izabel, a house-maid who sometimes helped in the kitchen. A sharp-tongued young woman, as mean as Alice, and someone even Ambrose took pains to avoid.

When Mawde arrived back at the kitchen, Alice was describing the hanging in gory detail to the delight of all the kitchen servants. Even Cook was struggling to hide his interest.

'As for that one,' Alice jerked her head towards Mawde, 'she couldn't bring herself to look. I've never seen anyone so squeamish. She even ran away and threw up.'

All eyes turned towards Mawde. A searing heat crept from her neck to her face.

'I saw you spilling your guts in that alleyway. Reminded you of something, did it?'

Mawde's mouth turned as dry as ash. 'What do you mean?'

'Heard you lost your home in a fire.' Alice leaned so close to Mawde that she could smell cloves on Alice's breath. 'Is it true?'

Mawde nodded.

'Did anyone die?'

Mawde nodded again.

Alice's sneer faded. 'In that case, your reaction makes sense.' Alice rapped the table with her knuckles to turn all eyes back towards her. 'As sure as eggs is eggs, off she went afterwards to look for her idiot friend.'

John and Alice had titbits of news to share about other members of the household staff, some bordering on scan-dalous, and others wildly exaggerated. Cook, Ambrose and the butcher boys were relishing the gossip and so Mawde decided the time had come to add her juicy tale.

'Guess what I saw today?' Mawde challenged their

curiosity with a beaming smile. 'A couple rutting in the woods.'

John leaned towards her. 'How much did you see?'

'More than I wanted to. They put on quite a show.'

'Tell us everything,' Alice said. 'Don't spare any details!'

Cook picked up a large knife and started carving bread.

Mawde mimicked the grunts and moans of the amorous couple until the servants cried with laughter. At last, she felt as if she belonged among them, with Alice begging her for more details.

'Time for supper,' Cook said, when the laughter subsided. 'Alice, fetch some ale.'

Alice disappeared into the buttery and returned with the brewer. They each carried a large pitcher.

'You didn't tell us who they were, your lovers in the woods.' Alice passed a cup of ale to Mawde.

'It was a stable groom. Philip, I think his name is.'

'Oh, he's wonderful,' Alice said, turning dreamy-eyed. 'And the girl? Did you recognise her?'

'Oh, yes. She's a housemaid.'

Alice gasped. Ambrose looked uncomfortable and excused himself from the table.

'Which one?' John asked.

Mawde put her finger to her lips. 'I shouldn't say.'

'Please, Mawde, tell us,' Alice wheedled. 'It's the best gossip we've heard!'

Mawde waited for a dramatic pause before saying, 'It was Izabel!'

Smiles froze on horrified faces. Cook sent a large pewter dish skidding over the flagstones. Mawde suddenly felt cold despite the heat of the kitchen as Cook strode towards her. He stopped in front of her, eyes wide and upper lip twitching, then struck her hard across her cheek.

'The kitchen is not a gossip parlour.' Cook glared at each servant. 'None of you are to speak of this slanderous filth again. Another word from any of you, and you'll get a whipping for your insolence.' His angry eyes were fixed on Mawde as he pointed towards the far end of the kitchen. 'Get out of here!'

'Come, help me in the buttery,' the brewer said kindly.

Mawde massaged her cheek as she followed her out of the kitchen.

The brewer closed the door behind them and put a comforting arm around Mawde. 'There's something you should know,' she said, stroking the livid imprint of Cook's hand on Mawde's cheek. 'Izabel is Cook's daughter.'

CHAPTER TWENTY-ONE
SEPTEMBER 1527

A BUTCHER BOY pushed a large wooden casket towards Mawde. She shovelled salt inside and pressed it down firmly, taking care to cover all the pork. She tried to slide the casket towards a groom who was waiting to secure the lid in place, but it was too heavy. The groom sniggered and watched her try a second time before he reached across and dragged it away. All too soon, another casket appeared in front of her.

Coarse grains of salt had become embedded into tiny cuts in Mawde's skin. Her palms burned and her fingers were swollen. She wiped her hands on her apron and grimaced.

Cook's menacing shadow darkened the doorway. When he drew beside her, he said, 'After that's done, I want you pickling and preserving.' He had been frosty towards her since the day of the hanging.

'I'll come now, Cook. We've just salted the last pig.'

Grateful to be back in the kitchen, Mawde curled her stinging fingers around the handle of a knife. Her mind wandered while she peeled and chopped. Three years had elapsed since her uprooting from Roseland and she had changed from a child to a fourteen-year-old young woman. She wondered if her mother had altered at all, if her hair had streaks of silver. Did she have creases beneath her eyes and were her joints stiff in the mornings? As for little Agnes, Mawde knew she would not recognise her at all. She scooped chopped apple into a pot before starting on a pile of onions.

'Look at you, smiling at a vegetable and daydreaming.' Cook's face was so close that his breath warmed her skin.

Mawde took a small step backwards and noticed he was on tiptoes.

'What are you smirking at? Tidy this mess!' Cook picked up an unpeeled onion and rammed it against the tabletop. The skin split and the onion bled pungent white juice. Cook waited for Mawde to wipe it clean before calling all staff members to congregate by the table. 'I've received word that Sir William and Lady Courtenay come home tomorrow and are bringing guests, so you'll have to finish the preserving today. No one leaves the kitchen until it's done. Understood?'

'Yes, Cook,' came the collective reply.

Murmurs of discontent rippled through the kitchen, followed by a subdued silence. Mawde was secretly rejoicing because she was confident that Sir William would want to impress his visitors with subtleties. She quickened her pace with her chopping knife and contemplated ideas for her next sweet creation.

'Lady Courtenay's going to be fuming when she gets home,' Alice declared, smacking Adam's hand away as he plunged his finger into a pot of cooling damson jam. 'Two housemaids are with child.'

Mawde glanced at Cook. Not even a flicker of reaction showed on his face.

'Which two?' the brewer asked.

'Jenett and Marie.'

'Jenett? Are you sure? Marie doesn't surprise me, but Jenett?'

Cook brandished his favourite wooden spoon. 'It's not so hard to believe it of either of them. Whenever Sir William and Lady Courtenay go away, this place degenerates into a harlots' den.'

Mawde was stunned by Cook's words. There was still a chance Izabel might be with child too. 'What will happen to Jenett and Marie?'

'They'll have to return to their families, I suppose,' the brewer said. 'Unless there's talk of marriage.'

Alice shook her head. 'When they named the fathers of their babies, both men denied it. I always knew those two would get themselves into trouble.' She pushed a few peeled onions across the table. 'You sense it with some people, don't you, Mawde? You know they're rotten inside.'

Mawde felt Cook's eyes boring into her. She swallowed and raised her head to meet his gaze. 'Perhaps it was Jenett or Marie I saw in the woods that day? I must have been mistaken when I said—'

'I'm sure you were.' Cook's stern expression softened. 'I overheard a gardener say there are penny buns in the woods. A mushroom sauce will go well with tomorrow's dinner. Mawde, Alice, take a break from the kitchen. Find the penny buns and bring plenty back with you.'

'That's enough.' Alice dropped a full basket next to Mawde. She split a thin twig and used the fine end of one half to gouge dirt from beneath a fingernail. 'I saw fool's funnels earlier.'

'Aren't they poisonous?'

'They are. Ever seen one before?'

Mawde thought for a moment. 'Don't think so.'

'Shall I show you?'

'Please. Then I'll know what to avoid in the future.'

Alice bent forward and retrieved her basket. 'They're back towards the house.'

The lane emerged from woodland with pasture to one side and the orchard wall to the other. Turning towards the pasture, Alice pointed to a clump of mushrooms nestling in lush grass.

'There, see? Each one has a dip in the middle and looks like it's had a dusting of flour.' She used the tip of her shoe to tilt the mushroom. 'It's got white gills underneath.'

Mawde studied it, imprinting it on her mind so she would never mistake it for something edible. A plump pigeon landed on a fence post. It ruffled its feathers as if warning Mawde to take care.

Alice shooed the pigeon away. 'Have you ever wanted to poison someone, Mawde?'

'Goodness, no!'

'I wouldn't blame you if you had. Some of us have given you a hard time since you arrived.'

'You have, but even so, I wouldn't poison anyone. What about you?'

Alice widened her eyes. 'Me? Course not! There's been the odd time when I've wished someone dead, but only because I was angry or something. I'd never actually kill someone.'

Mawde felt a cold shiver pass through her. Alice had a habit of making comments a little too close to the truth. She thought back to her grandmother's mean scowls and barbed comments, and the sounds and smells of the fire.

Alice was crouching, prodding the fool's funnels with a stick. 'Be easy though, wouldn't it?'

'What would?'

'To slip a slice or two into a pottage or gravy.'

'I suppose so, if you were that way inclined.'

Alice straightened up and steered Mawde towards the lane. 'We'd better hurry. Cook'll have us working late enough as it is. By the way, don't think that doing this together has made us friends. If you repeat anything I've said, I'll make your life more miserable than you can imagine.'

'Don't worry, Alice.' Mawde gave a wry laugh. 'I would *never* mistake you for a friend.'

CHAPTER TWENTY-TWO
SEPTEMBER 1527

THE TRUG'S contents shimmered in the autumn sunlight. There were bright blue cornflowers for sugar-coating and orange calendula to garnish Cook's delicious baked fish. Nestling alongside were sprigs of fragrant lavender with pale purple flowers, and bright yellow pansies stained with splashes of deep burgundy.

Satisfied she had all she needed to decorate a Garden of Eden subtlety for a feast later that day, Mawde hooked her arm through the handle of her trug and left the kitchen garden. Something darted in the periphery of her vision and set her heartbeat pounding. She stopped and turned, expecting to see a strutting peacock or a cat slinking into the shadows, but saw only Sir William a long way off in the distance, shouting for his steward to join him in the rose garden. To her right, in the courtyard, a groom ran his hand over the legs of a palfrey, checking for hidden injuries. Another groom was brushing the horse's coat to a high gloss, preparing him for a hunt. Chastising herself for startling too easily, she continued towards the kitchen. Foot- steps echoed behind her. The unmistakable scuffing of wooden soles against uneven cobbles in the courtyard. Mawde's shoes had leather soles, so she knew it couldn't be the echoes of her own footsteps. She whirled around. A brief flare of dark cloak disappeared behind an open stable door. She dismissed her paranoia for the footsteps of a groom.

'There you are!' Cook said, as Mawde entered the kitchen. His face was flushed and sweating, and the delicate skin at the outer edge of his right eye flickered and twitched. He blinked hard. 'Too many guests coming to this banquet! I'm running out of pots. Go to the forge. I ordered new pots weeks ago. The blacksmith should have them ready by now.'

Mawde hesitated. The final touches to her Garden of Eden required a slow and steady hand. Time was not on her side.

'It's not like Mawde to ignore the chance to take a break,' John quipped.

Mawde placed the calendula in front of Cook and looked towards her workbench against the far wall. 'I've too much left to do to finish that,' she said, spotting a miniature apple tree that looked as if it might topple.

'God's blood!' Ambrose said, throwing a ball of dough onto the tabletop. 'We all have a lot to do. Why's your work more important than anyone else's? I'll admit you create things that look pretty, but the rest of us actually feed Sir William's guests.'

Mawde kept her cool. 'They eat my sugar work, too. You know how tasty it is, Ambrose. You sample it often enough – already twice today.'

Ambrose's cheeks turned as rosy as Mawde's tiny sugar apples.

'Someone must go,' Cook said, raising his voice.

Gregory, the latest addition to the band of butcher

boys, had his hands inside a peacock's skin, preparing to stuff it with layers of roasted meats. 'I'd go, but I've got to pluck and stuff another two of these. You'd think it was Christmas the way Sir William's carrying on with all this feasting.'

'Dear Lord, please let him spend Christmas at court this year,' Alice said. 'We're exhausted. Can't someone slip something into his dinner to put him off food for a few days? We all need a rest!'

Mawde raised her eyebrows but kept her gaze fixed on her workbench.

'Alice!'

'I'm sorry, Cook. I was only jesting. Didn't mean no harm.'

'It'll have to be you, Mawde.'

She spun around to protest but Cook had his palms raised.

'I know you'll say you've more to do, but that garden looks complete to me.'

'But I have to place all the flowers!'

'There'll be no need for any of it if the main courses aren't ready on time, and for those, we need more pots.'

'Can't one of the boys go?'

'They could, but you'd have to turn the spit or clean out the skin of another bird. You don't fancy that as an alternative? I thought as much. Everyone has an important job to do, but yours is the only one that can wait. Go!'

Mawde folded her apron and left the kitchen. She gathered her skirts in her hand and ran along the lane, stumbling over ruts and stones. Her foot caught in a divot, and she fell forward, sprawling across the dusty track. Crows fluttered up from the trees and whirled around in a squawking cloud of black. Mawde wondered what it must feel like to fly and glide through the air. A thin brittle twig snapped beneath her palm. She startled and drew her hand away. After chastising herself for becoming so jumpy, she clambered to her feet and continued on her way.

Something rustled. It sounded like clothing catching on a branch. Mawde slowed her pace, listening for the sound again. A gentle wind sighed between the trees, plucking withered leaves and dropping them to the woodland floor. Autumn was fast approaching.

Mawde was certain someone was following her. Sweat dampened her palms. Her neck prickled. 'Don't be a fool,' she murmured, glancing up and down the lane. Reassured she was alone, she continued towards the forge, treading carefully to avoid another tumble.

Mawde rounded a bend, and the roof of the forge came into view. A steady plume of grey smoke rose from a tall chimney, thinning and fading to nothing as it reached towards the sky. Mawde quickened her pace and heard the rapid footsteps of a person moving among the trees. She slowed her pace. A brief delay, then the other person slowed too.

'That's enough!' she shouted. She considered running, but a man would soon catch up with her. She hoped the forge was close enough for the blacksmith to hear if she screamed. 'Show yourself!' Mawde's legs shook beneath her skirts. Leaves rustled. Mawde twisted towards the noise. Something dark moved beyond the gnarled trunk of an aged oak tree. Mawde's heart was pounding. Her breaths were shallow and fast.

Her pursuer emerged into the light, head lowered and concealed by the hood of a long, black cloak. Their movements were slow and sinister, but as wooden-soled shoes scraped over stones, Mawde's fear ebbed away. The pale brown weave of a skirt peeked through the opening at the bottom of the cloak. A female.

Mawde stepped towards the stranger, eager to see her face, but her pursuer scuttled backwards towards the gloom of the trees.

'Don't be afraid. I mean no harm.'

The stranger lowered her hood. Locks of shimmering red hair spilled across her cloak.

'It's you!' Mawde giggled with relief. 'For a moment, I thought you might leap out and attack me!'

The girl lowered her gaze and fidgeted with the ties of her cloak.

'Will you walk with me to the forge?' Mawde asked, keeping her tone soft. 'That's where you live, isn't it?'

The girl raised her head. The corners of her mouth lifted into a shy smile.

Mawde beckoned to her. 'Please, walk with me. You've no need to hide in the trees.'

The girl did not move.

'I'm sorry,' Mawde said, holding out her hand. She made sure the young girl could see her lips when she spoke again. 'I forgot you can't hear me.'

The girl sucked in her bottom lip as she contemplated Mawde's proffered hand. Then she stepped forward and placed her fingers against Mawde's palm. Mawde gave her a gentle squeeze. They continued along the lane, hand in hand, the blacksmith's daughter skipping and grinning as they drew nearer to her home.

The blacksmith raised an eyebrow as the girls entered the forge. 'Good morrow. What brings you here?'

Mawde had seen the blacksmith before, but only from a distance. He was the tallest man she had ever encountered. His arms were broad and muscular, and rope-like veins bulged beneath his grimy skin. But his charcoal-dappled face glistened with kindness, framed by a mane of unruly golden hair.

'Begging your pardon, sir, but I'm from the kitchen at Powderham. Cook sent me to find out if his pots are ready.'

'Aye, they're ready, but you won't be able to manage them alone. They're heavy.' The blacksmith looked beyond Mawde to his daughter, then back to Mawde. 'Elsebeth will help you. You can carry two each.'

The pots were bulky, the handles too thin to carry comfortably in the crook of an arm. Mawde had no choice but to grasp the handles with her fingers and carry one pot in each hand. Her muscles burned from the weight of them. Her shoulders ached. Exhausted, she lowered her pots to the ground, and flexed and straightened at her elbows. Elsebeth lowered her pots too and giggled.

Mawde smiled. 'You must be used to lifting heavy things, being the blacksmith's daughter. Spending so much time on dainty sugar work has made my muscles soft.' Mawde settled on a boulder covered with moss. 'Here I am, chattering away like a fool and you unable to join in.' She fiddled with the hem of her kirtle. 'I wish you could. I spend every day in a crowded kitchen, but I feel so alone. You'll understand what that feels like because you're different too and people are cruel to us both.'

Mawde stood and retrieved her pots. 'I should get back or Cook's going to yell at me for taking too long.'

They moved forward along the lane, side by side and in matching steps. 'Sir William's fondness for feasting is making life unbearable in the kitchen. Tempers are fraying because we're all exhausted.' Mawde readjusted her hands on the pot handles. 'The other day, Alice suggested giving Sir William something to put him off his food for a while, just to give us all a break. You should have seen Cook's reaction.'

When they reached the gate to the stable yard, Elsebeth stopped and dropped her pots and hooks. She pointed towards the kitchen and shook her head.

Mawde shared Elsebeth's reluctance. 'Not to worry, I'll manage from here. Thank you for your help. I've enjoyed being with you.' Mawde reached for Elsebeth's fingers and gave them a gentle squeeze. 'I hope we can call ourselves friends now.'

Elsebeth fixed Mawde with an honest gaze, then turned and walked away.

Mawde could hear Cook bellowing in the kitchen, and she wondered what had riled him this time. Undeterred, she grasped two pot handles in each hand and staggered across the yard. As soon as the pots were delivered, Cook gave Mawde a list of tasks to complete before she could add the finishing touches to her subtlety. She accepted the instructions without protest and gave Cook a gracious smile. No matter how hard she had to work, she had received the precious gift of friendship, and no one could take that from her.

CHAPTER TWENTY-THREE
APRIL 1528

AFTER FOUR YEARS AT POWDERHAM, Mawde still found Master Davey's presence unsettling. Sir William's steward was a rare visitor to the kitchen, and his appearance in the doorway was a sign that something was terribly wrong. He tapped his right foot against the step, the leather sole of his shoe making a soft scuffing sound on the stone.

'How much longer?'

Cook stirred a small pot of steaming liquid. 'It's almost ready.' Mawde sensed his agitation despite any effort he might be making to conceal it.

The steward pressed his fingertips to his temples. ''Tis awful to see Sir William writhing in his bed and crying like a baby. He's been like this for two days now, with no sign of it abating. The physician's adamant it's a case of poisoning even though it started within an hour or so of eating. Now, Lady Courtenay insists one of us tastes everything first. You can't blame me for watching you prepare this, rather than take my chances when it's sent up to his chamber.'

Cook turned to face the steward. 'Am I accused?'

'Goodness, no. I wasn't suggesting——'

'I should think not. Over twenty years of loyal service...'

Mawde felt the tension building in the kitchen.

'Who would do such a thing?' Ambrose's hand trembled as he placed his paring knife on the table.

The brewer dragged a three-legged stool from beneath a workbench and sat with her head and shoulders hunched forward. ''Tis unthinkable. I feel faint at the thought of it.' When she lifted her head, her face was the colour of raw pastry.

Master Davey stepped further into the room. 'He's deteriorating fast, so it must be poison. No one else has felt unwell since dinner, so it's not like he's eaten something that's turned, or others would be falling sick, too.' His expression hardened. 'Which means someone in this room purposely added something to his food.'

'Not necessarily!' Cook drew himself to his full height. 'Anyone in the hall could have slipped a drop of something into his ale or sprinkled a powder on his plate. Even you! Don't point your finger at members of my staff unless you can prove your accusation.'

Mawde pictured Sir William, knees drawn to his chest and rolling around with pain. She wiped her sugar-coated hands on her apron and approached the steward. 'Master Davey, a tisane of chamomile might settle Sir William's stomach. My grandmother used to swear by it.'

The steward peered down his nose. 'What insolence is this? Will your chamomile do better than the physician's prescribed powders?' To Cook, he said, 'The astrologer is studying the charts now, so we'll soon know if Sir William will recover.'

Mawde retreated towards her workbench and resumed

grating a cone of sugar. She doubted she would ever understand the preference for astrological charts over remedies provided by nature.

The kitchen cat jumped down from the window ledge and stood with hackles raised. He pounced towards a rat that dared to emerge from a hole at the bottom of a wall. The cat clamped its teeth around the rat's neck, dragged it towards the steward and draped it across his shoe.

'Disgusting!' The steward lifted the rat by the tail and flung it through the door that opened onto the courtyard. 'I don't know what's worse, a mangled rat or that unholy cat.'

'An unholy creature he might well be,' Cook said, shooing the cat into the courtyard. 'But he's a fine mouser and rat-catcher.'

Mawde turned her attention to the moulds stacked in neat little piles on shelves above her workbench. It had swelled into an impressive collection thanks to Lady Courtenay gathering new moulds every time she visited London. Seeking a particular shape, Mawde spotted a mould out of place. It was teetering on the edge of the narrow top shelf instead of stacked with others of a similar size on a lower, wider shelf. As she moved the mould into its correct position, a folded slip of paper dropped onto her bench. Thinking it to be an old sketch she had used to make a subtlety, she hooked up a corner of her apron to create a fold and stowed the paper inside.

It was a hot day for spring. Mawde dabbed her brow with her apron, worried that beads of sweat might drop into the comfits that were slowly growing in the pan. The paper packet fell out from the fold. Mawde retrieved it and pushed it between her chemise and kirtle, while swirling the comfits in the pan with her other hand. She would look at the sketch later and stow it with the others kept flat beneath her mattress. Her early sugar work had been crude compared to recent offerings, but all the early drawings were suitable for adapting into elaborate confections.

Adam, the spit-boy, was struggling to cope with the heat from the fire. His eyelids drooped and his head lolled forward. Mawde dropped a spoon to rouse him with the clang of pewter against stone. Adam looked about, dazed and disorientated. He caught Mawde watching him and the colour drained from his rosy cheeks. Mawde tapped her fingertip on her lips to reassure him his nap would be their secret. He mouthed his thanks and turned to stoke the fire.

The kitchen door flew open, banging hard against the wall.

'Stop what you're doing and stand in a line with your hands held out in front of you. Now!'

Three of Sir William's men burst into the kitchen and took up positions by the doors, guarding the exits to the great hall, courtyard and scullery.

'Move!'

The servants exchanged nervous glances. Mawde's heartbeat galloped as she lifted her pan away from the hot coals to stop the comfits from burning. She placed it by the hearth, hoping several hours of work had not been in vain, then rushed to the other side of the table to join the line.

The steward entered the kitchen and stood at the head of the table. His flinty eyes studied each servant. 'Sir William has deteriorated, and now he's gravely ill.' He waited for the gasps and exclamations to settle. 'This is a serious matter.' He walked along the line of staff, staring into the eyes of each person and holding their gaze for several seconds before moving on. 'He complains of pains in his chest and is struggling to breathe. The physician is adamant that someone tainted Sir William's food with some form of poison.'

'No!' Cook crossed himself. 'No one from my kitchen would ever consider such a thing.'

'Then who? He's eaten nowhere but here for the last three days.' The steward stepped in front of Mawde and leaned towards her. 'Was it you?'

Mawde recoiled from his warm, stale breath. 'No!'

'Sir William's always praising your fancy sugar work and expects every new creation to be better than the last. Is it too much for you, I wonder? One of your "natural reme-dies" would soon silence his demands.'

'I relish the challenge, and I would never harm anyone on purpose.' She fell silent and lowered her gaze.

'Shake out your apron.'

'Master Davey?'

'Your apron! Remove it and give it a good shake, so anything hidden will drop out.'

Mawde did as he ordered and registered his look of disappointment when nothing tumbled from the folds.

'Your pocket,' he said, pointing to the pouch tied at her waist. Mawde loosened the drawstring and held it open for Master Davey to peer inside. He raised an eyebrow at her small carving of the Madonna and Child, then gestured she could close it because there was nothing else inside. 'Toss the kitchen!'

'No!' Cook glowered at the steward, his jaw muscles tense as pots and plates were swept from shelves and uten-sils flung to the floor.

'It'll be the death penalty for sure, if they catch the poisoner.' Ambrose picked at the edge of a scab on the

174

back of his hand. He cursed when he picked too hard and drew a trickle of blood.

Alice sidled up to Mawde. 'Looks like your little corner's next.'

Mawde flinched as her equipment clattered to the flag-stones. Old wooden moulds cracked and splintered. Metal moulds clanged and skittered across the floor.

'They won't find anything.'

'You sure about that?'

Mawde met Alice's gaze. 'Of course, I'm sure. I have nothing to hide.' She looked back towards her corner. The guards had already moved on.

Bemusement rippled across Alice's brow.

'You look disappointed?' Mawde said.

'No,' Alice replied. 'Why would I be?'

Mawde rested her head on the pillow, grateful the day was drawing to a close. An owl gave a melancholic 'hoo, hoo' as rain started falling and large drops tapped the window. Mawde's back ached and her head was pounding. She retrieved the folded paper from between her kirtle and shift and started opening the folds. Her candle flickered beside her, the flame threatening to die. Mawde pushed herself up to sitting and reached up to close the window, but it was already as tight as it would go, a mottled glass barrier against an ominous charcoal sky. Shielding the candle from the draught, she studied the folded paper by the dim light of a faltering yellow flame. The paper was of a poorer quality than the sheets she used for sketches. This paper was coarse, like the wrapping used by the local apothecary for dispensing powders and herbs. There was a ragged edge along one side, suggesting someone had ripped it in a hurry. Mawde's stomach twisted. Something wasn't right.

'Dear God, no!' Her heart lurched. She pressed her fist against her lips, terrified the slightest sound would bring Sir William's guards rushing to apprehend her. She stared at slivers of dried mushroom resting on her lap. Fool's funnel. Poisonous. Deadly.

The shadowy walls seemed to close in towards her. She had observed Master Davey give Cook the apothecary's packet and instruct him to make a tisane. The steward had watched Cook prepare it and would have seen if he had added anything. Had the steward added the poison before entering the kitchen? Mawde screwed her eyelids shut, forcing herself to think. No. That was not what happened. She recalled the gentle crack of splitting wax when Cook broke open the sealed packet. Not the steward, then. Nor Cook. And anyway, Sir William was already unwell when Master Davey entered the kitchen to ask for the tisane. Someone must have retrieved the paper after Cook had discarded it, then used it to wrap the left-over poisonous flakes. That left one possibility. Someone had intended for Mawde to take the blame by hiding the package among her moulds.

An intermittent creak from the wooden staircase cut through the silence of the night. Someone was climbing the stairs. Mawde folded the paper and thrust it back into the hiding place between layers of her clothing. She knelt on the floorboards and busied herself with her mattress, plumping the straw as if preparing for sleep. The room was soon abuzz with chattering housemaids and dairymaids who shared the attic space. Mawde joined in, feigning a keenness to gossip about the day's events. Theories passed back and forth but were rapidly discarded.

At last, conversations gave way to fatigue. Mawde

removed her kirtle, taking care to keep the package nestled
in its folds. Those around her drifted off to sleep, while
Mawde tossed and turned. She rolled onto her back and
stared towards the muted light filtering through the
window. The rain clouds had moved away, leaving a pearly
moon and sprinkling of stars. If her mother was awake
and gazing at the night sky, she would see the same moon.
It was as if God had hung it there as a way of keeping
them connected. 'Oh, Mamm,' she said in the softest of
whispers. 'One day, I'll find my way home.'

Something rustled under her mattress. Mawde snapped
her eyes open and slid her hand towards the edge of her
blanket, expecting to feel a mouse or a rat. But her hand
struck something larger. She clenched her fingers and felt
them slip over soft human skin. Keeping a tight grasp, she
sat up and waited for her eyes to adjust to the gloom.

'What were you doing?' she hissed.

'I know you found the packet of mushroom flakes,'
came the whispered reply. 'Please, get rid of it. Burn it, or
something.' A stifled sob. 'They found the rest of the paper
under my mattress, so if they find the rest of it, they'll
know it came from me.' The whispering grew more urgent.
'Please get rid of it, Mawde. I shouldn't have... I wasn't
trying to kill him, but I want to go home for a few days. My
mother's not well and I thought if we weren't so busy, he'd
let me go.'

'Why didn't you ask?' Mawde said. 'Sir William would
have understood.'

'Because last time I asked, I lied. I didn't think I'd get a
second chance.' Another sob. 'What have I done? If they
find—'

Fists pummelled against solid wood. The door flew
open, and two guards entered, each man carrying a
blazing torch.

'It was her,' a housemaid said, pointing an accusatory finger. 'She's your poisoner. She even confessed!'

'No!' Mawde turned rigid with panic. 'I didn't—'

'Not you, Mawde,' the maid interrupted. 'Her.'

Mawde stared at the young woman whose arm was still in her grasp.

It was Alice.

CHAPTER TWENTY-FOUR

APRIL 1528

A WARM SPRING breeze pushed soft white clouds in front of the sun and blew delicate ripples across the river. Mawde shivered. Sir William was recovering well from his near-death experience – but she was not. Panic had seized her several times during the night, soaking her chemise and dampening her sheet. It would be her swinging from the gallows later that morning if she had not spotted the misplaced mould on the shelf. Not Alice.

Lady Courtenay cancelled her early spring banquet and requested all visitors to leave the manor. With only family and staff members to cater for, Cook took the opportunity for a spring clean. Floors were scrubbed, walls washed, windows polished, and shelves dusted. A poor harvest the previous year had left the storerooms almost empty, so Sir William had dispatched two of his men over-seas to source reliable supplies of flour, spices, oranges and oil. Cook had received word that their return was immi-nent. He instructed Mawde to wait for the delivery while everyone else attended the hanging.

'Funny how things turn out, isn't it?' Mawde plucked narrow white petals from a lawn daisy. 'Alice taunted me for my dislike of a public hanging while deriving great pleasure from it herself. Now, it's her turn to entertain the crowds. I can't believe she tried to make it look like the poisoning was my fault! Ambrose said Alice tried to give someone fool's funnel once before – her father, would you believe? She convinced everyone it was accidental, but now we're not so sure.' She threw the depleted bloom to the ground and reached for Elsebeth's hand. Mawde thought she sensed a slight squeeze before Elsebeth withdrew her hand and shielded her eyes against the sun-dappled water. She stood and leaned forward, squinting into the distance.

'What is it, Elsebeth? What do you see?'

Three ships were making their way upriver towards Topsham, while another was heading towards the open sea.

'None of those are coming this way. We've still a while to wait.' She turned her back towards the river and looked at the rose garden. In a matter of weeks, it would become a blaze of yellows, reds and pinks, and a delicate perfume would scent the air.

Elsebeth tugged Mawde's sleeve.

'Another ship?' Mawde asked, turning to look.

Elsebeth had a broad smile. She bobbed up and down on her toes, pointing into the distance. She clapped and waved, her face bright with joy. A ship was tacking towards them, and Sir William's pennant fluttered at the top of the tallest mast.

Mawde watched her friend's smile broaden. 'Look at you! Anyone would think you had something arriving on the ship.'

A high spring tide allowed the ship to dock alongside the Powderham jetty. The cargo was offloaded with swift efficiency, and Mawde directed sailors to carry the crates and casks to the scullery and buttery. After the final crate came ashore, Elsebeth ran towards the jetty.

'Elsebeth, where're you going? The unloading's finished so we can do something else now.'

Elsebeth broke into a run.

'Elsebeth, come back!' Mawde hurried after her, but soon pulled up short. She watched, confused, as Elsebeth hurled herself into the arms of a handsome young man. He had an engaging smile, neat hair tied with a ribbon, and a clean-shaven complexion. His clothes were smart despite many days at sea, and his eyes shone with affection for Elsebeth. He swept her off her feet, spinning her in a circle and calling out her name. When he set her down, he kissed her twice on each cheek. Elsebeth patted his forearm and pointed towards Mawde.

Mawde stiffened under the young man's intense gaze but could not take her eyes off him. Something shifted deep in her chest and her heart fluttered. The young man doffed his felt hat and bowed. Mawde looked around to see if anyone was watching. Relieved his antics were of no interest to other people, she studied the young man before her. She estimated he was four to five years older than her. His saffron coloured jerkin was fastened with thick laces and the sleeves were trimmed with elegant embroidered cuffs.

Elsebeth was beaming. Her eyes shone with love. Mawde wondered how a deaf and mute girl had caught the eye of a man of such substance, then felt guilty for harbouring such a mean thought.

''Tis a pleasure to see you again, Mawde.'

His dark blue eyes glittered like a starlit night. His hair was the colour of wheat and glowed in the midday sun.

Mawde furrowed her brow.

He gave Elsebeth a playful nudge. 'My return has rendered your friend speechless.' He pointed to a bench that faced the river. 'Let's make ourselves comfortable there. Too long has passed since we were last together.'

Mawde's mood dropped like a stone in water. She had been looking forward to an hour or two with Elsebeth before returning to work. 'I'll bid you both farewell and leave you to catch up.'

Elsebeth shook her head and gestured for her to sit.

'Join us, Mawde. I insist,' the young man said, cocking his head a little to one side. 'I'm sure we have much to talk about.'

Mawde eyed him uncertainly. That was the second time he had used her name.

Elsebeth linked her arm through Mawde's and guided her towards the bench. Mawde and Elsebeth sat on the seat while their companion settled on the grass in front of them.

Mawde could contain herself no longer. 'Forgive me, but who are you? And how did you and Elsebeth become so well acquainted?'

'What do you mean?' His eyes danced with merriment.

Mawde took a moment to choose the right words. 'Elsebeth's the blacksmith's daughter, and you're...' She struggled to find the right words.

'The blacksmith's son,' he finished for her.

'His son? So, you're Elsebeth's brother? But I thought—'

He chuckled. 'You thought my fondness for my sister was romantic in nature?' He grinned at Elsebeth. 'We've always been close, but only as siblings. We share little resemblance, but that's because we have different mothers.' His expression turned serious. 'Mine died in childbirth.'

'I'm sorry, I didn't mean to pry.' Mawde could not reconcile the well-dressed, articulate young man with his claimed parentage.

His smile returned. 'We share a wonderful father.' He turned his face towards the sun and closed his eyes. 'And I am fortunate to enjoy Sir William's guardianship. My mother was Sir William's niece—'

Mawde cut him short. 'You've no need to explain. It's none of my business.'

'But I'm happy to share this with you.' He regarded her intently. There was something alluring about him, and she returned his gaze with equal intensity. 'My mother was a romantic. For every suitor presented to her by my grand-parents, she found faults that warned of an unhappy marriage. She insisted she would only marry for love. Her parents were aghast, naturally, but gave her the choice – marry a man of their choosing and benefit from the family connection, or marry for love and find herself banished for good.' His expression softened. He plucked a blade of grass and slit it in two with his thumbnail. 'She chose love.'

Mawde felt compassion towards his mother. She must have been so courageous to sacrifice her family and lifestyle for the man she loved. She smoothed out imaginary creases in her kirtle. Elsebeth's brother had shared personal infor-mation and must have been blind to her uniform of a lowly kitchen maid. He might be the blacksmith's son, but he had elevated his status.

'My great-uncle adored my mother,' he continued. 'When the local blacksmith died, he insisted she move here with her new husband. No one opposed the idea – the blacksmith had no heirs, and his young apprentice lacked the experience needed to run a busy forge. My mother couldn't have been happier.'

Mawde gasped. 'So, you're related to Sir William?'

Nicholas raised his hands as if in surrender. 'Guilty, as charged. When my mother died, he approached my father and offered to take me in as his ward. I joined his own sons in their schoolroom and lived with them as part of the family – a similar arrangement that would have occurred if my mother had married according to the will of her parents. Sir William didn't want me to miss out. A black-smith's son has limited career opportunities, so my father accepted, and I have the freedom to visit my true home whenever I wish.' The young man smiled. 'Turns out, I have a head for numbers. Sir William appointed me as a junior secretary. I help manage his investments and trade deals, and now he wants me to travel further afield. The best thing about that is I'll be able to spend more time at home between trips.'

''Tis a remarkable story.' Mawde was struggling to process the revelations. 'But I think you may have shared too much. I'm a servant, not one of your peers.'

'I fear you've missed the point of my story. Did it not show how any of us can achieve our dreams? For many, wealth is the goal, for others love.' A pink tinge rose in his cheeks. 'For me, it is both.' He fell silent for a long moment, then looked at Mawde. 'I would say the shift in your circumstances has opened up new possibilities for you.'

Mawde stiffened. 'What would you know about my circumstances?'

The young man was unperturbed by the sharp tone of her voice. 'I was there, Mawde, the day you left Roseland.'

'You're Nicholas?'

'The very same.' He gave her a warm smile. 'Sir William tasked your uncle with broadening my education, and I worked with him in Exeter for close to eighteen months.' He switched his gaze to Elsebeth and then back to Mawde. 'My sister said you've shown her great kindness.'

'She's my one genuine friend here.'

'And you are hers.'

Elsebeth's face was glowing with adoration for Nicholas.

'When did she tell you that?' Mawde asked.

'When she ran to greet me after I stepped ashore.'

Mawde contemplated her mute friend. 'How did she tell you?'

Nicholas waggled his finger at Elsebeth. 'Come now, Beth. Mawde is your dearest friend, but still does not know your secret?'

'She can't hear you,' Mawde said. 'As her brother, you should know that.'

'I can hear perfectly well, thank you.'

'Elsebeth?' Mawde thought she might have imagined Elsebeth's light and musical voice.

Nicholas grinned.

'I've heard every word you've ever said to me.'

Mawde's shock turned to rage. 'Then why did you never tell me you could speak?'

Elsebeth reached for her hand, but Mawde brushed it away. 'How could you?'

'Dearest Mawde, forgive me. I should have told sooner, but as time passed, I found it harder to reveal my true self to you.'

Mawde's anger evaporated, leaving her bewildered. She stared into the distance, wondering why anyone would pretend to be deaf and mute and subject themselves to other people's cruelty.

After a long uncomfortable silence, Nicholas said, 'Very few people know Beth is as talkative as you and I. Our father knows, of course, and her mother. And Sir William.'

'Sir William?' echoed Mawde. 'Why does he encourage you to keep up this pretence?'

A noisy crowd of servants gathered near the jetty. Elsebeth looked alarmed.

'Don't worry, Beth,' Nicholas said. 'they're not interested in you, and they're too far away to see or hear you speak.'

Elsebeth took a deep breath. 'I had a twin sister called Elis. She died when we were four years old. My mother said we chattered to each other all the time, but when Elis died, I felt crushed by grief and ran out of things to say. Several months later, Nicholas took me to the stables to see a newborn foal. Sir William joined us and opened the stable door. I pointed to the foal and said "Elis". After that, I rediscovered my voice but would not speak to anyone outside the family other than Sir William.' Elsebeth's expression became desolate. 'By then, the gossipmongers had branded me "dumb", and I lacked the courage to prove them wrong. People are unkind, you know, especially when they think you can't hear them. But, thanks to my secret, I'm able to pass on important information to Sir William. In return, he allows me to exercise Elis.'

Nicholas stood and brushed dust and grass from his breeches. 'I'd better go to my uncle. By now, he'll know I'm here.'

'He'll be pleased to see you,' Elsebeth said. 'He's still recovering from his dose of poison.'

Nicholas raised an eyebrow. 'Poison? No doubt, he will tell me more.'

Elsebeth waited for Nicholas to disappear from view. 'I

shouldn't have kept my secret from you, Mawde. When I knew I could trust you, I should've said something. Forgive me? Please?'

'We're the best of friends, Elsebeth.' Mawde smiled. 'There's nothing to forgive.'

CHAPTER TWENTY-FIVE

Powderham
25 October 1528

DEAREST MAMM,

 I pray this letter finds you well, and little Agnes, too. I think of you both every day and wish I was with you in Roseland. Four long years have passed since I arrived here, and it has taken all this time to find someone I trust to write my words to you. I wonder who you will choose to read aloud my news. Aunt Mary, perhaps, or the pastor after church?

 When I left the farm, my heart broke in two. One day, I will return. Being a kitchen maid has made it impossible so far, but I will find a way to make my way back to you. I will smell the sweet fragrance of Cornish heather again, and taste the salt of a fresh south-westerly breeze.

 I found it hard to settle here. The Cornish people are not well-liked, and the other servants teased me for my accent. But it will please you to know I'm settled now. Be proud of me, Mamm. I have grown strong of spirit and am determined to make something of myself one day. Yesterday, I was gathering herbs when a little robin hopped about in front of me. It was so close that I could have reached out and stroked its feathers. It looked so frail, yet it was fearless, watching me as I worked. I want to be like that robin – strong of character and resilient, despite my delicate frame.

Lady Courtenay is a kind mistress. You would like her. She's elegant of dress and refined in her manners, but she appreciates everything her servants do for her. She encouraged me to develop the skills required of a confectioner. I wish I could show you the decorations I've prepared for Sir William's feasting tables. I've made castles and pleasure gardens, woodlands and animals, all sculpted from sugar and almond paste. To think we rarely saw sugar at home, and here it's used to make fanciful decorations! It's not a simple task, though. It takes many hours to grind sugar cones to dust, and make syrups and sugar paste, marchpane and candied fruits. If you knew the cost of all that sugar, it would give you sleepless nights!

Be assured that I am well. Lady Courtenay provided me with two comfortable wool dresses and a new pair of sturdy shoes. My apron has my initials embroidered on it, and I have two spare linen shifts. I don't even have to wash my own clothes! Mind you, the days are too busy to even contemplate such a thing.

I'm paid a wage for my work in the kitchen. Every three months, we line up in front of Sir William's table and take our turn to receive our coins. Mine are stowed and rarely spent, so I may give them to you when I make it home. I plan to save enough money to return without becoming a burden to you, and I want to buy a special dress for you to wear on Sundays, and one for Agnes too.

I've made a good friend here. She's called Elsebeth and is the daughter of the blacksmith. Nicholas, her brother, is writing these words. Perhaps one day, I'll learn my letters, then I won't need someone to write on my behalf.

Elsebeth is a magnificent horsewoman. Sir William allows her to exercise his horses when he's away from home. Sometimes, Sir William attends the Royal Courts. Imagine, Mamm – my master in the same room as our King! He says he'd prefer to spend less time at court, but I don't think Lady Courtenay would agree. They have a house in London and occasionally take the children there. As much as I like my master and mistress, I prefer life when they're away from Powderham because we're not so busy in the kitchen and can enjoy a few hours of leisure.

So much has happened in the last four years – too much for a single letter. A few months ago, a maid was sentenced to hang. She tried to poison Sir William. It was a shock to us all because he's a kind master, even if he does expect too much from us sometimes. Preparing for feasts is gruelling. I work on confectionery most of the time and spend many hours leaning over my workbench. Some nights, it's difficult to get comfortable because my back and legs ache so. But I'm not grumbling. I eat well. I have a comfortable bed in a room I share with other maids. And I have Elsebeth.

Mamm, please think of me from time to time. I look at the moon before I go to sleep and imagine you looking at it too – a giant pearl in the sky, binding us together. I yearn for a letter from home, so if you can find someone willing to write it for you, it would be so warmly received.

Your daughter,
Mawde

CHAPTER TWENTY-SIX

St Mawes
1 December 1528

D*aughter*,

Your letter brought such joy, but how my heart aches with a
longing to see you. Forgive me for not finding a way to write sooner,
but so much has happened during your absence and it's hard to know
where to begin.

Three years ago, Vintner and Mistress Wyn employed me as their
housekeeper. With a run of poor harvests, I was a burden to my sister
and her husband and could no longer ask for their charity. The vintner's house is comfortably furnished, and Agnes has settled well here.
Two years ago, Mistress Wyn died. After the vintner was widowed, a
fondness grew between us. I am no longer Widow Hygons, Mawde.
Now, I'm known as Goodwife Wyn. It surprised us both that we
should develop such affection for one another, and we married in the
spring. He provides well for me and Agnes but, dearest Mawde, there's
nothing for you here. There is a bed where you may lay your head and
food and wine aplenty, but the village cannot offer you any kind of

wage. St Mawes is no longer prosperous. The manor rots behind its low stone wall, and my husband cannot always find customers for his wines. The village needs a twist of fate to prosper once again. Until then, I urge you to make the best of any opportunities you have there.

I wish we could call upon you, but Agnes would not travel well. She had consumption after you left. She has a weak constitution and suffers recurrent bouts of coughing. I fear I cannot leave her unattended and make the journey alone. I pray you understand.

Uncle William is no longer with us. He suffered dreadfully when the plough overturned and ripped through his leg. The damaged flesh turned rotten and robbed him of his life. The farm passed to Henry, what with him being the eldest son, but my sister and her children continue to live and work there. Henry is a fine young man, loyal to his family. He wed a Gerrans lass and they expect their first babe to arrive any day. My sister is eager to welcome her first grandchild!

You may have heard about my brother, although it's probably news your master would prefer not to share. Thomas fell in with undesirable types and ran up debts from gambling. They say he fell to thievery to pay for food and bills. Sir William had no choice but to end his employment and throw him to the mercy of the people of Exeter. I've heard nothing since and fear the worst. His poor family.

Christmastide approaches. My husband has promised Agnes that we will bring in the green and decorate the house with holly, mistletoe and ivy. We will enjoy a feast on Christmas Day with veal and wedges of cheese, washed down with a fine French wine. The house will be full, as we have invited many guests, including family members from both sides. Henry said he'll bring a small pig for roasting. As merry as we shall be, dear Mawde, my thoughts will be with you.

You may be wondering who is writing this letter on my behalf. Vintner Wyn is putting pen to paper, but the signature is my own! I'm learning my letters and can already spell a few words. One day, we might write letters to each other with our own hands!

I'm pleased you have a special friend. You must always treasure

Elsebeth. We all need a special person to lift our spirits when things aren't going our way.

Keep looking at the moon, dear daughter, because it's something we can do together and know we are thinking of each other.

Sending my love and prayers for your health and happiness,

Mamm

CHAPTER TWENTY-SEVEN

MAY 1529, WHITSUN

A SWARM OF MAIDS, grooms and gardeners shattered the tranquillity of the rose garden as they processed along the path running along its edge towards the jetty, eager to board the next boat for Topsham. Sir William and Lady Courtenay had sent word of a delay on their journey home from London, and with the daily chores completed, the servants were eager to enjoy a few hours of leisure time.

Mawde and Elsebeth settled on a bench seat in a small fishing boat that reeked of saltwater and the morning's catch, even though its owner had scrubbed every surface. The sail flapped as the fisherman cast off from the jetty, and the girls were quick to duck when the boom hurtled towards them. The sail snapped, taut with wind, and soon they were gliding across the water, propelled forward by a brisk easterly breeze.

John called to Mawde from across the deck and pointed at Elsebeth. 'What do you see in her? It must be like having a small child with you.'

Mawde linked arms with Elsebeth and squeezed gently.

Elsebeth remained impassive, staring at the wake trailing behind them.

'Elsebeth's company is more rewarding than yours,' Mawde said.

John snorted. The woman next to him whispered something in his ear, and they both laughed. Mawde thought nothing of it. The woman was the carpenter's wife, known for her love of rumour and gossip, and unpopular because of her loose tongue.

The fishing boat soon arrived at Topsham quay, and the eager pleasure seekers disembarked. Hot meat pies and malty beer fragranced the air, and cheerful music beckoned from the town square. Mawde and Elsebeth pushed their way through the crowd, eventually emerging breathless with anticipation. Three musicians greeted them with smiles while beating a rhythm on their tabors. Their two companions swayed from side-to-side, cheeks puffed, forcing air into bagpipes. A ring of dancers glowed with joy, moving as one in a circle. A ruddy-faced woman beckoned to the girls. Elsebeth stepped forward.

Mawde froze. Images of Tamsin flooded her mind, the memories of a previous Whitsun, leaving her winded and miserable. Mawde dropped to her knees and buried her face in her hands, hating herself for a moment of cold hesitation. Tamsin was dead because of her.

Elsebeth crouched beside Mawde and put an arm around her. Mawde lifted her head a little to show Elsebeth her gratitude, but her friend's kind face, so full of love and concern, triggered another bout of weeping.

Elsebeth nudged her. 'Mawde, whatever has upset you?' she whispered.

Mawde shook her head, struggling to get her words out between sobs. 'I can't say.'

'Let's go somewhere less crowded.'

Elsebeth eased Mawde to her feet, then walked in front of her, clearing a path through a throng of people. They continued along a narrow street and entered a deserted churchyard. Settling against a high stone wall on the far side of the red sandstone church, Elsebeth held Mawde's hand and waited for her to speak.

Minutes passed.

'I once did a terrible thing,' Mawde said, breaking the silence. 'Two people paid dearly for my sin.' She stared up at a stained glass window. It appeared dull from the outside, but inside it would be bright and colourful from the sun shining through. Mawde withdrew her hand from Elsebeth's. 'I'm not worthy of your friendship, Elsebeth.'

'You made a mistake and still punish yourself for it. That doesn't mean we should not be friends.' Elsebeth pulled a square of linen from her pocket. She dabbed Mawde's cheeks, then pressed the linen into her hand. 'In case you need it again.'

Beyond the church, musicians struck up another jolly tune.

'You should join the dancing,' Mawde said.

'You forget – I can't hear the music.'

Mawde's eyes darted towards Elsebeth. Both girls giggled.

Mawde's mood soon sobered. 'I'm serious, Elsebeth. Bad things happen to those who get close to me.'

'I'll hear no more of that silly talk.' She scrambled to her feet and reached her hand towards Mawde to help her up. 'It's rare for us to have an entire afternoon together, so let's not waste it by feeling sorry for ourselves.'

Mawde allowed herself to be pulled to her feet, grateful Elsebeth had not pressed her to explain.

As if reading her thoughts, Elsebeth said, 'Your past is your business. You've been nothing but kind to me and forgave me for keeping a big secret from you. Whatever you did, I have no right to judge you.'

'I can't believe you've ever hurt anyone!'

'I believe I have. I told Sir William what you said about Alice wanting to hurt people she disliked. Don't you see? I made him suspect her of poisoning him and sent the search in her direction.'

'Sir William almost died because of Alice!'

'I know. But is it right to retaliate and hurt the people who hurt us? Do we not commit a similar crime by doing so?'

'I don't know.' Mawde kicked a small stone with the tip of her shoe. 'It's always been that way.'

'Enough of this maudlin. Let's join the dancing,' Elsebeth said. 'We'll allow the music to calm our troubled souls.'

Mawde immersed herself in the spirit of the moment and felt her troubles ebb away. Although she had done something terrible, her mistake was in the past and she would not let it define her.

The girls danced until they were giddy. As they withdrew from a circle of dancers, Mawde spied Powderham servants heading their way. She nudged Elsebeth. Elsebeth lowered her head, and they made their way in silence to a large group of stalls. They bought spiced biscuits, pies and ale, then settled on a mound of grass to watch a troupe of performers act out a play.

'Thought I'd find you somewhere near here.'

Mawde's heart skipped a beat. It was Nicholas. Several months had passed since the day he read her mother's letter to her. Elsebeth hurried to her feet and threw her arms around him. Mawde stood more slowly, feeling flustered in his presence. She brushed crumbs from her skirt and offered him a biscuit. He accepted with a broad smile.

Full of news about his recent exploits in London, Nicholas led the girls back towards the dancing. Mawde lingered behind, feeling awkward in his presence.

'Come,' Nicholas said, turning and beckoning to her. 'Don't be shy.'

'I'm not,' Mawde replied in a voice that sounded unusually high. Her cheeks flamed. 'Sir William and Lady Courtenay might be home by now. They'll be wanting something to eat. I should go back to Powderham and help prepare something for them.'

Nicholas shook his head. 'They won't want anything. Not for a while yet. Anyway, they can help themselves to a supper of bread and cheese.'

'No!' Mawde imagined their reaction to finding the kitchen devoid of staff. 'It wouldn't be right.'

'They won't be in a rush to return home because they know everyone's here today. Sir William's bound to have secured rooms at an inn. You can stop fretting.'

The drummers raised their batons, ready to beat their tabors. Nicholas offered Mawde his hand. She took it, caught unawares by the heat in his fingers. His warmth seemed to spread through her, rushing up her arm and across her chest. She accepted the hand of a stranger standing to her other side, then the circle moved at a slow pace, but gathering speed with every rotation.

The dance finished. Mawde broke away from the ring of dancers, smiling and gasping for breath. She looked around for Elsebeth. There was no sign of her.

'Where's Elsebeth?' she cried, her heart galloping in her chest.

'She saw our father and her mother and went off with them.'

Mawde's joy evaporated, leaving a well of emptiness. 'I should go, too.'

Nicholas enclosed her hand in his. 'One more dance,' he said. 'I insist.' His pupils were wide, his lips parted in an affectionate smile.

'Very well. One more dance, but then I must go.'

When the music stopped, Mawde and Nicholas turned to face each other. Nicholas studied her, his eyes unblinking. A feeling passed through her, similar to a shiver, but not unpleasant. It was unfamiliar and thrilling.

'I really should go now.'

Nicholas angled his head a little to one side. 'Very well, but on the condition that you allow me to escort you home.'

'I don't want you to go to any trouble.'

'It's no trouble. Have you forgotten that the manor is on my way home?'

They set off at a slow walk and they had taken several steps before Mawde realised they were still holding hands. She slipped her fingers from his grasp and threw him a shy glance. He took her hand back in his and returned her gaze, his eyes sparkling like sun-dappled water.

They found a ferry bound for the village of Starcross. Nicholas negotiated an unscheduled stop at Powderham and paid well for the ferryman's trouble. The little boat was overcrowded, the passengers pressed tight together. Mawde could feel the heat radiating from Nicholas's body as they sat thigh-to-thigh, arm-to-arm, wedged between strangers. She longed for him to wrap his arm around her and draw her closer. She wanted to run her fingers over the contours of his face, trace the angles of his chiselled jaw. Ashamed of herself for harbouring wanton thoughts, she angled herself away from him to watch the shifting scenery of the shoreline.

The boat approached the Powderham jetty. Nicholas stepped up onto the seat, then the gunwale, and jumped to the jetty steps, lithe as a cat. He turned and held out his hand to Mawde.

They lingered at the top of the steps and watched the ferry continue on its way.

'Thank you for escorting me home,' Mawde said.

'It was my pleasure. I hope you enjoyed the afternoon?'

'I did. Especially the dancing.'

'Good.' Nicholas smiled. 'Farewell, Mawde.'

He reached for her hand and bowed. Mawde hoped he would raise her hand to his lips, but he lowered it to her side and stroked her cheek with his fingertip. He turned and walked away, striding towards the forge without a backward glance.

It had been a magical day, but the spell was already broken.

CHAPTER TWENTY-EIGHT

MAY 1529

'I HAVE something for each of you.' Lady Courtenay gestured for a groom to heft a bulky package on to the kitchen table. She untied the string and, with a flourish, drew out a white linen apron. 'Look at this!' she said, pointing to an embroidered emblem. 'Our reputation is on the rise, so it's only fitting that you should wear aprons bearing the Courtenay crest. Every servant at court is liveried. I want similar standards here. Soon, you'll have new jerkins, breeches and kirtles, too.'

'Forgive me, my lady, but white's not a practical colour.' Cook used his forearm to mop sweat from his flushed face. 'We'd be constantly worrying about staining the linen with hart's blood, blackberry juice, gravy or wine.'

'I understand your concern, Hugh. There are new grey aprons, too. You will wear grey whilst working in the kitchen, then change into a clean white apron if you have reason to come into the hall. We are raising our standards at Powderham.' Lady Courtenay stepped aside to allow two pages to deposit a heavy crate onto the table. 'We have new tankards, plates and bowls as well.' She looked at each servant in turn. 'I have a third offering which I know will be more to your liking.' Her eyes lingered on Mawde. 'My husband and I have excellent servants here at Powderham. My husband's penchant for feasting has tested you all repeatedly, and every time, you've done us proud. Therefore, Sir William has reviewed the household accounts and has decided to give each of you a small increase in wage.'

Mawde suppressed an urge to embrace her mistress. She had tried to save coins since her arrival at Powderham, but the contents of her purse were stubbornly lean. The news of a wage increase helped her feel a little closer to home. It would be a long time before she would have the funds to return to Roseland, but her dream was becoming more of a possibility.

Nods and grins rippled through the kitchen.

Lady Courtenay beamed. 'Sir William will discuss the finer details with you soon. Now, get back to work, except you, Mawde.' She beckoned with her finger. 'You're to come with me.'

'Yes, my lady.' Mawde followed her out of the kitchen and to a trestle table positioned at the far end of the hall. Almost the whole surface was covered with clothes, sheets and bales of cloth. Lady Courtenay selected a folded piece of fine woollen cloth and held it out to Mawde. 'You've achieved things far beyond my expectations, and I've never heard you grumble or complain. Take this. You've earned it.'

Mawde opened the fabric and caught her breath. It was a thin blanket, the wool soft and almost cool to the touch, with little orange flowers embroidered along one edge. Mawde took care to fold it and placed it back on the board. 'Thank you, my lady, but I can't accept. The maids will make my life a misery if they see something as fine as that on my bed.'

Lady Courtenay retrieved it. 'I insist you have it. Say your mother sent it as a gift. You haven't seen your mother for a long time, so I cannot believe they would begrudge you a gift from home?'

A reasonable enough explanation.

'Thank you, my lady.' Mawde bobbed a curtsey, then scampered up the servants' stairs to give the blanket pride of place on her bed.

Mawde took her time to select a large handful of unspoilt borage flowers. The sky-blue petals resembled stars and would make the perfect finishing touch for her subtlety. She stood up and looked around, hoping to see Elsebeth, but there was no sign of her. Mawde left the herb beds and walked a little way down the lane towards the forge, scanning the vegetation. To her delight, she spotted a bountiful clump of sweet white violets nestling by the edge of the woodland. She plucked one and twisted the hairy stem between her fingers while admiring the petals. The violets would be delicious with a coating of crystallised sugar. Better still, she would keep a few back and set them over a clear jelly so that it would appear as if the little blooms were floating on a moonlit pond.

Mawde heard a twig snap somewhere behind her, followed by the crunching of stones underfoot. She spun around to see who was approaching.

'Mix violets with lavender and you'll attract your true love. That's what my sister would tell you, anyway.'

'Good morrow, Nicholas.' Mawde bent to place her trug on the verge so Nicholas would not see her blushes. 'How is Elsebeth today? I was hoping to see her.'

'She's in good spirits, thank you. Riding with my uncle, regaling him with the latest rumours, no doubt.'

'Doesn't that raise an eyebrow or two? Her riding with Sir William?'

'I don't think so. Most servants know of my link to his family through my mother, so they probably think he pities her. Truth is, he's very fond of her. She's a competent rider and excellent conversationalist – not that many people know that!' Nicholas adjusted a lace on his jerkin. 'Walk with me a while?'

'I can only spare a few minutes.'

'Then I shall have to make do.' Nicholas pointed to a bend in the lane. 'To there and back?'

'Perfect.'

Mawde fell into step beside him, and they set off at a slow pace, walking in silence. Mawde smiled, her cheeks aflame as she was overcome with shyness.

'It seems we've run out of things to talk about,' Nicholas said amiably.

'We only saw each other yesterday and nothing of interest has happened since. I'm sorry Elsebeth left Topsham early, leaving you to entertain me.'

'Don't be sorry about that.'

Nicholas stopped and put a finger to his lips. He pointed to a jay taking flight from a fallen branch, a shock of blue on each wing shimmering in the afternoon light.

Nicholas reached for Mawde's hands and ran his thumbs over her fingers. 'I asked Beth to leave us. I wanted you to myself for a while.'

Mawde gazed at their intertwined fingers. 'I enjoyed your company,' she said, hoping she didn't sound too forward.

Nicholas dusted her knuckles with featherlight kisses.

'Beth talks about you all the time. I feel like I know you so well.'

'I love her as if she were my sister,' Mawde confessed. 'Even when she didn't speak, I felt I was in the presence of someone who cared about me.'

'Her affection for you doesn't surprise me. You captured my heart the moment I stepped off that ship.' Nicholas spoke softly, his tone sincere. 'It's hard to reconcile you with the troubled child plucked from the bosom of her family. I can't imagine how hard it was for you to adjust to living here. I know this sounds selfish, but I'm glad your uncle delivered you from Roseland.'

'Do you mean that?'

'I do.' Nicholas released Mawde's hands and smoothed his palms across his immaculate jerkin. 'Tell me, Mawde, do you think you could ever have feelings for me too?'

Mawde stifled a nervous giggle. 'I already do! But Nicholas, your lifestyle is different from mine. I fear your interest in me will fade.'

Nicholas shook his head. 'It won't. Not in this lifetime. My mother understood the draw of love. I believe I share that understanding.' His pupils were wide, his eyes darting from side to side as he waited for her to say something in return.

Butterflies danced inside Mawde's stomach. Words failed her. Eventually she said, 'Cook will be angry if I stay out too long.'

Nicholas's expression turned serious. 'Of course. We'll find another opportunity to spend time together. But please, let it be soon?'

'After Sunday service? I'm allowed three hours to spend as I please every other week.'

'After Sunday service,' confirmed Nicholas. He kissed her brow, then gently pressed his lips to hers.

Mawde closed her eyes, wishing the delicious moment would last forever.

When they drew apart, Mawde counted the days on her fingers. 'Six days until we meet again on Sunday.'

'Six days will feel like a lifetime.'

'For me, too.'

Mawde retrieved her trug and headed back to the kitchen. Her ears pricked at sounds coming from all around her. Squirrels chattered. Branches creaked. A wren trilled in a tree. And Nicholas was singing.

CHAPTER TWENTY-NINE
APRIL 1530

MAWDE REMOVED her coif and stretched out on a blanket of celandines, her hair fanning out like a glossy black halo. Nicholas settled beside her, propped on one elbow, and ran his fingertip over her brow, nose and chin. He traced the contours of her jaw and neck, then paused in the little dip above her breastbone.

'You're as radiant as the sun,' he said, his voice thick with desire.

Heat coursed through Mawde's body. She closed her eyes, willing his finger to continue its journey. Her skin tingled beneath his touch and deep inside she felt a longing, a desperate need to press her body against his and to possess him with all her being until they merged as one. A screeching crow fell silent, as if holding its breath and willing them on. Mawde reached up to Nicholas. She cupped her hands around his cheeks and drew him towards her until their lips touched. The solid ground beneath her seemed to melt away, and she felt as if she was floating, cradled in the arms of a man she adored. She rolled

Nicholas onto his back and sat astride him, pinning him to the carpet of yellow-gold stars.

During the long winter months, Mawde had noticed changes to her reflection in the mirror. Her breasts now swelled pleasingly at the neckline of her bodice. She had a confident poise, and long dark lashes framing seductive eyes. The scar above her eyebrow was her only minor imperfection, and even that was difficult to discern. The dashing new stable groom took every opportunity to flirt with her, and even Ambrose had dropped his hurtful jibes. But she had eyes for only one man. Mawde felt a part of Nicholas stir beneath her. She arched her back and moved her body back and forth, driven by an unfamiliar instinct. Her body was a riot of confusing sensations, intense, yet compulsive and thrilling. Nicholas watched her through hungry eyes, his gaze drifting to the exposed swell of her breasts. His hand burrowed beneath her and fidgeted with his codpiece. Mawde had heard maids whispering under the cover of darkness, describing the antics they had performed with the grooms. Now, she was eager to experiment for herself. Nicholas had almost freed himself and Mawde raised herself up a fraction and splayed out her skirts. And then, in her head, she heard Grandmother screeching, warning Mawde to be careful and not ruin her life. Her lustful thoughts dwindled to nothing and her good sense returned. Unmarried pregnant servants faced a future of hardship, a lifetime of regret.

The fire in Mawde's belly turned to ice. She felt confused and ashamed. She rolled off Nicholas and cursed her grandmother's ghost for extinguishing her passion. If Grandmother had not perished in the fire, Mawde would not be at Powderham, nor have fallen in love with a perfect young man, only to have him snatched away by the rules of decorum.

Nicholas sat up and furrowed his brow. He pulled the heads from celandines and cast the naked stalks to one side.

'I'm sorry,' Mawde said. 'It's only... I can't... I can't risk—'

'It's not that! I'm glad you have a sense of modesty about you.'

'Then what is it?'

Nicholas stared into the distance. 'I'm not sure how to break this to you...'

Mawde felt a sense of foreboding. 'I know what you're going to say. We've enjoyed time together over the past few months, but now it's time for all this to end.'

Nicholas hesitated. 'Not exactly. I must leave Powderham for a while, but I can't bear the thought of us being apart.'

Mawde toyed with a lock of her hair and wound it so tight around her finger that her skin blanched. 'You'll get used to it.'

Nicholas forced a smile. 'Sir William wishes to reward me for my hard work, but the reward comes at a high price.'

A cloud covered the sun. Mawde shivered.

'I have to leave Powderham to take advantage of a magnificent opportunity to secure a comfortable future.'

'I'm pleased for you,' Mawde said, resisting the urge to cry.

'You don't sound pleased. Think back to last year. When we were first reacquainted, I had been overseas with a merchant to assess investment opportunities for Sir William. Turns out, I did rather well, and that same merchant is expanding his empire and importing exotic goods to London. He even has an arrangement in place to supply the royal courts! Sir William is considering investing in the venture and has commissioned me to accompany the merchant and determine the level of risk involved.'

'Where will you go?' Mawde was struggling to imagine a Sunday afternoon without a walk in the woods holding his hand, or a snatched kiss behind the kitchen garden wall.

'Spain. Portugal. Places I've not heard of, and some far away. I don't know how long I'll be gone. It could be months, or more than a year, but if things go well, I'll be handsomely rewarded with the means to furnish a comfortable home in which to raise a family and even start a business of my own.'

'So, this is the end of our time together?' Mawde felt as if the earth might drop away from beneath her. 'With you, I tasted true happiness and I'll always be grateful for that.' Mawde buried her face in her hands, fighting a tide of sorrow.

'No! Mawde, what are you saying?' Nicholas prised her hands from her face. 'I love you with all my heart. When I return to Powderham, it will be you I look for first.'

A wood pigeon called to its mate in a melancholy tone. Mawde feared she would break apart.

'I have something for you.' Nicholas fumbled inside his shirt and pulled out a small oval-shaped wooden box, inlaid with delicate marquetry.

Mawde took the box and stroked the smooth wood. It was warm from resting against his skin. 'It's beautiful. Thank you.'

'Look inside.'

Mawde lifted the lid. 'Oh, my!' A pendant nestled on a blue velvet cushion. It was in the shape of a dainty flower, with each of its four petals rounded at the tip and inlaid with mother-of-pearl. A small disc of pale blue glass joined them at the centre, and the flower was secured to a length of grey ribbon. Nicholas lifted it from the box and draped it around Mawde's neck.

'I give you this gift as a token of my love.' Nicholas kissed Mawde's forehead. 'I've been carrying it around, waiting for the right moment to give it to you. This isn't how I imagined it would be, but you must have it before I leave.'

Mawde caressed the smooth surface of a petal. 'I have nothing to give you in return.'

'Oh, but you do.'

'I have nothing, Nicholas. Not even a tiny trinket with which to declare my love.'

'The only thing I want from you is your promise to wait for my return.'

'You have my promise.'

'Dearest Mawde, that's enough for me.' He pulled her into an embrace and held her tight against him. When he released her, he said, 'Will you wait for me for as long as it takes, saving yourself only for me?'

A squirrel jumped from one branch to another, then stood as still as a garden statue. His beady eyes were fixed on Mawde, as if waiting for her answer.

'I will.'

'You understand what I'm asking? I intend to gain sufficient means to return and set up my own home and business, and of course, to make you my wife.'

'Yes. I'll wait for you.' Doubt pricked at her conscience. 'Shouldn't you speak to your father first? And Sir William?'

'My father knows of my feelings for you, and I know he'll not object. How could he? As for Sir William, I'd rather not tell him yet.' Nicholas knelt in front of her and clasped both of her hands. 'Sweeting, before God, I declare I'm yours, and yours alone.'

Mawde's lips parted into an adoring smile. 'Dearest

Nicholas, before God, I declare I'm yours, and yours alone.'

Nicholas drew her into a passionate kiss. 'We'll declare a public betrothal as soon as I return and consummate our pledge. We'll have a small church wedding – inside, not at the door – and I promise to be a good husband.'

Mawde was giddy with emotion. 'Can't we declare our betrothal now?'

Nicholas checked the position of the sun. 'Not today. Alas, it grieves me to tell you my departure is imminent. I sail on this afternoon's tide.'

'No!' Mawde's knees buckled, causing her to stumble.

'Think of me every day,' he said, holding her steady. 'Pray for my safe return.'

With slow, reluctant steps, they advanced towards the courtyard gate. Exchanging sad smiles, they said farewell to each other, then Mawde drew away from Nicholas.

'God speed, my love. May the Lord keep you safe until the moment you return to me.' With her head held high, she walked towards the kitchen, pressing her fingers to the pendant nestled against her skin.

The merchant ship glided towards the middle of the river, then changed tack towards the open sea. Mawde withdrew to the shadows of the scullery, her breaking heart held together by the gossamer threads of a promise.

CHAPTER THIRTY
MAY 1532

Two years had passed since Nicholas's departure. Two long years without any news. Mawde knelt on the grass verge bordering a herb bed, picking rosemary and lovage sprigs and layering them in her trug. An owl's hoot made her look towards the trees beyond the garden wall. An owl hooting in the middle of the afternoon! A small team of gardeners continued digging on the far side of the garden, oblivious to the owl's call when it hooted again. Mawde glimpsed a movement among the branches of a tree. She smiled. It was Elsebeth, and she was beckoning Mawde to join her.

By the time Mawde had left the kitchen garden and followed the wall towards the woodland, Elsebeth had climbed down from her hiding place in the branches and was running towards her.

Her face appeared flushed, and her eyes were bright with joy. 'Nicholas has written, Mawde. Nicholas is well! He's been to France and Italy and is now heading towards Spain. He hopes to return home before autumn.'

Mawde threw her arms around Elsebeth and shed tears of joy as the two friends held each other tightly.

'I was so worried, thinking he'd perished in a storm.' Mawde released Elsebeth and dried her cheeks with the back of her hand. 'But even as the months crept by, I never gave up hope.'

'He said in his letter, it took all this time to find someone who could carry a letter to London and deliver it to the King's court. Sir William brought it home with him yesterday and summoned my father to his office to tell him the good news.' Elsebeth stroked Mawde's arm. 'Nicholas really does love you, you know. He talked about you constantly before he went away.'

Mawde smiled. 'I know. My heart flutters every time I think of him, even after all this time. Dear God, how I long to see him again!'

'I wish I could feel that way about someone, even if only for a day.'

'You'll have your turn, Beth. I'm sure of it.'

Elsebeth shook her head. 'Not with the secret I'm forced to keep. Imagine the uproar if the truth was revealed. I'm a prisoner of Powderham, serving my sentence as a silent victim of ridicule.'

Mawde felt a rush of love for her dearest friend. If Nicholas returned with even half of the wealth he had dreamed of, there might be a way to let Elsebeth live a normal life. 'One day, I'll take you away from here, Beth. I promise.'

The kitchen was in chaos by the time Mawde returned.

'What took you so long?' Cook was pacing the floor

and clenching and unclenching his fingers. Many months had passed since Mawde had seen him so out of sorts.

Mawde gazed around the room, noting the angst on the faces of the other servants. 'Has something happened?'

'You could say that! Sir William announced this morning that he's expecting an esteemed guest, and insists we prepare the finest dishes fit for a king's banquet. He wants a subtlety, too.'

'When for?'

'Today.'

Mawde's stomach clenched. 'I need a few days to make something appropriate, not a few hours!'

'Shall I leave it to you to tell Sir William he can't have what he wants?' Cook's expression turned to one of sympathy. He had softened towards Mawde during the two years since Nicholas left Powderham, and he often praised her for her hard work. 'Why don't you trim the pies and jellies with a few of your prettiest floral decorations? That might be enough to stop them from noticing the absence of a proper subtlety.'

John pushed a bowl of cherries towards Mawde. 'They've got stones in, but can you do something with them?'

Mawde pictured them sparkling with sugar crystals and tiny flakes of gold leaf. 'I have an idea,' she said, gratefully accepting them.

The brewer poured a cup of cool ale and passed it to Mawde. 'I overheard the steward talking about the guest. His name's Thomas Cromwell. He's an important man, by all accounts, and has the ear of the King. That's probably why Sir William's so intent on impressing him.'

'A politician then?' Mawde drank thirstily from the cup.

'Don't think so. More like a legal man, or something similar.'

Cook huffed and puffed. 'If this Cromwell's as powerful as the rumours would have us believe, we can't have anything go wrong with this dinner – let alone something that could shame Sir William.' He thumped a large ball of pastry on to the kitchen table, bringing the conversation to an end.

Adam was turning a swan and a small pig on the spits. Mawde watched a rivulet of sweat trickle down the side of his florid face and soak into his shirt. He perched on a stool and used his feet to shuffle it away from the heat of the fire. He yawned and buried his face in his hands. Soon after, he was snoring. Cook cuffed him above the ear, making him jerk upright. Mawde took pity on him. As soon as Cook's back was turned, she passed him her cup of ale. He thanked her and pulled a face, causing Mawde to chuckle.

'Mawde!' Cook looked apoplectic. 'This is not the time for silliness. This is your moment to impress an important guest.'

Mawde turned her attention back to the cherries, and dreamed of a day when she might leave the life of a kitchen maid well and truly behind her.

Sitting near the end of the trestle table shared by the servants, Mawde craned her neck to get a better view of Sir William and his guest. Sir William was in high spirits, making flamboyant gestures with his hands, telling entertaining stories and making those around him laugh. All except one man.

The gentleman seated to the right of Sir William laughed at something when Sir William addressed him directly. Afterwards, his eyes roved around the great hall, scanning the faces of all those present. Then his gaze settled on Mawde. Intense. Unsettling. She shuddered and lowered her gaze to her trencher. She broke off a small mouthful of pork, placed the succulent meat in her mouth, and chewed. When she dared to glance back at the guest, the pork turned dry in her mouth. He was still looking at her, his brow ridged with thought. Mawde tried to swallow, but the meat stuck in her throat. She panicked and struggled out from her position on the bench, knocking against Ambrose and standing on John's foot. She dashed into the kitchen, her heart thumping, her head pounding. She coughed up the meat, and then staggered into the courtyard where she fought to catch her breath.

By the time she returned to the table, Thomas Cromwell's interest had shifted elsewhere. Mawde pushed her food around her trencher and took a small sip of ale. Something about this guest unsettled her. He was of portly build, immaculately groomed, and wore jewelled rings on his fingers. But his fine black clothes drained him of colour, and he looked like an angel of death.

CHAPTER THIRTY-ONE

SEPTEMBER 1532

SUMMER PASSED with a steady stream of visitors to the manor, and Mawde had plenty of time to practise her confectionery skills, making small sweet treats and subtleties without the pressure of having to create elaborate new designs. She felt more settled in the busy kitchen, her fellow servants now generous with their compliments and treating her as one of their own. She finished shaping miniature pastry acorns and set them on a tray with neatly cut oak leaves, then slid the tray across to Ambrose.

'Beautiful,' he said, giving Mawde a broad smile. 'But I fear I might ruin such intricate pieces with my indelicate hands. Do you mind?'

'Not at all.'

Mawde set about covering his spiced pork and apple pie with her elegant pastry decorations, while Ambrose left the kitchen to fetch more flour.

There was a sudden commotion in the courtyard. Hoofbeats clattered over cobbles then drew to an abrupt halt. Dogs barked. Boots thumped across the unforgiving ground. Everyone in the kitchen thronged towards the windows, eager to see who had arrived with such a racket.

Mawde caught a flash of apprehension ripple across Cook's furrowed brow. Unsettled, she returned to the worktable.

'Did you see who it was?' Ambrose asked, returning to the kitchen dragging a large sack.

The brewer glanced at Cook before answering him. 'Bouchier, the vintner.'

'The vintner? What brings him at such a gallop?'

Mawde immediately thought of her mother. Her last letter, received before Nicholas departed, had reported Vintner Wyn's rapidly failing health. Mawde assumed Vintner Wyn had passed soon after the letter was sent. With no one to write or read for her or her mother, the fine thread of contact had broken. Mawde tried to suppress all thoughts of home and concentrated on the conversation taking place around her.

'Whatever the reason, he's not happy about it.' The brewer sounded anxious.

Angry words drifted through the open window. Cook wiped his hands on his apron and opened the door to the courtyard. He listened to a heated exchange then leaned against the doorframe, his usually florid cheeks drained of all colour.

'Cook? What is it?' She had never seen him look so beaten.

''Tis the beginning of the end.'

'How so?' said the brewer, wringing her hands together.

'The vintner accused Sir William of not settling his account. If that's true, other merchants will come calling.'

'Hugh Dillon, how dare you suggest such a thing!' Master Davey stepped out from the shadows of the corridor connecting the kitchen to the great hall. His face contorted with rage. '*You* are the last person I'd expect to stoop so low. Wait 'til the master hears about your idle gossip.'

Cook seemed unruffled as he ambled towards the steward. 'We'll soon see if it be idle gossip.' He prodded the steward in the chest. 'And don't go thinking you're any safer than the rest of us.'

The steward's lips curled at the corners. 'What are you implying?'

'I've seen you strutting about with your head up your ass.'

Mawde and John gasped in unison. Mawde braced, anticipating the steward's reaction, but he stood in stony silence while Cook railed at him.

'Think about it! There hasn't been a feast for three or four months, and I heard Lady Courtenay was refused her allowance for new robes. Signs that times are hard, wouldn't you agree?'

Mawde racked her brain, desperate to recall her last grand subtlety and prove Cook's fear to be wrong. And how long ago had she been told there was no gold leaf because it was suddenly difficult to get hold of? She gathered empty bowls and headed to the scullery, needing a quiet moment alone to gather her thoughts.

If Sir William had accrued large debts, what future would Nicholas have as his junior secretary? And what of their future? Nicholas had made it clear they would not marry until he had sufficient means to support her. She thought back to the news about his letter. Nicholas was engaged with Sir William's business ventures, and that was why he was still away from home. Could his efforts put everything right again for Sir William? Determined to believe all would be well, Mawde took confident steps back to the kitchen.

She had lived through difficult times before, and whatever the outcome of this latest situation, she would get through it again. Somehow.

CHAPTER THIRTY-TWO
JUNE 1533

HOUSEMAIDS FUSSED in the kitchen like bees swarming over nectar. They were in unfamiliar territory and getting in the way. Preparations for a grand banquet were in full swing, to honour Thomas Cromwell and his appointment to the role of Chancellor of the Exchequer.

Ale flowed freely from brand new pitchers, and servants no longer feared for their futures. The buttery was piled high with cases of fine wines. Jars of spices, pickles and preserves crowded every shelf. Most encouragingly of all, Mawde had taken delivery of six cones of sugar and a generous supply of gold leaf. Confident Nicholas was somewhere at the heart of this change of fortune, Mawde set to work creating her finest subtlety yet.

Lady Courtenay enthused over Mawde's sketches for a sugary interpretation of Heaven. The project was ambitious – angels playing harps while swaying on candied swings; fluffy clouds floating above rivers of shimmering silver; trees bearing golden fruits and miniature deer roaming in lush meadows. Mawde was adamant she had the skills for such a detailed masterpiece, complete with an edging of miniature Tudor roses.

Mawde stepped back to assess her handiwork and iden- tify sections needing last-minute adjustments. It was the most exquisite piece of artwork she had ever crafted. Sir William would be thrilled.

The door creaked open. Music wafted into the kitchen, competing with the hubbub of a hundred babbling voices. Housemaids adjusted their coifs. Mawde and the brewer smoothed down their kirtles. Following Cook's lead, they swapped soiled grey aprons for pristine white ones, then assembled in line behind Sir William's gentlemen server, a yeoman server, and four grooms, ready to carry platters and dishes to the hall for Sir William and his guests. It had been a gruelling time in the kitchen, but Mawde was proud of all they had achieved. Pastries had been baked to crisp perfection, and the breads were evenly shaped. Baked fish retained the succulence of tender flesh, and steam emanated from side dishes fragrant with spices and herbs.

Platters of appetisers went out heavily laden and returned empty after being picked clean. As servants helped each other raise heavy trays upon their shoulders, a fanfare of trumpets announced the imminent arrival of the main courses to the great hall. Mawde sensed Cook's tension. With it being a Friday, he had not been able to showcase his skills with meat. Instead, he had created an array of tempting dishes using mackerel, eels and perch. Roasted onions had been separated into layers, cut into petal shapes and reassembled as savoury flowers. Salted cod basked in a rich red wine gravy, while whole trout lay on platters waiting to be dressed in a tantalising cherry sauce.

Mawde poured cherry sauce for one guest after another at the lower tables in the hall, returning to the kitchen twice to refill her jug with more. The hall thrummed with competing conversations, laughter and guffaws. Guests sat crammed together on narrow benches, shouting across tables, exchanging opinions and news. Acrobats tumbled at the centre of the room while jugglers shimmied between diners, entertaining with comical tricks. Mawde scanned the hall for a glimpse of Nicholas, hoping he had planned to surprise her with an unannounced return. Her optimism soon evaporated. Nicholas was not there.

At last, it was time for the final course. Adam and John lifted Mawde's sculpture from the table and onto the yeoman's outstretched arms. Mawde fussed over it, resisting the urge to adjust the positions of the tiny sugar sculptures. After a deep breath to steady her nerves, she stepped away to allow the yeoman to process towards the hall.

Mawde held her breath as the yeoman placed her tableau of Heaven in front of Sir William. He studied it carefully, pointing and talking to his guest. He looked up at the yeoman and smiled. Mawde turned her attention to Thomas Cromwell. He puckered his brow and his lips turned down as he studied Mawde's perfect creation. Other guests seated at the top table clapped with raucous applause, but Cromwell interlaced his fingers and rested his hands on the table. Sir William's eyes roved the lower end of the hall until his gaze fell on Mawde. He leaned towards Cromwell, smiled, and pointed at her. Cromwell fixed his sombre eyes on Mawde, responding to Sir William with only a slight dip of his head. As he continued to stare, she lowered her gaze. The hairs rose on the back of her neck, and she turned and fled to the sanctuary of the kitchen.

'Sir William wants to see you.' Master Davey peered down his nose, appearing aloof and intimidating.

'Do you know why?' Mawde asked politely, while stacking clean dishes on a shelf.

'It's not for us to question his instructions. Stop what you're doing and come at once.'

Cook prompted her to remove her sugar-spattered apron. Mawde quickly released the ties and handed it to him before following the steward out of the kitchen.

The hall was empty of guests apart from a small gathering huddled at one end. Trestles and benches had been stacked at the sides and rushes lifted from the floor. House servants busied themselves with sweeping, too far away to hear what Sir William had to say. Mawde curtseyed, and Sir William raised her with a smile. She glanced at Lady Courtenay who had her head lowered and was frowning at her lap. Thomas Cromwell stood at Sir William's other side and fixed Mawde with a probing stare.

Sir William cleared his throat. Mawde interlocked her fingers and grasped them tightly, willing them to stop shaking.

'Don't look so tense,' Sir William said. 'I'm the bearer of good news.'

Mawde caught Lady Courtenay throw him a sidelong glance.

'An opportunity has arisen for you to travel to London,' Sir William continued, 'to work for my esteemed friend.'

'That's not—'

Sir William silenced Lady Courtenay by raising his hand.

'London?' Mawde's chin wobbled. She imagined large crowds, noisy streets, and a warren of alleyways where she might easily become lost. 'How long will I be absent from Powderham?'

'Permanently,' Sir William said.

'No!' Lady Courtenay threw Mawde a look of sympathy. She leaned towards her husband and spoke in a harsh whisper that was loud enough for Mawde to hear. 'Must you trade our only confectioner to repay a foolish debt?'

Sir William glowered at his wife. 'You begrudge a servant such a fine opportunity? Thomas will pay her well.'

Lady Courtenay shook her head and excused herself from the hall.

'Sir William and Lady Courtenay admire your work.' Cromwell's voice was as smooth as velvet, but his eyes were cold and flinty. 'Personally, I find your efforts amateurish. However, under the guidance of the right mentor, I'm sure you can be trained. I'm willing to sponsor you and give you an opportunity to develop your skills. We'll soon discover if you have what is required to become a truly skilled confectioner.'

Sir William murmured his approval of Cromwell's proposition. 'As much as I'd like to keep you here, I cannot match what Master Cromwell is offering. With the right teacher, you'll earn a reputation in greater circles than could ever happen here.'

Cromwell twisted a cumbersome ring around his podgy finger. 'You will join the team of confectioners who work for His Majesty, the King. You will remain under my employ throughout your time with them, and as such, I may recall you from the court confectionary at any time. You should consider this an honour, and an opportunity to become a skilled artisan.'

The words pummelled Mawde like a violent hailstorm, cold, hard and stinging. It was too much to take in. She would be leaving her kind mistress to work for a man whose aura was as dark as his clothes. The reality of her situation struck her like an axe. She would soon be far from

Elsebeth, and even further from her mother. Would Nicholas know where to find her? Mawde closed her eyes, desperate to calm her swirling thoughts. Of course, Elsebeth would tell Nicholas when he returned. She would run to the forge to find Elsebeth and share her disappointing news.

Mawde swallowed and addressed Sir William. 'Master, may I be excused?'

Sir William waved her away. 'Of course. Off you go and gather your possessions.'

'Now, sir? But I thought I'd have time to—'

'Regrettably, there's no time for you to do anything other than gather your belongings. You sail within the hour.'

Powderham faded into the distance, shrinking into a miniature version of itself. A flock of gulls circled overhead, squawking and shrieking at one another. One bird separated from its companions, heading back towards land with a lamenting call. The other gulls wheeled around, responding with a dance of sorts. Then all the birds flew away, leaving the air empty and still.

The pitiful screeching echoed in Mawde's mind for several minutes afterwards. It was as if the voices of the dead were calling out a warning, but about what, she could not say.

PART THREE
GREENWICH

CHAPTER THIRTY-THREE

JULY 1533

THE MIDDAY SUN beat down on Greenwich Palace, illuminating its red brick facade and glinting on large glazed windows. The building was large and regal, its reflection rippling on the river water and reaching towards the ship.

Cromwell loomed at Mawde's side, his presence dark and ominous. 'You'll get used to it,' he said. He turned to Ralph Sadler, his secretary, and lowered his voice. 'Ralph, when you get to Austin Friars, be sure to update the ledger. Record Sir William's part repayment and adjust the date for final settlement to six months hence.'

'It'll be the first thing I do, Master Cromwell. Does Sir William have the means to repay the debt?'

'Hard to say.' Cromwell turned his back towards the riverbank and fanned his florid face with his hat. 'Whatever happens, he won't cajole me into another foolish arrangement like this.'

Mawde felt a flush creep from her neck to her face. She felt like a calf traded on market day, a commodity bartered and paid for. She caught Ralph studying her, his bottom lip caught between his teeth. He looked as if he might say something but thought better of it.

Cromwell continued speaking. 'It might prove worth-while on this occasion, but we'll see. Meanwhile, I'll trust Sir William to honour the remaining terms.'

Cromwell moved across the deck, his gait awkward and lumbering. Mawde cleared her throat to speak, but Ralph put a finger to his lips and shook his head.

'Some things are best left unsaid. Take no heed of Master Cromwell's words – for your own sake.'

'Whatever's occurring between him and Sir William is no business of mine.' Mawde paused. 'Your expression a moment ago suggested you felt sorry for me. Why?'

Ralph turned and stared towards the jetty where men were gathering to unload the ship after it docked alongside.

'Please tell me,' Mawde said. 'Master Cromwell snatched me from Powderham giving me very little warning and no time to bid farewell to my dearest friend. At least help me understand why I'm here.'

Ralph hesitated. 'Master Cromwell's done you a favour. You should be glad he recognised your potential and agreed to bring you with him. He's difficult to impress, but work hard, Mawde, and learn everything you can about making confectionery. Make him proud. The greater the reputation you earn for yourself, the better it will reflect on him, and you'll reap the rewards.'

'But why did he employ me? He spared me no praise at Powderham. The opposite, in fact.'

Ralph stroked his immaculate beard. 'That's his way. He's not one to instil arrogance. No matter how accomplished we become, we always have more to learn, and he likes us to be open to the wisdom of others and not assume we know everything already. If Master Cromwell thought your skills were lacking, you wouldn't be here now. He's placing you in the King's confectionary at his own expense, so although Sir William gave you to Master Cromwell to repay a debt, you come at a significant cost. Master Cromwell's investing in you and your future and expects great things in return. You'd be wise to avoid disappointing him.'

'Easy for you to say. You're not being passed around like an unwanted trinket.'

As the ship drew closer to the jetty, Greenwich Palace grew in grandeur. It was gargantuan compared to the manor at Powderham and would need a large kitchen to cater to a building of such magnitude. Houses spread from the sides of the palace, strung out along the edge of a narrow road. A large hill rose behind, with a glimpse of an orchard on its lower slopes beyond the palace. Two riders on horseback galloped towards the brow of the hill, kicking up pale clouds of dust as they raced towards the top. Mawde thought of Elsebeth and smiled.

'That's more like it,' Ralph said. 'Embrace the change of scenery and, dare I say it, an exciting opportunity to make something of yourself.'

His words were reassuring. No one at Greenwich knew her, therefore Mawde could start afresh. With Cromwell paying for her to work in a royal kitchen, she would strive to become the best confectioner London had ever seen, and eventually free herself from servitude. Together, she and Nicholas would earn sufficient money to buy fine clothes and live in a comfortable home while saving for the most prized reward of all – the return to her beloved Roseland.

A smiling sailor reached down towards her. She grasped his hand and pulled herself up on to the gunwale of the ship and stepped with confidence onto dry land. A warm breeze dragged the pungent smell of river water across the jetty, filling the air with the odours of mud, effluent and decay. Mawde tucked stray strands of hair beneath her coif and cap and gazed up at the palace windows.

'Mawde Hygons has arrived,' she announced to anyone who cared to listen. She gathered her belongings and hurried after Cromwell.

Despite his bulk and awkward limp, Cromwell moved swiftly along one corridor after another, his black robe billowing like a raven's wings.

Cromwell stopped two perspiring butcher boys dressed in bloodied aprons and struggling with the bulk of a large boar. 'Which way to the confectionary?' he asked.

'Down there, second on the right, sir,' replied the taller of the boys, jerking his head towards another corridor. 'There's no one there, though. They're at York Place and won't be back for weeks.'

Mawde's confidence wavered.

Cromwell grunted. 'Everyone?'

'Think so.'

Cromwell fixed his mean grey eyes on Mawde. 'We'll have to find something to occupy you until they return.'

'The clerk's in his office across the way,' said the other boy. 'He might be able to help you.'

Cromwell muttered his thanks and charged towards the clerk's office. The room was small. Ledgers and papers cluttered shelves, and a portly clerk hunched over a writing table, squinting at a document. The clerk looked up as Cromwell knocked on the door.

'Master Cromwell! Enter, please.' The clerk scrambled to his feet and bowed. 'How may I be of assistance?'

Cromwell beckoned Mawde to step forward. 'This is Mawde Hygons. She's to work at the confectionary, but I hear the confectioners aren't there.'

'Correct, Master Cromwell. They were called to York Place after the coronation. No one told me to expect an addition to the confectionary.'

'I sent word to the cofferer. Perhaps he did not mention it because I will pay her board and wages.'

The clerk dipped his head. 'As you wish. She could work in the bakehouse until the confectionary reopens, if that pleases you?' To Mawde, he added, 'I presume you can bake?'

'I can,' she replied.

Cromwell thanked the clerk and turned to leave. He paused in the doorway and looked over his shoulder at Mawde. 'I omitted to tell you about your lodgings. At dusk, visit the laundry and ask for Widow Foxe's daughter. Widow Foxe has agreed to take you as a lodger.'

Before Mawde could reply, Cromwell had gone.

'I'd better show you to the bakehouse then.'

The clerk escorted Mawde out of the office and pulled a large brass key from his belt to lock the door behind them. Mawde struggled to keep pace with his nimble strides and had to run every few steps to keep up with him. They hurried through a maze of corridors, passing a confusing variety of kitchens, storerooms and cellars until they reached the bakehouse. A small pile of bricks propped the door open, permitting the delicious aroma of baking bread to spill from inside.

A tall, flushed man was kneading a mass of dough. The clerk spoke to him, but his words were drowned out by the clanging of pots and general din of the crowded room. The man smirked at the clerk, then looked at Mawde, his eyes shining with lust. Mawde looked away, scanning the bakehouse, hoping to find a friendlier face. Pot boys scurried this way and that, reacting to the barked instructions of master bakers. Not one person showed any interest in Mawde. And they were all men.

Once again, she was alone among strangers, and vulnerable.

CHAPTER THIRTY-FOUR
AUGUST 1533

AFTER FIVE WEEKS of hot bread ovens, lewd stares and suggestive comments, Mawde was glad to put the palace bakehouse days behind her. Now she endured a different scrutiny. She recognised the signs – a grimace of disgust, wariness in the eyes, and the sigh of bitter disappointment. Resentment.

The two women eyed each other with suspicion. Mawde held her head high, but she was unsettled by the older woman's penetrating gaze.

'Why?' One clipped word was enough to infer that Mawde was an imposter in this woman's domain.

Master Dawes, yeoman of the confectionary, maintained his cool composure. 'She's Cromwell's. He wants her to learn from the best. Won't hurt to have an extra pair of hands here, will it?' He drew closer to Mawde. 'Ignore Widow Cornwallis. She gives the impression of having a mean streak but give her time and she'll be fussing over you like a mother hen.'

Widow Cornwallis plucked a clean apron from a large cupboard and tied it around her waist. She pointed to a groom carrying a large copper pan. 'Show us what you can do. Make a batch of comfits.'

Disappointed, Mawde passed a side table laden with decadent jellies and tarts. Her sleepless night had been in vain – hours of tossing and turning, imagining intricate designs she might use to showcase her abilities. The groom passed her a small bowl of caraway seeds and set a swinging pan over a large dish already glowing with hot charcoal. He placed a pot of syrup within her reach, then set about preparing another pan for his own use.

Widow Cornwallis wagged a misshapen finger at Mawde. 'Don't forget those comfits must be fit for the King.'

Mawde wanted to reply, but words failed her. Making comfits had become her simplest task at Powderham, but making comfits for the King was a different matter. She laboured over her pan, not daring to look away for a moment. She added syrup one small ladleful at a time while keeping the contents moving with her other hand.

Master Dawes peered over her shoulder. 'It's a fair effort, but we can't serve them like this.' He picked out a handful of seeds that appeared ragged compared to the others. 'They all have to be smooth.' He swapped the syrup pot for another. 'Use this for the final layers.'

Mawde ladled some of the new syrup into the pan, noting its yellow hue. As the syrup hardened, the yellow intensified and the coated seeds resembled little balls of sunshine.

Satisfied every comfit shell was smooth, Mawde removed the pan from the heat. Widow Cornwallis bustled over and picked out some yellow beads. She screwed up her eyes to squint at them, then dropped them back into the pan. She wiped her fingers on her apron and beckoned to Master Dawes.

'It's a fair effort, Stephen, but they can't go to the King. Good enough for his men, though.'

Mawde caught a reassuring smile from the groom. She returned his smile, grateful for his silent camaraderie. It was already a better start than her first day in the Powderham kitchen. Her smile faded when she realised Widow Cornwallis was watching her. Mawde dared to look into her eyes, but not wanting to appear insolent, she was the first to look away.

'You did well,' Widow Cornwallis said with an air of superiority, before moving away to inspect the groom's offerings.

Mawde gathered up her dirty dishes and followed the groom out of the confectionary.

'Who's in charge here?' Mawde asked, rubbing dried syrup from her fingers. 'Is it Widow Cornwallis?'

The groom chuckled. 'Absolutely not, though she'd like you to think so.' He scrubbed a copper pan that was already gleaming. 'Sergeant Barker's in charge, but he spends most of his time sorting rosters, orders, and that type of thing. Widow Cornwallis has been here longer, though, and the King's rather partial to her custards – as she often reminds us. He sends down requests for her to make them, asking for her by name. But she's not the only one to receive the King's praise. He's partial to the sweets and desserts the rest of us make, too.'

'Do you like her?'

'I do. Your turning up ruffled her feathers a bit, and she's lost the honour of being the only woman in the kitchens. Most of the time, she's pleasant. Caring. If you take an interest in something she's making and show some admiration, she'll soon warm towards you.'

'What about Master Dawes? What's he like?'

'I like him, but many don't. Provided you always try

your best and don't complain when we're busy, he'll leave you be. Watch out if you vex him, though. It's not unknown for him to fling a pan at you if you make him angry. He's been controlling his temper better of late, though.' The groom checked the door to make sure no one else was within earshot. 'He got into trouble with Sergeant Barker last week and was warned about his temper. He hurled a copper pan at my head, but I ducked so the pan missed me. It hit a shelf and knocked off a load of moulds. Broke or dented most of them. Had his wages docked to pay for replacements.'

'How did you make him so angry?'

'Burnt some syrup. Been out revelling the night before, hadn't I? Only shut my eyes for a moment. Fell asleep, I did. Standing up, too! I tipped forward and struck my head against the wall. That soon brought me to my senses, but it was too late. Syrup had caught. I tried to hide it, but Dawes could smell the burning. I was lucky they didn't dock my wages for the wasted sugar, but I suppose the damaged moulds took their minds off what I did wrong.'

They stacked the clean dishes and carried them back to the confectionary.

'What's your name?' asked Mawde, paying attention to where the groom stowed the pots and pans.

'Anthony,' he said. 'You?'

'Mawde.'

'Pleased to meet you, Mawde.' Anthony's hazel eyes glowed with kindness. 'The confectionary's not that bad a place to work. It's cooler than the other kitchens, and we get to showcase our artistic talents. Gets fraught sometimes, especially if there's banqueting going on, but we try to help each other out. Where're you from, anyway? I can't place your accent.'

'Cornwall,' Mawde replied. 'One day, I'm going back

there.' She touched the pendant hanging around her neck. 'God willing.'

'I wish you well with that, Mawde.' He reached for a pile of jelly moulds and passed two to her. 'Let's make a start on these. At least they're more interesting than swirling comfits in a pan.'

As she stepped onto the cool tiled floor of the confectionary, Mawde's spirits lifted. Sir William had been right. She would enjoy working at Greenwich Palace, after all.

'You seem 'appier today. What's put such a big smile on your face?'

Mawde stopped and stooped to pet a tabby cat basking on a neighbour's doorstep. She loved the silken feel of his fur and the way he tipped his head while purring at her touch. 'The confectionary's reopened and I'm working where I'm supposed to be.' She stood and beamed at Nan. 'I believe I'm going to enjoy it, too.'

'I'm glad. Was worried about you, you know.' Nan pinched Mawde's cheek. 'You're pretty when you smile. Should do it more often.'

Mawde gave Nan a playful shove and followed her into the house. Nan was the youngest of Widow Foxe's four daughters, and the only one still living at home. Mawde and Nan worked similar hours and walked to and from the palace together almost every day. Nan revelled in flirting with young men, drawing their attention with flirtatious poses and returning their stares with her intense brown eyes.

Widow Foxe emerged from the kitchen. Worry lines ridged her brow. She pulled Nan to one side and spoke to her in a lowered voice. 'I'm sorry, love, but you'll have to go out for me later. I know I said I wouldn't ask again, but something's come up.' She looked at Mawde. 'Forgive me, love, but do you mind leaving us so we can talk in private?'

Mawde excused herself and climbed the stairs. She crossed the corridor with heavy footsteps so Nan and her mother would know she was out of earshot. Then she tiptoed back to the top of the staircase, taking care to avoid the floorboards that would give her actions away. Nan had been out on several errands lately, but whenever Mawde enquired where she went and why, Nan steered the conversation onto other things. Eager to hear what was being said downstairs, Mawde held her breath and listened.

'I promised him I was good for the money,' the widow said in a wheedling voice, 'but he won't wait, not even one more day. Please, love. I'll do what I can to make sure it's a while before I ask again.'

'Oh, Ma, you said that last time. Fine! I'll do it, but I want a bigger cut for meself.'

'Course, love. That's only fair.'

'Not just this time, Ma. *Every* time.'

'Fine! Just give me what I need. Keep the rest for yourself.'

Mawde tiptoed away, wondering what Nan did that involved taking a cut. She hoped it wasn't thieving. Mawde slipped into her small bedchamber and rushed over to the window. In the narrow street below, men and women hurried home, treading carefully to avoid slop-filled gutters while dodging horses and carts.

Nan pushed open the door, as Mawde knew she would.

'Gotta run an errand for Ma,' Nan said. 'Shan't be long.'

'I'll go with you,' offered Mawde.

'No!' Nan checked her reflection in a small mirror and pinched both of her cheeks. 'I'll be quicker on me own.

When I get back, you can brush me 'air for me, like you promised. I've been looking forward to it all day.' She gave a shy smile. 'It makes me feel like a proper lady when you brush me 'air.'

'I'll see if your mother wants help while you're gone.'

Nan kissed Mawde on the cheek. 'You're an angel, you are.'

Mawde hung her head. 'I'm no angel.'

Nan backed away towards the door. 'Shan't be long,' she said, grinning like an excited child.

Nan's shoes clip-clopped down the stairs. The slam of the front door confirmed her departure. Mawde watched her from the window as she scurried along the street heading towards the docks.

When Mawde returned to the kitchen, she found Widow Foxe's mood had improved. The widow stopped kneading a ball of dough to pour them each a small measure of wine.

CHAPTER THIRTY-FIVE
OCTOBER 1533

MAWDE MOISTENED the tip of a tiny coney tail that had been shaped into a delicate point and gently touched it against a corner of a cut section of gold leaf. With a steady hand, she lifted it away from the plate.

'Careful now,' Sergeant Barker said, his voice little more than a whisper.

Mawde held her breath so as not to blow on the thin sheet of gold or distort it any way. She positioned the leaf on a dampened section of her sculpture, then swapped the moist coney tail for a dry one and smoothed the leaf into place with slow sweeping movements of the brush.

The sergeant stepped back and let out his breath. 'Perfect, Mawde. You've given it a beautiful even finish. There's not a crease or tear in sight. You don't need me watching over your shoulder, so I'll leave you to finish it alone.'

A bubble of joy rose in her chest. 'Really?'

'Yes, I trust you to finish the task unsupervised. I couldn't have done it better myself. I'll prepare the last few pieces of gold leaf for you. Don't be tempted to rush, though. Although there's very little left to do, you must continue with the greatest care right to the very end.'

Once the final pieces had been brushed into place, Mawde stepped back and admired the sculpture. It was magnificent. The golden feather tips of a large gyrfalcon shimmered as if the bird might take flight at any moment.

'His Majesty will adore it.' Widow Cornwallis nodded her approval. 'I hear the King is in sad humour these days, so a likeness of his favourite hunter is sure to lift his spirits.'

Mawde's stomach twisted. It was the first time one of her subtleties would grace the King's table. Even Master Dawes had given a rare nod of approval. Her skills had improved significantly under his tutelage. Now she understood why Master Cromwell had described her efforts as amateurish back at Powderham.

How she longed to be summoned to Cromwell's kitchen to prepare something for one of his banquets and impress him with what she had achieved in such a short time. He might even give her an extra coin or two if she created something splendid. Mawde felt for the purse suspended from her waist. It contained a total of nine shillings. Not a huge sum, but significantly more than she had arrived with. And Cromwell had sent over two new kirtles of soft lilac-grey, the best quality clothing she had ever possessed. Mawde drew great pleasure from running her fingers over the finely woven wool, and feeling the weight of the money in her purse. Her circumstances were improving. But she wanted more.

The air stank of fetid waste spilling from the gutters. Nan adjusted her cloak and yelped. A bead of blood bubbled up from a crack on the back of her hand. It doubled in size, then spilled across the knuckle, staining the dry skin in its wake.

'You need a salve for that,' Mawde said.

'I ain't got no money for a salve,' Nan countered, watching another bead of blood break the surface. 'Ma needs every penny. With the cost of our lease going up, and you being our only lodger, times are 'ard. Costs a lot, you know, to live in an 'ouse like ours. Once upon a time, the 'ouse was so full, we'd 'ave shared a chamber.'

'I would have enjoyed that,' Mawde said. 'I never had a room to myself before I came here. It's taking a bit of getting used to.'

'Can imagine it does. I would've 'ated to share with me sisters, mind. They'd 'ave snored like pigs and kept me awake all night.'

'It wouldn't have bothered you if that was all you had ever known.' Mawde pointed to a low moss-covered wall. 'Let's see if there are snails over there. The weather's mild, so if we're lucky, we might find one or two before the sun goes down. The slime will soothe your skin.'

Nan pouted. 'I ain't got time to do that, Mawde. Ma wants me to run errands again tonight.'

'That'll be the third time this week!' Mawde feared for her friend. If she was caught stealing, she'd suffer a whipping and might even be sentenced to hang.

Nan licked a patch of raw skin on the back of her hand. 'Me spit'll have to do for now. 'Unting snails ain't gonna pay the bills, but I'll try not to stay out too late.'

When they reached the house, Mawde stood between Nan and the door. 'Tell me what you do when you go out in the evenings.'

Nan avoided looking her in the eyes. 'This and that. Little things to earn a bit of money.'

'Like doing chores for other people?'

Nan prodded Mawde in the chest. 'Ain't you the nosey one?' She gave a strange smile. 'Chores sounds about right.'

Mawde felt a little reassured and moved out of Nan's way. 'Well, take care of your hands, and try not to put them in water for too long. I'll see if I can find a snail or two ready for when you come home.'

After a quick supper of bread and cheese, Nan excused herself and left Mawde to clear away the dishes. Widow Foxe was nowhere to be seen. Nan suggested her mother might be out visiting one of her other daughters.

Hearing the click of the closing door, Mawde abandoned the kitchen and snatched her cloak from a hook on the wall. She pulled the front door ajar and peeped outside. Once again, Nan was heading for the labyrinth of alleyways leading towards Deptford Docks. Mawde pulled her hood low over her head and scuttled after her. She reached the top of the road she had seen Nan turn into. A flutter of yellow caught her eye – Nan's kirtle – and all too soon it disappeared when Nan turned off the main thoroughfare. Mawde quickened her pace. She was jostled by burly young men and forced to step aside into murky puddles as she fought her way through a throng of dockworkers eager for entertainment after a hard day of work.

She stumbled and fell against a smartly clad man. As she mumbled her apology, he grasped her by the arms and lifted her to one side. 'Out of my way, whore!' He spat a gobbet of phlegm which landed on the toe of her shoe. Mawde stared after him, but a strong pair of hands shoved her aside again. She retreated and stood with her back to a wall as men of all ages surged along the street towards the taverns. The jagged edges of roughly cut stone dug into her arms and back. At last, the street emptied of all but a few stragglers, and Mawde resumed her pursuit of Nan.

Mawde stared at a forlorn collection of dilapidated houses, the windows of their upper storeys reaching towards each other from opposite sides of a narrow street. The buildings were so close they almost touched at their uppermost levels, blocking out the light from the late evening sun. It took a while for Mawde's eyes to adjust to the gloom, but then the scene in front of her became all too clear. The seedy street was littered with women. Some perched on stools with their skirts pulled high, revealing flesh above their ankles. Other women leaned against walls or preened in doorways, smiling suggestively at any man willing to spare them a glance. A few solitary figures wandered down the centre of the road, taking their time to look from one side of the road to the other, studying the women on display. Others walked in pairs or groups, teasing one another and calling to the girls with lewd gestures and comments. Mawde slunk back into the shadows. She had strayed into the stews.

Close to Mawde's hiding place, there was a young woman sitting on a low stool. Her bare feet were planted wide apart on the filthy ground, and her soiled hem was pulled up to her knees to display her shapely calves. A young man approached. A clerk, thought Mawde, based on his neat but faded attire. The woman lifted her skirts a little higher, revealing a glimpse of milky skin on her inner thigh.

'Is that your button there, good sir?' She leaned forward as if to retrieve something from the dirt while lifting her breasts with her other arm. 'My mistake. It's a little round stone.' She peered up at the man and fluttered her eyelids.

Words were exchanged, but Mawde could not hear them. The woman rose from her seat and reached for the man's hand, then guided him through a doorway.

Mawde had heard gossip about places like this and knew she should have been appalled. Instead, she was curious and wanted to see more.

She startled at the sound of a man clearing his throat as loud and clear as if he was standing behind her. She spun around, but there was no one there. A grimy window sat slightly ajar, and more noise came from inside.

An autumn breeze set leaves swirling at Mawde's feet. A sign swayed and creaked. She looked up at a picture of a suckling pig, which seemed appropriate for the street she was in. Another building had a sign emblazoned with a bishop's mitre, and its neighbour a painting of a storm-tossed merchant ship. So many taverns and inns crowded into one space. And brothels. She sensed a movement somewhere behind her. Tearing her eyes away from the gaudy tavern signs, she turned and caught a brief glimpse of a deep blue cloak and a very fine pair of shoes.

'What are you doin' 'ere?' It was Nan's voice.

Mawde spun around and threw her arms around her friend's neck.

'Thank goodness,' Mawde said, releasing Nan. 'For a moment, I thought you were earning the odd shilling here.'

A bemused expression crossed Nan's face.

Mawde chuckled. 'I tried to catch up with you, but you were too fast for me.' She reduced her voice to a whisper. 'Then I stumbled across all this, and I couldn't help but watch the people here. Anyway, where are you headed? I might as well go with you now you've found me.'

'No, Mawde. There's a reason I've come down 'ere and, trust me, you don't want anything to do with it.'

'Please, Nan. I know Master Cromwell pays my rent, but you and your ma are good to me. You treat me like part of the family. I can clean, launder and stitch, so whatever it is you do here, I can help.'

'I said no.' Nan's face looked stern. 'If she learns you're interested in what goes on down 'ere, she'll have you tainted in a heartbeat.'

'Who? Your ma?'

Nan shook her head. 'Not me ma. Promise me you'll go straight 'ome, Mawde, and forget about this?'

'I don't understand.'

Voices pulled Mawde's gaze towards two women loitering at the opposite corner of the street. They were better dressed than the other women Mawde had been watching, but their intentions were clearly the same. One of them called Nan's name.

Mawde swivelled her eyes back to Nan. 'No, Nan. Not you. Please tell me you're not one of them?'

Nan looked defeated. 'I don't do it just for the rent. Ma's got a taste for coins. At first, it was to spare us begging on the streets after me da died. Then Ma wanted the odd luxury, like a new kirtle or a better cut of meat. Then I got a taste for the money. What girl doesn't like a new pair of stockings or a decorative trinket for her wrist? Then I got to thinking, if I save all me extra coins, there might come a day I won't have to work in the laundry. Then my hands will soften like a lady's and not bleed at the slightest thing.'

Mawde understood the lure of money, but the risks for Nan were high. 'But what you're doing, Nan, is it safe?'

'Depends on what you mean by safe. Most of these poor wenches live 'ere and spend hours on their backs or servicing gentlemen in damp dark alleys. I'm one of the lucky ones. For a reasonable fee, I get to use a chamber, and I'm sensible enough to not drink meself to death. Every night, I say me prayers and beg God to keep me womb empty.'

'Must you do this? There must be something else you can do with less risk?'

Nan gestured to her companions that she would not keep them waiting any longer. 'My work in the laundry isn't glamorous like yours, Mawde. Look at the state of me 'ands. Even me gentlemen complain at times, telling me that me 'ands is too rough to 'andle their delicate parts. This is me only chance of a better life. The oldest career in the world, they say. Even me ma had her turn when she was still a looker. But you don't belong 'ere, so please, go 'ome. I'll only be an hour or two behind you.'

Mawde watched Nan walk towards a brothel some way down the street. Not wanting to humiliate her friend by watching her pick up a customer, Mawde turned away and started walking back towards the outskirts of Greenwich. As her feet pounded the cobbles, she wondered how much money the Deptford whores earned for each customer, and what exactly they had to do to earn their fees. Nan seemed willing enough to rent out her body and had admitted she frequented the stews by choice.

Mawde had a few spare hours she could use to earn extra money. The stews were tempting, and it sounded like easy work, but there were dangers that could not be ignored. And she had promised to wait for Nicholas.

CHAPTER THIRTY-SIX

NOVEMBER 1533

'Do you like it?' Nan danced in a twirl, her pale skirt fluttering around her like a flock of doves.

'It's beautiful.' Mawde reached out to touch the soft wool cloth after Nan came to a breathless halt. 'You were the best dressed woman in church today.'

Nan gave a coy smile. 'No, that honour goes to Ma.'

Widow Foxe preened in her ochre-coloured sleeves and kirtle, and a gown the colour of sage.

Mawde dreamed of owning a kirtle and gown of such quality – hardly worn and not a stain in sight. Her own kirtles were either work attire or dotted with neat repairs. Even her Sunday gown was speckled with stitches – they were small and difficult to discern, but they were there. Reaching for her pocket, she felt the weight of coins within it. Enough to buy fabric for a new dress if she wished. But no. She must resist temptation. Frivolous spending would scupper her dream of returning home to her mother.

Mawde helped herself to a ladleful of fragrant stew and tipped it into her trencher, taking care to avoid splashing her clothes with gravy. She tore off a chunk of bread, used it to soak up some of the juice, then relished the rich mutton flavour as it coated her tongue. The quality of food had been more consistent of late, no doubt a consequence of Nan's forays to the docks.

Conversations flew back and forth across the table, but Mawde remained silent, analysing the curious lives of the women who shared their home with her. She felt out of place. The worst dressed person at the dinner table. Even the two new lodgers were better dressed than Mawde. But Mawde was the only one who did not rent out her body for the pleasure of paying guests.

'I want to go with you.'

Nan swivelled on the stool at her dressing table and brandished her comb at Mawde. 'No, Mawde. You've seen what it's like in the stews. It ain't no place for you.'

'Doesn't bother you.'

Nan lowered her gaze. 'I was damaged goods from an early age, so I 'ad nothing to lose. You 'ave an opportunity to build a decent future, so don't spoil it by defiling your- self!' Nan removed her Sunday kirtle and wriggled into an older one.

Mawde's thoughts strayed to Nicholas. Three years had passed since she had seen him, and more than a year since Elsebeth had reported he was safe and well. Nicholas was expected at Powderham soon after, so why hadn't he come to find her? He must be dead. That was the only reason- able explanation. If he were alive and truly loved her, he would have tracked her down. Sir William would not have kept Mawde's location a secret from Nicholas, of that she was certain. His persistent absence could mean only one thing – she had lost him.

A future without Nicholas loomed bleak and uninviting. She had no desire to spend the rest of her days living in Greenwich or London. She craved the clean air of the Cornish coast, the loving embrace of her mother and the companionship of a sister she had barely known. There was only one future she would consider without Nicholas, and for that, she needed to go home.

'Please, Nan, take me with you.'

Nan looked aghast.

'My future doesn't lie in Greenwich or London,' Mawde said, fixing Nan with desperate eyes. 'Roseland is where I belong. I need money so as not to be a burden on my family, and there's no other way to earn it but to do the same as you. Please, help me, Nan, I beg you.'

Nan moved to the window and pressed her forehead to the glass. 'Thing is, Mawde, when you've done the deed the first time, there ain't no going back.' She turned and fixed Mawde with a solemn gaze. 'You're a good person, kind and decent. You don't belong in the stews. No respectable man'll want you after 'e finds out what you've done, and a good man'll know, believe me. As your friend, I'm telling you, don't do as I've done. I 'ad no choice. I ain't got special skills, but you 'ave. You're talented and beautiful, and best of all, you're pure. Don't throw it all away for the sake of a few grubby coins. One day, your confectionery skills could take you to places you never dreamed of, but things are different for me. I ain't going to find a decent life with me arms immersed in soiled linen.'

The grey light of dusk faded to darkness. A low fire cast shadows in the room.

A heaviness settled in the pit of Mawde's stomach. She perched on the edge of Nan's bed and stared at the flickering flames. 'I so badly want to go home. I miss my mother so much. My little sister, too. I thought it would get easier as time passes, but if anything, it's getting worse. You're a wonderful friend, Nan, and your ma tries to make me feel as if I belong, but I feel so lonely.' Mawde failed to keep her tears in check, and they spilled onto her cheeks. 'I need my mamm.'

Nan grasped Mawde's shoulders and dug her fingers in hard. 'Calm yourself, Mawde. You're whining like a child and this ain't like you. The comfort you seek ain't by the docks.' She jabbed Mawde in the chest. 'What you're looking for is in there. I know me and Ma were showing off new dresses today, but you can't imagine what I did to pay for that privilege. I've walked a path to 'Ell and back several times over, and sometimes I 'ate myself for the things I've done. I'm telling you, Mawde, the stews ain't the place for you.'

Mawde blotted her cheeks with her sleeve and took deep breaths to calm herself. She hated the bustle of Greenwich, the pong of the river, and the filth that clogged the gutters. She disliked living near a busy dockyard, being harassed by beggars and jostled in the streets. The salty air of Roseland and the green expanse of Cornish fields seemed to belong to a different lifetime.

Nan was still protesting, but Mawde grew more determined. 'If you can do it, so can I.'

Nan's lips puckered into an ugly grimace. 'You sure there ain't no changing your mind?'

'I'm sure.'

Nan gave a half-hearted shrug. 'Well, 'tis your decision, and I 'ope you don't regret it. Better take off your Sunday best. Don't want to ruin the only decent dress you own. Borrow one of mine.'

Nan helped Mawde into a brown kirtle, faded and softened with age. She pulled the laces so tight that Mawde feared her ribs would snap. Nan looked her up and down, then plunged her hand beneath Mawde's shift and fondled both of her breasts.

'What are you doing!' shouted Mawde, slapping Nan's hand away.

'What's up? Don't you like a woman touching your paps?' Nan sneered. 'If you can't handle my gentle touch, you won't like the gluttons of the stews mauling and slob-bering all over you.'

Mawde perched on the edge of Nan's bed and traced her finger along the twirling leaf pattern on Nan's comforter. The thought of a stranger touching her body caused her to shudder.

'Getting second thoughts?' Nan said. 'Don't blame you if you are. I told you, it ain't for you.'

The lure of money was intense, and Mawde was not ready to concede defeat. 'You took me by surprise, that's all. If you can handle it, I can too.'

Nan lit a candle and studied her face in a mirror. She had a small sore to the side of her mouth and concealed it with a layer of powder.

'I've an idea,' Nan said. 'There are certain men who desire untouched girls and pay a premium to deflower them. You won't be able to keep all the coins you earn because you'll 'ave to pay Mistress Walker for using of one of 'er rooms, and a commission for introducing you, but I'll see she's fair. What do you say?'

Voices drifted up from the street, followed by cackling laughter.

Mawde took a deep breath. 'I'm ready.'

'My dears, what a delightful proposition. I have the perfect client in mind, and he's already here waiting for me to send in his evening's entertainment! My goodness, he'll be thrilled.' Mistress Walker's eyes glinted with greed as she grasped Mawde's chin and looked her up and down. She traced her fingertip along the thin pale line above Mawde's eyebrow. 'An application of powder will soon conceal that.' She released her grip, silver chains jingling as she lowered her wrist. 'He's offered a healthy little bonus if I find him a young virgin. How old are you, dearie? Seventeen? Eighteen?'

'In my twenty-first year, I believe.'

Mistress Walker clapped her hands. 'A fully grown woman who's untouched! A rarity in these parts and I predict we'll all do rather well from it.'

Mawde glared at Nan. 'All of us?'

Nan twitched one shoulder. 'I get a cut for introducing you to Mistress Walker.'

'You're supposed to be my friend!'

Nan raised her palms in a placating gesture. 'I am, Mawde. Don't forget, I did me best to talk you out of this.'

Mistress Walker snorted. 'Seems you two need to talk.' She bustled from the room, leaving a cloud of sickly-sweet perfume.

Nan waited until her footsteps faded. 'I'm going to give my cut to you, silly,' she said.

Mawde had a throbbing headache. She pressed her cool fingers to her temples and massaged gently to try and ease the pain. 'Nan?'

'Yes?'

'I'm scared.'

'Course you are.' Nan's voice was smooth with understanding. 'We all are the first time.' She pinched Mawde's cheeks and stepped back to look at her. 'That's better. Now you look flushed with passion, not white with terror.'

Mistress Walker reappeared at the door. 'All set?'

'All set.' Nan reached for Mawde's hand and gave it a reassuring squeeze.

Mawde's stomach turned with a wave of nausea. She ran from the room, stumbling against her skirts in her desperation to be outside in the cool night air. As she stepped outdoors, the contents of her stomach rose into her mouth, and she managed only a few steps before vomiting onto a pile of horse dung in the middle of the street. The back of her throat burned. The smell of vomit filled her nostrils. She dry-heaved from an empty stomach, feeling the strain in her muscles and wishing there was more to bring up.

'You poor thing,' Nan said in a tender voice. 'I did that afore my first time, too. It gets easier.'

Mawde felt several pairs of eyes on her, whores and their clients watching from both sides of the street.

'Think of the money,' Nan said, her friendly concern replaced by a business-like tone.

'I can't do it,' Mawde said. 'You were right. I shouldn't have come here. I'll make my way home and wait for you there.'

'Oh, no you won't.' Nan wrapped her fingers around Mawde's arm. Mawde tried to shrug her off, but her grip tightened like a vice.

'Nan, you're hurting me.'

'Ain't my intention.' But her grip remained firm. 'The time for backing out was before we left 'ome. You're 'ere now and arrangements are in place. Don't keep Mistress Walker waiting. She don't like it, and she'll take it out on me.'

'No, Nan, I can't! I won't!'

A loud noise erupted further down the street. Both women looked to see what was happening. Men and women stepped aside to make way for a horse and rider.

Nan dragged Mawde towards Mistress Walker's front door and bundled her inside. Mawde heard the soft thuds of shoes against the earthen road, and the deep voice of a man, but the door closed before she could make out any of his features.

Mistress Walker's face was red and taut with rage. She slapped Mawde across the cheek. 'How dare you!' she said, shoving Mawde backwards and sending her crashing against the unforgiving oak stairs.

Someone started banging on the front door, the knocks loud and persistent .

'Now who might that be?' Mistress Walker pointed at Mawde and then to the upper floor. 'Take her upstairs, Nan. Knock sense into her if you must. Our generous patron has agreed terms and will wonder where she is.'

A weight settled across Mawde's chest. She fought to catch her breath.

'Try not to fret, Mawde,' Nan said quietly. 'It'll be over before you know it, because when a man's pent up with expectation, 'e just can't 'old it back. You'll see. A minor discomfort, then quick as a lightning flash, the deed's as good as done. A day or two from now, you'll wonder what you were fussing about.' Nan reached for Mawde's hand. 'Come. The man who's paying for you knows me well. I'll ask 'im to be extra gentle.' Nan lowered her voice to a whisper. 'I'll be right outside the door. If I 'ear anything untoward, I'll intervene.'

The colour drained from Mawde's cheeks as she strug-gled to make sense of what was going on around her. Nan had a firm grip on her hand, leading her upstairs, and was behaving more like a merchant than a friend. Their easy companionship had been destroyed by a moment of greed – her own followed by Nan's. Mawde dragged herself up the stairs, one uncertain footstep after another, resigned to her fate. Her only consolation was that in time, with more experience, she would become as relaxed as Nan and would hoard enough coins to make her dream come true.

'Wait!' Mistress Walker said. 'Come back down here.'

'But—'

'Now,' said Mistress Walker, cutting Nan short.

'As you wish,' Nan said, her voice thick with sarcasm.

Mawde took her time to turn around, unsettled by the sudden change of plan. As she began her descent, her frown deepened. An exquisitely dressed gentleman stood at Mistress Walker's side, his quilted pink doublet shimmering in the light of a lantern. His breeches were silvery-grey, cut with neat slashes to reveal narrow panels the same colour as his doublet. He wore a dark blue hat and leather boots that rose as high as his knees, and he stood a full head and shoulders above Mistress Walker. His skin was brown, the colour of horse chestnut seeds, but most striking of all was the deep blue cloak slung across his shoulders. Mawde had seen it before.

The gentleman smiled at Mawde, his eyes bright with kindness. Unable to help herself, she smiled back.

'This gentleman has bid a much higher price for you,' Mistress Walker said. 'It would be madness to turn him away.'

A breath caught in Mawde's throat. Her smile died. The gentleman stood with his head held high, his shoulders wide, and cocked his head a little to one side. He raised an eyebrow and his cheek twitched as if he suppressed a laugh. Her fear lessened. She was glad of his mirth, and soon forgot about the gentleman waiting in the bedchamber upstairs, robbed of his virgin prize.

'Ain't seen 'im afore now, but 'e looks a decent sort,' Nan whispered. 'I doubt you'll come to any 'arm with 'im.'

Mawde gave a barely perceptible nod. Her palms were

clammy, her heart racing. She hoped Nan would still listen at the door.

'This gentleman has paid a premium to take you else-where for the night,' Mistress Walker said, staring at a leather pouch resting on her palm.

'He can't do that!'

Mistress Walker silenced Nan with a glare. 'He's already paid my fee, and yours too, Nan. Mawde, you will get yours when he's finished with you. Be sure to make him happy.'

Mawde feared her knees would give way and grasped the banister to descend the stairs. When she reached the bottom, the gentleman opened the front door and invited her to exit before him. Mawde pulled her shawl tight around her and slipped outside. The night air was chilly and damp. Mawde shivered.

'Do not be afraid. I won't hurt you.' The gentleman's voice was as soothing as a cooling balm, yet confident and strong. 'My name is Master Robert Perris. I already know your name is Mawde. Please, accompany me this way.' They walked in silence to the end of the street and out onto the main road, turning in the Greenwich direction. A few minutes later, Master Perris stopped. 'This is far enough,' he said. 'We will part company here.'

'Part company? But I thought…'

Master Perris reached beneath his jerkin and pulled out a golden angel. Mawde stared at it, wide-eyed.

'May this coin keep you safe and protect you from the evils that fester in the stews,' he said. 'You have no place there. Do not go back. Put the coin somewhere safe and hide it until you need it.' He reached beneath his doublet and pulled out another coin. A crown this time. 'Whatever drove you here tonight, I hope this gift resolves it.'

'Thank you,' Mawde said, the coins tight within her

grasp. Relief washed over her like warm sunlight. He had given her a significant sum.

Master Perris bowed his head. 'Go now. And don't let me find you in this neighbourhood again.' He turned to walk away.

'Sir?'

He turned and raised his eyebrows. 'Yes?'

'I've seen you before. I recognise your cloak. Why show this kindness towards me?'

Master Perris clasped his hands in front of him. 'I cannot let you fall prey to the stews. I'm relieved I arrived in time to hear you cry out in the street. If I hadn't…'

'I'm grateful, sir,' Mawde said. She stared down at the crude pavement of cobbles and flint pressed into compacted earth.

'You have another question before we part?'

Mawde felt her cheeks redden. 'Forgive me for asking, but where do you hail from? It's the first time I've encountered a gentleman like you.'

Master Perris chuckled. 'Deptford,' he said. 'Don't let my appearance fool you. Neither of us is quite what we seem.' With that, he turned and strode away, leaving a faint aroma of spices in his wake.

CHAPTER THIRTY-SEVEN
DECEMBER 1533

THE GOLD-LEAF on the tableau looked exquisite, but the praise from Widow Cornwallis had done little to lighten Mawde's mood. She put away her brushes and sculpting tools, aware of her pocket bumping against her thigh as she moved. It wasn't as full as she would have liked. There would be no more coins until her next wages in another three months. With no other source of income, her savings were growing too slowly.

Her work finished for the day, Mawde reached for her cloak. As she tied the ribbon around her neck, a large dish of comfits caught her eye. She glanced out into the corridor. It was deserted. She closed her eyes and listened for the sound of distant footsteps. Silence. Mawde stepped back into the confectionary and rummaged along shelves and inside cupboards. Finding a pile of paper used for sketching subtlety designs, she took one sheet and moved to the table. Next, she scooped two handfuls of comfits onto the paper, then shook the bowl to even out those left behind. Satisfied she had not taken enough to arouse suspicion, Mawde folded the paper into a small parcel and stowed it between her shift and kirtle. She pulled the edges of her cape together and paused by the door. Glancing behind her to check the tables and shelves were tidy, she stepped into the corridor and collided with Anthony, the groom.

'Where are you off to in such a hurry?' he teased. 'Anyone would think you're up to no good!'

Mawde forced herself to return his smile. 'It's been a long day, and I finished later than expected. I promised Widow Foxe I'd be home in time to make minced pies. She's going to have a lot to do because she's invited so many guests.'

Anthony stepped aside and gestured for her to pass. 'Better hurry, then. Enjoy the rest of the day.'

'I will. You too, Anthony.'

It was bitter outside. Snowflakes danced and drifted to the tune of a northerly wind, and thick clouds promised heavier snowfall still to come. Mawde lowered her head, shielding her face from the icy chill. Her fingers tingled, her toes grew numb, but thoughts of a crackling fire drove her forward.

Mawde pushed open the front door and the aroma of roasting meat wafted towards her, making her stomach gurgle. Widow Foxe emerged from the kitchen.

'There you are, Mawde. I was wondering if you'd make it home at all! Nan's got us some lovely mutton for the minced pies. Everything's prepared except the pastry. Thought I'd leave that for you rather than have my heavy hands spoil it.'

Mawde saw that Widow Foxe had everything out ready for her to make the little pies. 'Perfect. I'll change first, but I won't be long. Is Nan home?'

'Upstairs, preening. You know how she is. Wants to look her best to greet the guests.'

Mawde felt apprehensive as she climbed the stairs. There had been a strain between her and Nan since her visit to the stews, and Mawde was eager to rekindle their friendship, but Nan had not made it easy and always found an excuse to be anywhere other than in Mawde's company. Mawde approached Nan's bedchamber. She knocked on the door and tried the handle, but Nan had turned the key in the lock.

'Nan?' Mawde knocked three times on the door. 'It's me, Mawde. May I come in?'

No response.

She knocked again. 'Please, Nan, let me in. I want to apologise for the way I've behaved. Nan? Are you there?'

The lock clicked, and the handle lifted. The door opened a fraction. An awkward pause, then Nan opened the door wider.

'Oh, Nan, I'm sorry. I don't know why I was so mad at you. I know you were doing what you thought was best for me, but I refused to heed your warning about the stews. Please forgive me and let us be friends again.'

Nan shrugged. 'It's alright for you 'cos you've got an employer encouraging you to make a name for yourself. What've I got? Nothing but filthy linen! I'm trying to make more of meself in the only way I know 'ow. I knew I shouldn't 'ave taken you with me, but you kept on. Then you stopped speaking to me after I gave in and did what you asked.' She paused, then added, 'If you want my cut from that night, I'm afraid you're too late.' She held the skirt of her russet gown and spun in an elegant twirl. 'I already spent it.'

'It suits you. You look beautiful.' Mawde smiled. 'I don't want money from you. I want to make peace. Here.' She handed the paper packet to Nan. 'This is for you. Mind as you open it because the contents might spill.'

Nan carefully lifted the folds of paper. When she looked up at Mawde, her eyes were bright with gratitude. But the smile soon crinkled into a worried frown. 'I know what you've done, and you could get into so much trouble. Did anyone see you take 'em?'

Mawde shook her head.

'Plenty 'ave lost their 'ands for less.'

'I know, but I thought you'd like them because I was told they're fit for the King!'

Nan pulled her into the chamber and closed the door. 'Whatever you do, don't tell Ma or she'll talk you into doing it again, and I won't allow it. Ain't worth the risk.'

Mawde perched beside Nan on the bed. 'Does this mean we're friends again?'

Nan snorted. 'Only if you promise not to go thieving again.'

'I promise.' She nudged Nan. 'Try one.'

Nan popped a comfit into her mouth, sucked briefly, then crunched it between her teeth. 'Ginger!' She held out the paper for Mawde to take one for herself.

Mawde grinned. 'It's one of the King's favourite flavours.'

The heavy thud of Widow Foxe's clogs on the stairs had Nan refolding the paper. She stuffed the package beneath her mattress. 'We'll share the rest later,' she said.

Mawde swallowed her comfit whole before Widow Foxe opened the door.

'You two look as if you're up to no good. I thought you'd have come downstairs by now.'

'I came to put things right between me and Nan,' Mawde said.

'About time.' Widow Foxe shook her head. 'I can't imagine why you two are ignoring each other. Best of friends you were, then not a word between you.'

'A misunderstanding, Ma, but 'tis all sorted now.'

Widow Foxe pointed at the snowflakes clinging to the window. 'I reckon we'll have a proper blizzard later. Come downstairs, the pair of you. I've got it warm and cosy.'

'We'll be right there, Ma.'

Mawde went into her bedchamber and shrugged off her cape. She smiled. The widow had placed a clean folded sheet and a new comforter on the mattress – a goodwill gesture for Christmas. She retrieved her pocket from beneath her kirtle, grateful Cromwell had put an arrangement in place to ensure she received her wages at the same time as the other servants. She tipped the coins onto her bed. Fifteen shillings, two pennies and a sixpence. Next, she slipped her fingers into a gap between the top of the doorframe and the wall, and eased out a small cloth bundle containing twelve shillings, a crown and the angel given to her by Master Perris. It was a reasonable sum by most standards, but it was nowhere near enough.

Mawde moved to the window and blew on the glass, watching her breath turn the air into mist. A thin wall of snow had accumulated on the window ledge. She wondered if it was snowing in St Mawes. Mawde returned to her bed and added ten shillings to her secret bundle before stowing it in its hiding place. She put the remaining coins in her pocket, changed into her best dress, then headed downstairs to join in with the preparations for the Christmas festivities.

As the afternoon gave way to evening, and the chatter and laughter of guests filled the house, Mawde's yearning for Roseland intensified. It was time to overcome her doubts and her shyness, and time to give pleasure to paying gentlemen. First, she needed to learn the secrets of the bedchamber, and the best teacher for that was Nan.

CHAPTER THIRTY-EIGHT
MARCH 1534

'THEY SAY the Queen's definitely got a boy in her belly this time.' Anthony paused his buffing of a silver salver. 'But how can they tell? They said it would be a boy last time, but we got a princess instead.'

Widow Cornwallis put a finger to her lips. 'Careful, Anthony, you'll get yourself into trouble with that loose tongue of yours. The King'll have spoken with his physicians and astrologers, and they have their ways of telling what's what.'

Frowning, Anthony selected a clean cloth and resumed rubbing the salver. 'I asked my ma if she knew what she was having each time she carried a babe. She said she was right sometimes, but not always. But with eight babies, she would guess it right sometimes, wouldn't she?'

Widow Cornwallis picked dried syrup from the rim of a mould. 'I gave birth to a daughter and four sons, and I couldn't say whether I'd have a boy or a girl. But the King's physicians are educated men, and their astrological charts don't lie. It's science they use for their predictions, not guesswork.'

Anthony placed the gleaming salver on the workbench in front of him and selected a small tarnished dish to work on next. 'I think they say what the King wants to hear and hope it's the truth. I wouldn't want to tell him news he wouldn't welcome.'

'My grandmother said you can tell by the way a woman carries whether it's a boy or girl,' Mawde said. 'She was adamant my mother would have a boy when she was carrying my brother, and she was right.'

'I didn't know you had a brother, Mawde,' Anthony said. 'What trade's he in?'

'He died when he was a baby.' Emotion clogged Mawde's throat.

Widow Cornwallis tutted. 'So many little ones taken before the end of their first year. A sad loss every time, but the good Lord must have his reasons.'

'Better hope the Queen's baby survives then,' Anthony said, 'seeing as the stars declared it's a boy.'

'That's enough!' Master Dawes loomed in the doorway, his face as pink as a raspberry. 'This is a confectionary, not a gossip parlour. Anthony, take the clean dishes back to the Jewel House, then fetch raisins and cinnamon from the spicery.'

Anthony layered squares of soft linen between the salvers he had buffed to a high shine, then lifted the heavy pile from the table, grimacing under their weight. 'You should hear what they say about the Queen,' he said, making his way towards the door.

'Bad things?' Mawde asked.

Anthony stopped as he drew level with her and cocked one eyebrow. 'Rumour has it, she enjoys pleasures of the flesh, and when the mood takes her, she's impossible to satisfy. They say she'd take several men a night if she could get away with it.' He lowered his voice. 'Picked up naughty tricks in France, so I'm told.'

Master Dawes strode into the room and gave Anthony a hefty slap across the back of his head. 'Go!'

Anthony pulled a silly face, but Master Dawes caught him. He grabbed a wooden pastry roller and brandished it like an axe, but Anthony was too quick and ducked out of the way, leaving Master Dawes swiping at the air. The top salver slipped, but Mawde rescued it before it hit the flag-stone floor. Anthony mouthed his thanks and scuttled into the corridor.

Widow Cornwallis stared after him. 'His tongue will be the death of him. Forget everything he said, Mawde. Idle chatter does none of us any good.'

Mawde replied with a nod, wondering if the Queen had performed any of the bedchamber tricks Nan had talked about.

'Take me with you this time.'

'No, Mawde. Not yet.' Nan pulled her laces tight, causing flesh to spill over the top of her bodice. 'Mistress Walker did well out of you that night, but you throwing up in the street – well, it was embarrassing for 'er and was the talk of the stews for days afterwards. 'Tis a blessing she's ignorant of the fact you didn't service that gentleman.' Nan pinched her cheeks and pouted at her reflection in the mirror. 'Mind you, if she knew you're still a virgin, she might give you another go.'

'I could rent a room somewhere else, though, couldn't I? You'd help me sort out some kind of arrangement in return for a reasonable cut?'

'Ain't that simple, Mawde. It's all about territory. The

mistresses are particular about their girls and where they ply their trade. Mistress Walker would hold a knife to me throat if she thought I was touting you to a competitor.'

Mawde blanched. 'A knife?'

'I don't know. Maybe. Anyhow, she specialises in untouched girls and has a reputation for it, so she's the best one for you. But not yet. Not until I'm certain it's what you want, because I ain't going to be the one responsible for spoiling you when it's not your true intention.'

Mawde thrust out her chin. 'It is what I want. I've been telling you for weeks now.'

'I don't believe you.' Nan checked her appearance in the mirror. 'If you were that sure, you'd 'ave found your own way into it by now. But you 'aven't, 'ave you? You're waiting for me to lead you by the 'and, and that bothers me.'

Nan was right. Mawde feared what the men might do to her. She recalled Nicholas pressing against her with his manhood stirring in his breeches, and her longing to feel his flesh deep inside her. But nothing happened between them, and she'd not experienced the same sensation since. The men in the stews were strangers, not lovers, and Nan's descriptions of the things she did to please them left Mawde confused and anxious. And there were risks.

'How come you've never had a babe in your belly, Nan?'

Nan gave a wry laugh. 'Dear Lord above, don't you know anything? You 'ave to get pleasure from it for that to 'appen. Believe me, there's no pleasure in being groped and rodded. Not for me, anyway. The main thing is that the men like it and bring their greedy yards back for more. I make them spill their seed all over the place – anywhere but inside me, if I can, just to be on the safe side. Don't always go to plan though, and if it does spill inside me, I stand up and let it trickle out so I can wipe it away with me shift.' She placed the flat of her hand across her belly. 'That and vinegar sponges seem to 'ave worked so far, and I've been in the business for a while now.'

Mawde pressed her cool fingertips to her face to draw heat from her flaming cheeks.

Nan laughed. 'I'm embarrassing you by talking like this, but I like your curiosity.' She considered Mawde for a moment. 'You know, I've got a regular who 'as a fancy for being watched. Says it increases 'is enjoyment when another wench watches 'im perform. Never gone along with 'is request before – left that to the other girls – but I don't mind doing it with you looking on, if it 'elps your education. 'E'd love a pretty thing like you in the room, especially with you being untouched. Mistress Walker would be 'appy – she'd charge him a right royal fee for the privilege. More than double, I expect.' Nan pressed her cheek against Mawde's burning face. 'I'll 'ave to tone down your rosy red cheeks with a few layers of powder.' As she drew away, she added, 'I'll 'ave a word with Mistress Walker, if you like?'

'But, Nan, what about you? Won't it be embarrassing to have me watching?'

'I'd do anything for you.' Nan planted a gentle kiss on Mawde's lips. 'Anything.' She smiled. 'Shall I set it up then? For tomorrow evening?'

Her heart racing and palms sweating, Mawde agreed.

20 MARCH 1534

Mawde grasped Nan's arm, pulling her to an abrupt stop. The night sky pressed down on them, but the stars were obscured by a layer of fog heavy with the stench of rotten food. There was a scuffle taking place somewhere nearby, and a mewling cat slinking along an alley.

'What is it?' Nan said. 'Nerves?'

'Shh,' Mawde whispered. 'Listen.'

'Can't 'ear nothing except your 'eavy breathing.'

Mawde closed her eyes and strained her ears to pick out the sound she thought she had heard earlier. She shrugged. 'Must have been my imagination.' They crossed the wooden bridge, then Mawde put out her hand again to bring Nan to a halt.

'Now what?'

Mawde ignored Nan and looked back towards the bridge. A hooded man, clothed all in black, stood holding the reins of a large grey horse.

'We're being followed.'

'Don't be ridiculous.' Nan followed Mawde's gaze. A couple of sailors shoved them aside, their footsteps echoing long after they passed. The man mounted his horse and rode away, heading towards Greenwich.

Nan tugged Mawde's sleeve. 'No one's following us. Come on. We need to get going.'

The young women continued on their way, diving to the side of the road as a horse and cart trundled past, throwing up splatters of mud.

'Stupid whoreson!' yelled Nan, wiping brown smudges from her face. 'Thank God I'm wearing a cloak. Imagine trying to seduce a man with your dress spattered with shit. On second thoughts, there's one or two clients that probably deserve it.'

They hurried on towards the stews. The thought of her purse growing heavier spurred Mawde forward.

'What do you think, then?' Nan asked, using her chemise to wipe between her legs. 'Not much to it, is there? Can you handle that?'

An urgent rapping at the door stopped Mawde from answering.

'Who is it?' shouted Nan, crossly.

'Open the door! I would speak with Mawde Hygons at once.'

The man's voice was familiar.

Nan adjusted her skirts and tidied the bed before nodding at Mawde to open the door. Ralph Sadler stood on the other side of the threshold.

'Ralph?' Mawde felt giddy with shame as she registered the disappointment on his face.

'I never imagined I'd find you in a place like this.' Ralph's attitude turned formal as he added, 'You're to come with me, this instant.'

'It's late in the evening. Where must I go with such urgency?'

'Master Cromwell demands your presence at Austin Friars.'

'Now?' Mawde's pulse thundered in her ears. If Master Cromwell knew where she was…

Ralph looked from Mawde to Nan, then back to Mawde. 'He instructed me to collect you on my way back from Greenwich.' He paused. 'I called at your lodgings, but you weren't there. The widow took a lot of persuading to tell me where I might find you.'

Mawde lowered her head. 'I'll need to collect some things.'

'No need. The landlady fetched your possessions from your bedchamber. We must go. It's already late for travelling across London.'

Mawde glanced at Nan. Nan gave a thin smile and waved her away.

'What about Master Dawes? He'll wonder where I am if I don't turn up in the morning.'

'Master Dawes will soon realise where you are. Remember who's paying your wages. We must leave. Now!'

Mawde felt a rising panic and caught her breath in shallow gasps as she followed Ralph down the stairs.

When the gateway to Cromwell's impressive home came into view, another horse and rider came trotting towards them. The rider doffed his hat to Ralph, then rode away.

Mawde stared after him. The horse was grey, and the rider dressed all in black, but his head was no longer covered by a hood. It was the same man who had watched her from the bridge. The quality of his clothes and the hue of his skin were unmistakable. It was Robert Perris.

CHAPTER THIRTY-NINE

MAY 1534

THERE WAS something about Thomas Cromwell's kitchens that put Mawde at ease. Although large by normal standards, the atmosphere was calmer than the kitchens at Greenwich Palace. Mawde had her own small room to work in. It was little more than a storeroom that had been cleared out, scrubbed from top to bottom, and furnished with a plain wooden workbench and a set of shelves. The master cook donated an old battered cupboard with sagging shelves and creaking door hinges, but it was ideal for storing sugar-work tools and moulds. The room was west facing, with two small windows admitting sufficient sunlight without overheating the room. As well as having a dedicated confectionary, Mawde had permission to wander among ornamental flower beds and the manicured kitchen gardens to select herbs and blooms to enhance her confections.

Mawde plucked a sprig of lavender from a raised border and rubbed the leaves between her thumb and finger. The fragrant perfume transported her back to her childhood to the times she made lavender bags with her mother. She sat on a bench, the stone warm from the heat of the early evening sun, and gazed towards the magnificent house, wondering what her mother would make of such a fine building.

A groom of the bedchamber forced open a first-floor window and shook out a bedsheet. He raised his hand in greeting, then disappeared. Of all the men on Cromwell's staff, Mawde liked him the most. Brian. A cheerful fellow with a rounded face, big green eyes and wild curly hair. He did not try to hide his affection for Mawde, but she felt no attraction towards him. His relaxed charm reminded her of Nicholas, reminded her of all she had lost. She closed her eyes, imagining Nicholas beside her, his arm draped across her shoulders, his thigh pressing against her skirt.

'Mawde!'

She snapped her eyes open and sprang to her feet. 'Yes, Master Thurston.' She retrieved her trug from beside the lavender bed and hurried across the garden. She had no wish to anger the master cook, who had shown her nothing but kindness since her arrival at Austin Friars.

'Master Cromwell wishes to see you.'

'Why?'

'He didn't say, but you're to report to him at once.'

Mawde felt a shiver of apprehension pass through her. It would be her first encounter with Cromwell since he delivered her to Greenwich Palace. His house was vast, especially since he had purchased neighbouring properties and instructed builders to remove dividing walls. Immersed in his business and house design plans, he rarely ventured near the kitchens.

'Master Thurston, how do I find his office?'

'You don't. Not alone, anyway. A clerk will come to escort you.'

Mawde removed her apron with trembling hands.

When the clerk loomed large in the doorway, Master Thurston gripped Mawde's upper arm. His meaty fingers pressed hard into her flesh as he pulled her closer. 'Be careful,' he whispered. 'You're a lamb among wolves here.'

'But I've done nothing wrong!'

'I know you haven't. Not in the kitchen, anyway. It's just that since his wife passed, his temperament has changed. He's become…' His voice trailed away.

'Hurry!' The clerk shifted from one foot to another. 'Master Cromwell is waiting.'

Mawde tried to steady her breathing as she followed him up a flight of narrow stairs. Cromwell was at a large writing desk with his chair angled towards the window. The fading daylight illuminated a letter in his hand. Thick brocade drapes darkened the room, their dark grey hue draining all colour and warmth. The clerk lit candles in sconces. Shadows danced along the long lines of bookshelves, licking at ledgers, books and furled scrolls.

Cromwell dismissed the clerk without lifting his eyes from the letter he was reading. When he reached the end, he folded the paper and placed it on the desk. He sat back in his chair and rested his hands on his ample lap. His hawkish eyes fixed on Mawde, assessing her. A nervous cough bubbled in her throat.

'There's no need to lurk by the door like an eavesdropper.' Cromwell's voice was deep and commanding yet gilded with a surprising hint of kindness.

Mawde took tentative steps towards his desk.

'You look like a rabbit in a snare, girl. Whatever's the matter?'

Mawde straightened her posture while keeping her gaze on the knotted carpet beneath her feet. The dark blues, greys and browns danced beneath her, disrupting the symmetry of a geometric pattern that someone had stitched with great skill. Mawde widened her stance, fearful she would swoon to the floor at any moment. She sensed Cromwell's eyes boring into her. The silence was as heavy as a storm cloud. After what seemed like an age, she lifted her gaze to look at him.

Cromwell leaned forward in his chair. 'I knew you'd find the courage to look me in the eye.'

'Forgive me, Master Cromwell.' Mawde dipped her chin towards her chest. Her legs shook, causing her skirts to tremble. She braced herself for an angry outburst, but Cromwell fell silent once more. Unable to stop herself, she risked another glance. His lips twitched into a thin smile.

'You're probably wondering why I wish to speak with you,' he said, resuming a serious air. 'Several weeks have passed since Ralph brought you here, but this is the first opportunity I've had to give your situation due considera-tion. I hear you've made quite a name for yourself.'

Cromwell retrieved a heavy ledger from the floor and dropped it on to his writing desk. The thud set the candle flames flickering. One almost blew out.

Mawde closed her eyes and uttered a silent prayer. Aloud, she said, 'Please forgive me. I only—'

Cromwell tapped his fingernail on his desk. 'You surprised me. I should have expected it, but I confess, I did not.'

Tears threatened. 'Master, I never intended to do anything that would reflect badly on you.'

Cromwell's brow furrowed. 'I think you misunderstand me. I'm referring to the impression you made on the King. He was full of praise for your gilded confections.'

Mawde swallowed her relief.

'I'm pleased to hear the King praised your work, but his admiration set me thinking. Tell me something.' Cromwell shuffled his chair closer to the desk and rested his forearms on the highly polished wood. 'Do you hear court gossip when you're in the company of other servants? I'm told Greenwich Palace is a hotbed of scandal.'

'I've heard nothing untoward about you, Master Cromwell.'

'Not about me! I keep myself above reproach.' He glanced towards the door and lowered his voice. 'I want to know what they say about the Queen.'

'Queen Anne?' Widow Cornwallis's warning pealed like a bell in Mawde's mind. 'I've heard nothing bad, Master Cromwell.'

'You're sure?' Cromwell looked disappointed. 'Nothing to raise an eyebrow?'

Mawde's eyes flitted from Cromwell to the bookshelves and a grand tapestry of a biblical scene adorning one wall. What was the correct thing to do, reveal or deny? She erred on the side of caution. 'Nothing, Master Cromwell.'

Cromwell looked defeated. He sat back in his chair. Surprised by his reaction, Mawde wondered if he had been hoping for gossip about the Queen. With tentative steps, she approached his desk.

'Master, if I did happen upon whispers and gossip, would you want me to report back to you?'

He peered at her with an expression that revealed nothing of his thoughts.

She tensed, unable to discern what Cromwell expected from her. 'Forgive me, I shouldn't have said that. It would be inappropriate for Master Cromwell's confectioner to engage in common tittle-tattle.'

Cromwell rose from his chair. Mawde held her breath as he made his way around the desk towards her.

He tilted her face towards him. Mawde tensed at his touch.

'It would be useful to have someone like you listening for rumours that make their way down from the apartments. Even the most loyal servant can struggle to keep a secret about their master or mistress. Surely the palace kitchens entertain such conversations periodically?'

'Yes, they do. But I'd attract Sergeant Barker's wrath if he caught me sharing such rumours. He'd banish me from the confectionary and destroy my reputation. And I wouldn't want to bring your name into disrepute, Master Cromwell.'

The sun went down. The room turned cold. Cromwell opened a wooden box and withdrew a flint and steel. He struck them together over a twist of charred cloth until a spark glowed between shallow folds. Cromwell selected a handful of wood shavings from a bowl and buried the glowing tinder within it. He blew gently until a low flame threatened to burn his thumb, then placed the shavings on a small pile of kindling, adding two logs when the fire took hold. He straightened up and brushed wood dust from his hose.

'I don't want you to engage in spreading rumours, but I'd like you to listen out for them and tell me what you hear. I'll reward your discrete attention with an extra crown.'

Mawde raised her eyebrows. 'A crown?' That was hardly sufficient recompense for risking her future.

'You consider a crown insufficient?'

'I'd have to speak to a gossip to be sure of the details if I'm to pass them on to you, sir. Of course, I would be careful, but I've no wish to be dismissed.' Mawde summoned the courage to ask for a bigger reward. 'I'd do what you ask in return for an angel.'

There was a firm rap on the door before a clerk

entered the room. Mawde caught a flash of agitation in Cromwell's eyes.

'What is it?'

'Forgive me, Master Cromwell, but Ambassador Chapuys has arrived a day early. I thought you should know right away.'

Cromwell flicked his eyes towards the door, instructing Mawde to leave. As she backed away, he said, 'I'm planning a feast for Whitsuntide. Impress me then, and I'll reward you generously.'

'Everything all right, Mawde?' Master Thurston asked when she walked into the kitchen.

'I think so.'

'What did he want?'

'He's hosting a feast at Whitsuntide and wants me to impress him.'

'You'll achieve that with ease, I'm sure.'

Mawde smiled. 'I'll certainly try my best.'

CHAPTER FORTY

MAY 1534

THE REPRODUCTION of the garden was magnificent. Delicate colourful blooms nestled among shrubs of various shades of green. A statue of Atlas bearing the world on his shoulders was an almost perfect replica of the original at the centre of Cromwell's neat garden. Mawde's attention to detail was faultless. The scene was accurate in all respects except her addition of angels perching on the garden walls, looking down on a tableau of Cromwell with his children. Her sparing use of gold leaf was masterly, having reserved it for the shimmering tips and edges of angels' wings. The subtlety was breath-taking.

It was almost time to parade into the dining hall. Mawde had a sensation of pebbles sinking in her stomach. She took a slow, deep breath.

'If that doesn't please him, nothing will,' Master Thurston said. 'It's exceptional, Mawde. Well done.'

Mawde muttered her thanks, more anxious about the subtlety reaching Cromwell in one piece than his opinion of it. Master Thurston and Brian lifted the subtlety from the table and positioned it across the forearms of

Cromwell's gentleman usher. Mawde fussed about the way he was holding it and urged him to avoid putting pressure against the marchpane wall.

A fanfare of trumpets sounded from the elegant dining hall where Cromwell entertained his guests. Mawde's pulse quickened. The usher and servers filed into the corridor, laden with platters and serving bowls. Mawde followed them as far as the entrance to the hall, her heart beating fast. Her creation was as impressive as anything sent out from the confectionary at Greenwich Palace, and she suspected Cromwell would brag about how he spotted and nurtured her potential. A smile played on her lips as praise and adoration rippled through the room. She caught whispered remarks such as 'simply stunning' and 'I've never seen anything so delightful'. She feasted on curious glances and envious stares that followed the subtlety towards Cromwell's table and the satisfied expression on her master's face.

As Mawde turned to head back towards the kitchens, she noticed a familiar face at the table nearest her. Robert Perris. He smiled and raised his hand as if greeting a close friend. Mawde felt a hot flush creep across her cheeks. She prayed the servers had not noticed – otherwise they would ask her questions she had no wish to answer.

Mawde spent the next hour assisting Master Thurston, organising serving platters and ensuring they left the kitchen in the correct order. She repositioned some items and added decorative garnishes to others, marvelling at the quality and quantity of the many courses. At last, it was time for the staff to enjoy the leftovers.

'You've barely touched a thing, Mawde. Are you ill?'

Mawde was moved by the concern in Brian's voice. 'No, Brian, I'm not unwell, but thank you for asking.'

'Too rich for you, perhaps? I can serve you pottage if

you prefer?' Brian drenched his own trencher with a thick creamy sauce. 'We eat well,' he said, between mouthfuls, 'but it's pauper's food compared to this.'

Mawde smiled. 'Enjoy it while you can. It's delicious, but I've lost my appetite. Exhaustion, probably. I had a run of late nights and early mornings to get that subtlety finished.'

'It was stunning, Mawde.' Brian gulped a large swig of ale. 'Shame, though. All that time and effort for something that graces a table for a mere hour or two.' He stuck out his bottom lip. 'If you're tired, does that mean I won't get to dance with you tonight?'

'I'm sorry, Brian, but not this time.'

An evening of dancing would have been enjoyable, but Mawde wanted nothing more than to rest on her bed.

One of Cromwell's housemaids shook Mawde by the shoulder to rouse her. 'Master wants to see you, Mawde.'

Mawde rubbed her bleary eyes, her head aching from the abrupt interruption of her sleep. 'Now?'

The housemaid nodded. 'Think so. I've been looking for you all over, so it's been a while since he sent me to fetch you. I didn't think you would have retired so early. Why didn't you stay for the dancing?'

'I was tired.' Mawde dragged herself into wakefulness. She pulled her kirtle over her shift and hurried down the stairs to Cromwell's study. She tapped on the door, but there was no answer. Muffled conversations crept beneath the doors to guest chambers, and the distant strains of music wafted from the servants' dining hall. Silvery light picked its way through a narrow window, cutting through the darkness. Mawde stared at a woman gazing down at her from an austere portrait and wondered what she should do.

A door creaked open. Cromwell stepped into the corridor.

'There you are.' He beckoned Mawde to join him, then retreated into the room.

Mawde swallowed and took tentative steps along the corridor. She hesitated in the doorway, surprised by the decor, a stark contrast to the austere masculinity of Cromwell's office. The oak-panelled bedchamber was warm and welcoming. Sumptuous tapestries adorned a canopied bed, the rich colours of woven flowers glowing in the candlelight. Cromwell was sitting on a cushioned chair with a small table in front of him. The table was laden with bread, cold meat and a flagon of wine. Two goblets. Cromwell poured wine into one of the goblets and broke off a large hunk of bread. He chewed, swallowed, then took a few sips of wine. Burning logs crackled and shifted in the grate, sending up a plume of orange flames. Mawde felt like an intruder in Cromwell's private space. Flustered, she lingered, unsure how to behave. Was the second goblet for her? Should she accept it, if offered? She watched Cromwell tear meat from a cold chicken leg and eat it with more bread. His pudgy cheeks glowed red from excessive drinking and feasting, and his eyelids hung heavy with fatigue. Mawde stifled a grimace, appalled by his overindulgence while people starved in London's streets.

Cromwell crossed one leg over the other and rested his hands on his thigh. 'You have become an accomplished confectioner whilst under my employ, and I believe I pay you well for your efforts.' He waggled his finger at her. 'You, however, think otherwise. Explain.' His words slurred, but their tone was as sharp as a dress pin.

Mawde tensed. 'You do reward me well, Master Cromwell.'

'That's not the impression you gave when you asked for an angel in return for relaying kitchen gossip.' Cromwell narrowed his eyes. 'And tell me something, what exactly was your business in the stews?'

Mawde broke into a cold sweat. 'Ralph told you.'

'He did. But he wasn't the first to bring it to my attention.'

'You were having me watched?'

'There was an unusual air about you at Powderham, a determination I don't see in other servants. I doubted your loyalty after I delivered you to Greenwich, so I had spies watching out for you. One close associate has business in Deptford, but not of the seedy kind, I hope.'

Robert Perris.

Mawde pressed her knees together to quell their trembling. 'It's not what you think.'

'Then what is it?' Cromwell's stare was cold and calculating, his tone sharp. 'You must have an exceptional explanation if you want me to believe it was something other than wanton behaviour.'

Mawde feared she was facing dismissal. Would Widow Foxe allow her to stay as a lodger if Cromwell stopped paying her rent? She had enough money to fund a month or two, but then what?

Deciding it was best to tell the truth, Mawde took a breath to steady her nerves. 'My dearest wish is to return to Cornwall to be with my mother and sister, but I need money to make it possible. I enjoy the same rewards as all of your servants, Master Cromwell, but for me, it's not enough.'

'You must have saved enough for a boat fare after all this time?'

'I have. But my mother's a widow and I intend to support her, not drain her limited resources.'

Cromwell's face softened. 'That, I respect.' He contemplated her for a moment. 'But why the stews?'

'I thought it the quickest and easiest way to earn extra coins but Ralph intervened before I serviced any gentlemen.'

'Gentlemen?' Cromwell said, raising his eyebrows. He rose from his chair and paced the room. 'It's probably against my better judgement, but I believe you.'

He stood behind Mawde and eased her coif from her head. Her long, dark tresses spilled across her shoulders and tumbled down her back. Mawde fought to keep her composure, fighting an instinct to duck away from Cromwell's touch.

'My wife had lovely hair.' Cromwell's voice fractured. He cleared his throat before saying more. 'Even after all this time, I can't accept she's gone.' He returned to his chair and gazed at a portrait above the fireplace, an image of an elegant young woman reading a book.

Thoughts tumbled through Mawde's mind. Memories of Nan sprawled on a bed, skirts pulled high, a customer grunting and thrusting into her. The transaction was complete in a few easy minutes, and Nan was none the worse for wear. She had wiped herself clean and straightened the bedcovers, ready to receive the next man eager to part with a coin. Mawde looked surreptitiously at Cromwell while he continued lamenting his wife's passing. Perhaps she could encourage him to part with an angel after all, if she gave him more than gossip. She closed her eyes, wondering how it would be. Could she go through with it? When she opened her eyes, Cromwell was looking at her, drinking heartily from his goblet of wine.

'You mocked me for wanting an angel for sharing gossip. What if I offered you more for that sum?'

Cromwell spluttered. 'I'd want something exceptional for the price of an angel, especially with so many rats at court who would happily feast on scraps from my table. What are you offering for such a princely sum?'

Mawde looked at the portrait of his wife and silently begged her forgiveness. 'I imagine a widower has unfulfilled needs. We could come to an arrangement.' Mawde felt detached from her body, as if watching a perfect copy of herself flaunt her flesh to this powerful man at court. She could hardly believe the words were spilling from her lips.

'You want to sate my carnal appetite in return for payment?' Cromwell looked appalled and amused in equal measure. 'I've no need for a common whore to taint the sheets on my bed.'

'I'm no whore,' Mawde said serenely. 'In fact, I'm still untouched.'

Mawde's breathing quickened. Her chest rose and fell seductively under Cromwell's gaze. She saw him swallow and knew he was considering her proposal. A return to Roseland drew tantalising closer – a departure from servitude, and a reunion with her mother. She straightened her posture, standing tall and proud, as feelings of intimidation gave way to determination and a desire to take full advantage of this influential and wealthy man. She rested her fingertips on the slight swell of soft creamy flesh exposed at the top of her shift, then looped a lace around her finger and pulled to loosen the tie.

Cromwell raised his eyebrows. She slid her fingertips towards her breast and heard Cromwell swallow. Nan had taught her well.

Cromwell cleared his throat. 'There are certain

comforts I have missed since my dear wife passed. I'll agree to an arrangement.' He refilled his goblet and fixed Mawde with a piercing stare. A prolonged silence followed. Her confidence wavered.

At last, Cromwell spoke again. 'If I find you pleasing in matters of the flesh, I'll reward you well, but I have two conditions. First, you are to listen carefully for any rumours regarding the Queen, including the briefest of whispers, and share them with me during our… assignations. Second, you will share a bed with no other man but me.'

Mawde suppressed her rising doubts. The lure of coins was overwhelming. 'I agree.'

'In that case, I suggest we start now.' Cromwell unlaced his shirt and loosened the ties of his breeches. 'Come to me.' His voice was deep and syrupy. 'I want to sample the goods.'

The features of the bedchamber faded to a blur as Mawde glided towards him. All she had seen and learned from Nan rushed through her mind in a dizzying whirl of images. Cromwell must find her pleasing – her future depended on it.

A handful of minutes felt like an hour, but at last, the deed was done. Mawde wanted to flee the room, unable to stomach the sight of Cromwell sprawled and sated. Bruised and sore, she knelt on the floor carpet and dried herself with her shift the way Nan had taught her. Thick smears of blood streaked across the fabric. Mawde recoiled in horror.

'So that really was your first time?' Cromwell seemed pleased. 'From the way you behaved, I was certain you'd known another man.' He sat up in the bed and reached towards a table. 'Next time, it won't hurt, and you'll find our coupling more pleasing.' Cromwell opened his purse and withdrew a gold sovereign. He gestured for Mawde to pick it up from where it landed on the coverlet. 'Don't expect one of those next time.'

Mawde took the coin and stowed it in her pocket. Tears drenched her cheeks, but not for her lost virginity.

Four long years after their parting, she had severed her vow to Nicholas.

CHAPTER FORTY-ONE

FEBRUARY 1535

ANOTHER GREENWICH BANQUET ENDED. The subtleties and confections were a success, and the mood in the kitchens was buoyant. It was late when Mawde left the confectionary. Her aching body craved the comfort of her flock topped mattress and a few hours of uninterrupted sleep. She pulled her new cape around her, relishing the thick weave of the wool, then tied the thick ribbon at her neck. The arrangement with Cromwell was working well. Her coin collection was growing, and so was her wardrobe. Mawde derived no pleasure from their couplings, and while Cromwell sought his pleasure, Mawde retreated to an imaginary world, rambling through meadows and collecting cockles from the beaches of Roseland.

Mawde entered the laundry and found a grey-haired washerwoman hard at work brushing a heavy brocade gown. A little girl stood on a stool in the corner, folding stockings and shifts and piling them on a bench.

The woman looked up as Mawde approached. 'Nan's not here, love. I take it she didn't walk in with you this morning?'

'Not today. I worked through the night in the confectionary because there was so much to do to before today's banquet.'

The woman gave a sympathetic nod. 'Well, I hope Nan's not sickening for something. She didn't look too perky yesterday. Tearful she was, and pale.'

Mawde bade the woman goodnight and hurried home. She ran up the stairs and flung open the door to Nan's bedchamber. Nan was on her bed, mumbling in delirium. Her face and neck were slick with sweat, her mouth swollen and blistered. She writhed on her mattress and drew her knees towards her chest.

'What's wrong with her?' Mawde pressed the back of her hand to Nan's fevered brow.

Widow Foxe wrung out a cloth and passed it to Mawde. 'Poisoning,' she whispered. 'Oil of savin, if I'm not mistaken.'

'How?' Mawde's voice was shrill. 'Who would poison Nan? She wouldn't hurt a soul.'

Widow Foxe shook her head. 'She did it herself, Mawde. I told her not to. Said there was no need to worry, that we'd work things out and get by, but she took it to her head that she'd be the ruin of us, and then this happened.'

Nan rolled towards Mawde and vomited over the side of the bed. Mawde recoiled in horror. Blood and green gunge poured on to the floorboards, splashing her new leather shoes.

Mawde peeled locks of matted hair from Nan's face. 'Send for a physician.'

Nan's breath was rasping.

'We can't.' Widow Foxe hung her head and wept.

'Of course, we can! I'll pay if money's an issue.'

'It's not about the money! What Nan did is illegal. When her courses didn't show and her breasts started swelling, she prayed it was a false alarm. But then she felt queasy and knew for sure she was carrying. She told me there was no way she would raise a bastard child in this cruel world.' Widow Foxe looked wretched, and her face sagged with lost hope. 'I tried feeding her milk, but the poor love couldn't keep it down.'

'She's with child?' Mawde's mouth turned as dry as parchment. 'But she was using vinegar sponges. She was adamant I should never let a man enter me without one in place. Did she forget?'

'Plenty of women get babes in their bellies, despite taking precautions. Oil of savin's supposed to end an unwanted pregnancy, but swallow too much and it takes the mother's life as well.'

Mawde had been using sponges to prevent Cromwell from getting her with child. If she fell pregnant, Cromwell would deny the child was his and she would lose everything she had strived for. Her coins had swelled in number of late, but she still did not have enough. She would have to keep taking her chances for a little while longer.

A feral cry from the bed caught their attention.

Widow Foxe leaned over Nan. 'Come on, love, open your eyes for me.'

Mawde held her breath, willing Nan to look at her mother. Nan's body tensed, then jerked from head to toe. Her lips turned blue and blood-stained saliva spewed from the corner of her mouth. Then she was quiet and still.

Widow Foxe tapped Nan's face. 'Nan! Nan, will you please look at me?'

Nan gave no response.

Mawde sank to her knees and buried her face in her hands. Nan, a dear friend, taken from her in such a cruel manner. Her dead grandmother's rantings whispered like a draught – accusations of her being cursed because of the timing of her birthing. Mawde could not help but wonder, had Grandmother been right?

CHAPTER FORTY-TWO

MARCH 1535

DARK CLOUDS THREATENED to unleash large drops of rain.

Three weeks had elapsed since Nan's passing, and the walk to Greenwich Palace seemed longer without her. Mawde missed her dreadfully. She often imagined she heard Nan calling her name or that she could hear Nan's clopping footsteps climbing the staircase to her chamber. Imagination was a cruel invention, repeatedly opening the wounds of loss.

Mawde pricked her ears, picking out sounds from the noisy street. Hawkers selling combs and ribbons, harassing maidservants and housewives as they scurried along the streets. Hoofbeats clattered on frost-coated cobbles, and wheels creaked as carts returned laden with cargo from the port. Mawde had a sense she was being followed. An echo of her footsteps that sometimes missed a beat, but whenever she looked to see who was behind her, she saw only melting shadows and strangers blending into crowds. Mawde longed for Cromwell to recall her to Austin Friars and remove her from the daily reminders that Nan had gone for good.

Three young women who rented rooms at Widow
Foxe's house loved chattering about finding husbands
among their patrons. They shared dreams of giving up
whoring in return for homes of their own. All three had
worked at the palace laundry, and all three had been
dismissed. Widow Foxe was flush with money and spent
liberally on dresses and furnishings. She had altered since
Nan's passing and favoured the company of the whores.
Mawde felt like a stranger and wondered how long
Cromwell's money would be enough to pay for her room.

Mawde quickened her steps and caught up with a
group of servants hurrying along the muddy road that split
the grounds of Greenwich Palace. A guard waved them
through the gate and into the stable courtyard. The
servants dispersed towards various doors leading to apartments, while Mawde continued towards the entrance to the
kitchens. A horse whinnied behind her, triggering the
excited barks of dogs. She turned to see a groom rush
forward and take the reins from a handsome gentleman
sitting tall in the saddle. A feather-plumed hat was set at a
jaunty angle, crowning the gentleman's russet brown hair.
His eyes were alight with mischief. The rider dismounted
and said something that made the groom laugh. He
slapped the groom on the back and gave him a coin before
striding across the courtyard.

A door flew open, and a woman burst forth.

'George!' The woman's brocade robe brushed against
Mawde as she dashed forward to greet the visitor. 'You're
here, at last!'

'Calm yourself, dear sister. We weren't apart for long.'
A broad grin illuminated the gentleman's face. 'How long
has it been? Six weeks? Two months at most?'

'I know, but it's always a thrill to see you.' The woman
flung her arms around her brother, hugging him close

despite her obvious pregnancy sitting awkwardly between them.

The gentleman returned the embrace before peeling her away. Mawde sidled to the side of the courtyard, mesmerised by a public display of familial affection.

'Pregnancy suits you well, Anne.' He opened her fur-lined cloak and rested his hand on the swell of her dress. 'Let us pray it's a boy child this time. The King must have an heir.'

A breath caught in Mawde's chest. For all the time she had spent at Greenwich, this was the first time she had been in such proximity to the Queen of England.

Hushed words passed between Queen Anne and her brother. They embraced once more, then drew apart, clasping hands and gazing at one another. The gentleman stooped and planted a brief kiss on his sister's lips. His gaze lingered on her back as she walked sedately towards the wing that housed her private rooms.

Mawde checked herself and averted her eyes as the Queen approached, but not before making fleeting eye contact. She dropped into a deep curtsey, resisting the urge to flee after being caught standing and gawping. The Queen bustled past in a cloud of rose perfume. She paused at the door and looked over her shoulder. Her eyes were as black as coal, yet radiant with happiness. Her hair, brown and lustrous, glowed beneath a pearl-trimmed hood, and her oval face culminated in a well-defined chin. She had a clear complexion of a slightly darkened hue, and a pale flush of pink adding colour to her cheeks. The Queen tilted her head a little, like a bird considering a worm. She smiled at Mawde, then disappeared through the doorway to a staircase rising towards the royal apartments.

Mawde released her breath and pressed her hand to the cool brick wall. The world seemed to tilt beneath her feet. It had been wrong of her to stare at the Queen like that, and she risked a punishment for her gall.

'You won't believe what just happened to me.' Mawde hung her cloak on a hook attached to the confectionary door. She took a clean apron from a pile on top of a cupboard and secured it around her waist. 'I saw Queen Anne in the courtyard, and she smiled at me.'

'Did she?' Widow Cornwallis said, raising an eyebrow. 'What was the Queen doing in the courtyard at this early hour?'

'Greeting her brother.'

'You're sure it was Queen Anne?'

'Of course, I'm sure! Her brother said her babe had better be a boy – an heir for the King.'

Widow Cornwallis lowered her voice. 'They say the Viscount Rochford is a very attractive man. Is he?'

Mawde smiled. 'I confess I found him rather appealing.'

'I've heard he's quite the ladies' man,' Anthony said, rolling out a thick sheet of marchpane. He looked at Mawde and Widow Cornwallis. 'And he has a taste for men, too.'

Master Dawes rapped Anthony across the knuckles with a small pan.

Anthony snatched his hand away and blew across his bruised skin. 'What was that for? I only repeated what other people have said.'

'You forget yourself.' Master Dawes stood with his hands on his hips, eyes bulging. 'You could lose your head for suggesting the Queen's brother engages in illegal activity.'

'Don't bother me what the fellow gets up to. I was only saying.' Anthony skulked back to his workbench and gave silent attention to a batch of marchpane.

'There are many poisons in the world, but words are the deadliest of all.' Master Dawes removed his apron. 'I don't want this matter raised again, by any of you. If anyone comes looking for me, I'll be with the cofferer reviewing budgets and accounts.'

'I saw them kiss,' Mawde said, breaking a silence that had stretched beyond an hour.

'That's not an offence,' Widow Cornwallis said. 'They're brother and sister and known to be fond of one another.'

'They kissed on the lips.'

Anthony looked up and raised his eyebrows.

'Passionately,' Mawde clarified, fuelled by his reaction. 'That's not right, is it? And he opened her cloak to put his hand on her belly.'

Widow Cornwallis crossed herself. 'Hush, Mawde, or you'll earn yourself a beating.'

The mood in the confectionary was subdued for the rest of the day.

CHAPTER FORTY-THREE

JUNE 1535

CROMWELL CLOSED his eyes and stretched out on his sumptuous feather mattress, his face relaxed, giving a glimpse of how he might have looked as a younger man. 'Any news from the kitchens?' he murmured.

Mawde pulled her shift over her head and fastened the laces. 'The mood's gloomy. News of the stillbirth shocked everyone.'

'What are they saying about it?'

'Words of sympathy for the King, and disappointment for the Queen.'

Lust reignited in Cromwell's eyes. He beckoned Mawde to return to the bed and lie alongside him. Mawde forced herself to smile and did as she was bidden. With every one of Cromwell's thrusts, she felt an increasing sense of shame for satiating his ardour for money. And Austin Friars was no place for secrets. Conversations stopped when Mawde entered a room. Servants muttered behind her back, and fragile friendships had shattered. She was as lonely as the day she arrived at Powderham. The only place where she felt accepted was in the confectionary of Greenwich

Palace, but her only hope of finding happiness lay at the bottom of Cromwell's purse.

Hoping to earn an extra sovereign, Mawde said, 'I hear the Greenwich pastry cooks are gambling at dice in the evenings.'

Cromwell appeared disinterested. 'A pastime enjoyed by many men. I'm partial to the occasional roll of a die, but it's not meant for the likes of them.'

'Why not?'

'The thrill of chasing a win can cause a man to lose everything, and then he and his family become a burden on society. That's why men of limited means are forbidden from gambling at dice.'

'Will the pastry cooks face punishment?'

'Maybe. But for now, there are bigger problems to worry about.' Cromwell rolled onto his side, his flaccid belly wobbling like an ill-set jelly.

'The Queen?'

Cromwell struggled to support his weight on his elbow. Beads of perspiration bubbled on his brow. 'Has something been said?'

'That she has an unhealthy interest in matters of the flesh.'

'So do you.'

If that's what he believed, she was fooling him well. 'Only for you, Master Cromwell.' When he didn't press for more information, she added, 'There are rumours the Queen needs more than the King to satisfy her urges.'

Cromwell snorted. 'Unlikely.'

'They also say she lies with her brother.'

Cromwell jerked his head towards her. 'Viscount Rochford?'

Thrilled to have his rapt attention, Mawde embellished her allegation. 'I witnessed their affection once, and it was far beyond what I'd expect to see between brother and sister.'

Cromwell's expression hardened. 'How did you come to be in the Queen's presence? Don't tell me she found herself lost in the kitchens.' His words were jagged and clipped.

'A chance encounter a few weeks ago, before she withdrew to her confinement chamber. I was on my way to the confectionary when Viscount Rochford rode into the stable courtyard. The Queen ran out to greet him and almost knocked me off my feet.'

'You're sure it was the Queen?'

'Her poise and elegance were unmistakable. I watched them embrace as fondly as lovers, and he even put his hand under her cloak to rest it on the swell of her belly.'

Cromwell sat up and slung his legs over the side of the bed. 'We all know she's fond of her brother, so we shouldn't read too much into an innocent show of affection.'

'There's something else.'

'Go on.'

'I forget the words he used, but he said something like "We must provide the King with an heir", as if the child was the product of his own seed.'

'You fool! He was merely stating the Boleyn family must provide an heir using Queen Anne as the vessel. It's the only way to secure that family's future.'

A candle on the nightstand had burned down to a stub. The flame died, leaving a brief curl of smoke. Another candle still burned, but with a feeble flame and cast an eery light beneath the canopy of the bed.

'I saw them kiss,' Mawde said. 'It was the lingering kiss of lovers, not a brief touch of lips.'

Cromwell looked old and troubled as he turned

towards her. 'You've made a serious accusation. Do you swear it's the truth? Retract the allegation now and I'll not punish your slanderous statements. However, if it's true, the consequences could be… unthinkable.'

Mawde held his gaze. If she retracted her statement, Cromwell would have no further use for her. She had no choice but to fortify the lie. 'I swear it's the truth, Master Cromwell. I swear it on my life.'

CHAPTER FORTY-FOUR
OCTOBER 1535

MAWDE AND ANTHONY were in a small scullery along the corridor from the confectionary. They worked in silence washing moulds and checking them for damage – the slightest imperfection would ruin the dramatic effect Mawde intended for her subtlety.

Anthony opened the door to check no other servants were within earshot. 'Heard the latest?'

Mawde shook her head.

'Word is, the Queen's behaving like a French harlot, rolling between the sheets with not one man, but two or three!'

'Who told you that?'

Anthony tapped the side of his nose. 'Never reveal the names of your sources. She lived in France for several years, you know, and French courts are different from ours. Giant pleasure palaces, and everyone's at it apparently – courtiers and servants.' He grinned. 'Wouldn't mind going to France to find out for myself.' He lowered his voice to a whisper. 'She told a couple of her ladies that the King can't... you know... do the business, and because he can't satisfy her, she's got no chance of giving him a son. That's why she takes pleasure from other men. Any son she bears, she can pass off as the King's. They say she's afraid he'll put her aside if she doesn't give him an heir, just like he did with Queen Katherine, so I suppose she has no choice.'

'But what if the King—'

'What are you two whispering about?' Widow Cornwallis breezed into the scullery with a pile of moulds and plates. 'Not gossiping, I hope?'

'Course not,' Anthony said. 'You know us better than that.'

Widow Cornwallis rolled her eyes. 'Indeed, I do.'

Anthony pointed out a small dent on the rim of a mould shaped like a rose. 'Can we get away with that?'

Mawde took it from him and ran her finger over the dent. 'It's a small nick, and it would be a shame to discard it for such a minor imperfection.'

Widow Cornwallis agreed. 'Put it at the back of the cupboard. One day, it might come in useful.'

They gathered up the clean moulds and carried them back to the confectionary. A short while later, Sergeant Barker arrived with a visitor. 'This is where all those magnificent subtleties come from,' he announced proudly, 'and Widow Cornwallis's heavenly custards so adored by the King.'

The visitor's gaze roved around the room and settled on Mawde. She smiled, charmed by his appearance. He was of similar age to her, dressed in a fine doublet of orange and black and his eyes seemed to sparkle with joy. Mawde's cheeks pinked when she returned his smile.

'He's a member of the Queen's household,' Anthony muttered in her ear. 'A musician, far too good for you, and no doubt already taken. The Queen will have sunk her fingernails into him by now.'

Mawde gave Anthony a dig in the ribs with her elbow. Sergeant Barker quelled their banter with a long cold glare.

'Mark Smeaton, as I live and breathe,' Widow Cornwallis beamed at him. 'What brings you to our humble kitchen?'

Smeaton doffed his hat and bowed. 'Always a pleasure to see you, Widow Cornwallis.' His voice was soft, almost feminine, and melodic.

'The King believes Queen Anne is out of sorts, and he's worried about her. Her melancholy will not shift, no matter how we try to please her.'

Mawde clamped her lips together and studied the flagstones while trying to ignore the twitching of Anthony's body as he struggled to suppress a snigger.

'His Majesty believes a sweet treat will lighten her mood. I said I'd visit you, dear lady, to request one of your delicious creations.'

Widow Cornwallis beamed at the young man. 'You flatter me, Master Smeaton.'

'It would be my honour to return later to collect the sweets,' he said. 'That way, I'll have the honour of seeing you again.'

Sergeant Barker snorted. 'You musicians and poets are all the same. Full of hot air and flattery. Go! Entertain Her Majesty with your lute and return to us at dusk. We'll have something ready for you to collect by then.'

Anthony stepped closer to Mawde. His breath tickled her neck as he whispered, 'So, that's what he's calling his instrument now. Perhaps he should encourage the Queen to pluck it?'

Mawde bit the inside of her cheek to compose herself and tasted the metallic tang of blood. 'Sergeant Barker, may I make something to send to the Queen? I've thought of something delicate and fragrant that might lift her spirits.'

'Please do, Mawde. I need Master Dawes and Widow Cornwallis to help me plan the desserts and confections for next week's banquet. Anthony can spend the day making comfits and assist you if you need an extra pair of hands.'

Anthony waited for everyone else to leave the confectionary, and said, 'You can pluck my lute, too, if you like.'

'What do you think?' Mawde placed a miniature posy of marchpane roses and spun-sugar violets on an empty chair in Sergeant Barker's office.

She had a pounding headache. The challenge of making something for the Queen at short notice had been more stressful than she envisaged. She had struggled to get the marchpane to the right consistency and battled crumbling petals and cracks in some of the leaves.

'It's beautiful, Mawde,' Widow Cornwallis said, placing a receipt book on Sergeant Barker's desk.

Sergeant Barker took his time to inspect it. 'Perfect.'

Mark Smeaton tapped on the office door. 'Am I too early?'

'Not at all.' Sergeant Barker beckoned him to approach the chair. 'See this elegant creation Mawde has made for the Queen?'

The posy nestled in a small silver bowl, the tiny flowers neat and delicate. Mawde had sprinkled a thin rosewater syrup over the top, the sheen and subtle fragrance making the blooms seem real.

Smeaton went to say something, but hesitated.

'You don't like it?' Mawde felt her heart sink in her chest. 'The Queen can pick a flower whenever one takes her fancy, and the rosewater fragrance will help to calm her troubled mind.'

'I like it very much,' the musician said. 'It's exquisite. But I was expecting something simpler. Perhaps a few decorative biscuits, or miniature fruits. This is more like a love token.'

Master Dawes cleared his throat. 'You told us you came on behalf of the King. A love token from a king to his queen is entirely appropriate, is it not?'

Smeaton avoided Master Dawes' piercing stare. 'The King's thoughtful gift will definitely please the Queen.'

Widow Cornwallis narrowed her eyes as the musician rushed away. 'I can't help thinking the King knew nothing about this. That young fellow had better tread carefully.'

Mawde excused herself from the office and retrieved her cloak from the confectionary. She needed to visit Austin Friars while the events of the day were fresh. Cromwell would feast on this.

The Queen's mood improved, but she miscarried again. The King was already in foul humour after a fall from his horse, and news that he had lost another son was almost too much for him to bear.

His misery and anger filtered through the palace, subduing the mood in the kitchens.

'Why does God deny the King his heir?' Widow Cornwallis persevered with making custard, even though she knew it would only go to waste.

Sergeant Dawes took the shaping knife from Mawde's hand. 'No point in continuing with sweets and subtleties. There'll be no feast tomorrow,' he glanced at her workbench, 'and the King won't want *that* on his table.'

Mawde stared at the incomplete tableau. It was her best creation yet – a perfect baby boy reclining on a cloud, surrounded by angels either singing or blowing golden trumpets.

'I can't help but fear for the Queen,' Widow Cornwallis said. 'The King will take this recent loss as proof she's incapable of giving him an heir.' She dipped a spoon into the custard, blew against a small curl of steam, then popped the spoon in her mouth. She rolled the custard over her tongue before swallowing and wiped the spoon on her skirt. 'The Queen will be eager to secure the royal line. My heart aches for her. To lose a child is dreadful. To lose a king's child is even worse.'

'Do you think God's punishing her for her sins?' Mawde asked.

'What sins? Lord knows, the gossips love spreading rumours of the Queen making potions and spells, but I don't believe a word of it. What queen would stoop so low? I'm sure Queen Anne has behaved above reproach and done everything possible to breed a healthy son.' Widow Cornwallis crossed herself. 'I pray she falls pregnant again soon and carries a son to term.'

CHAPTER FORTY-FIVE
APRIL 1536

CROMWELL SLIPPED a sovereign into Mawde's hand. 'No need to look so worried. I'll only ask questions about things we've discussed before.'

The fact he was pressing a coin into her hand instilled Mawde with dread. To receive a payment for services rendered was one thing, but to be paid upfront to answer questions in front of an audience was a different matter.

Ralph Sadler was at Cromwell's desk, poring over a ledger. He put it aside and rose to his feet when Cromwell opened the door. 'All set, Master Cromwell.'

'Thank you, Ralph. I'd like you to act as scribe and record everything said at this meeting.'

A groom knocked at the door and stood aside to allow a visitor to enter. Mawde could tell from the cut of his clothes and assured posture, this thin-faced gentleman was an important guest.

'Sir John, welcome. Thank you for coming here so quickly. I believe we may have everything we need to resolve our... situation. Please, sit by the fire.' Cromwell showed him to one of two cushioned armchairs on either side of the hearth. Both chairs faced the centre of the room rather than the low fire burning in the grate, an observation that set Mawde more on edge.

'This matter is of utmost importance. The sooner we achieve the outcome we desire, the better.' Sir John's voice was gruff. Deep worry lines furrowed his brow.

'Ralph, be sure to document that Sir John Seymour is present throughout this interview.'

Ralph nodded and started writing, scratching his nib across the parchment. Lightning flashed, slicing through a narrow gap in the curtains and illuminating the study. A few seconds later, a deep rumble of thunder set the floor vibrating beneath Mawde's feet. Rain pattered against the mullioned windows.

Cromwell settled himself in the other chair. 'So, let us begin.'

He instructed Mawde to step forward until she was in the middle of the room. It was as if she were about to face trial in a court. She clasped her hands together to steady her trembling.

'Now, remember what I told you, Mawde. I'll ask you a series of questions which you must answer to the best of your knowledge. Ralph will record everything you say.'

'Yes, Master Cromwell.' She looked at Ralph, hoping for reassurance, but he had his head bowed and was already scribing.

'First, have you ever been in proximity to our current queen?' Cromwell fixed her with a hard stare.

'Yes, master.'

Sir John sat forward, eyes wide with incredulity. 'Under what circumstances?'

'I was passing through the stable courtyard at Greenwich Palace when the Queen ran out to greet her brother. He'd just ridden in.'

'Then what happened?' Cromwell asked.

'Queen Anne threw her arms around him and embraced him. She was so full of joy to see him.'

'Did they speak?'

'They did.'

'What did they say?' Impatience showed in Cromwell's tone.

'Viscount Rochford said... something about... giving the King an heir.' She stumbled over her words as if each one might choke her. Why was Cromwell asking her this now? There had to be something sinister about it. Mawde bowed her head, reluctant to say more.

'Tell Sir John the rest! Tell him everything you told me.'

Mawde stared at the woven carpet covering the wooden floorboards.

'Have you lost your tongue, woman? I didn't bring Sir John all this way to watch you stand there like a fool. Tell him what happened!'

'Yes, Master Cromwell.' Mawde addressed her next words to Sir John. 'Viscount Rochford put his hand beneath the Queen's cloak to rest it on her belly.'

Sir John and Cromwell exchanged glances. Mawde thought she caught a flash of satisfaction from Sir John.

'Was there anything else remarkable about their interaction?' Cromwell asked.

Mawde felt a wave of regret for every word of gossip she had exaggerated to Cromwell.

'Well?' Cromwell was glaring at her.

'They kissed.'

Ralph looked up from his scribing. 'Are you sure?' His eyes were pleading Mawde to retract her statement, but that bit, at least, was the truth.

She lowered her head and nodded.

Sir John slapped his thigh. 'I knew it. No wonder His Majesty sought favour with my Jane.'

Cromwell was unruffled. 'Yes, but it's not uncommon for a brother and sister to exchange kisses, is it? Is that all it was, Mawde, a brief show of affection between siblings?'

The weight of the sovereign was like a rock in her pocket. She had trapped herself in a web spun from her lies. 'It was no ordinary kiss.' She said, knowing what Cromwell wanted her to say next. The lure of more sovereigns spurred her on. 'It was passionate. More like a greeting between lovers than a brother and sister.'

A smug smile brightened on Sir John's face. This revelation must have been of great importance to him now his daughter had the favour of King Henry.

Mawde pressed on. 'It was long and lingering.'

Sir John rose to his feet and paced the room. 'This is excellent news, Cromwell, precisely what we need.' He turned to Mawde. 'Were there other witnesses?'

Mawde thought for a moment, recalling what she had seen. 'There was a groom, but I can't say whether he witnessed the kiss. He attended to Viscount Rochford's horse. There was no one else.'

'You're sure it was a lingering kiss?'

There was a moment's hesitation before Mawde replied. 'Oh yes, sir. I swear, it's the truth.'

Sir John appeared delighted and returned to his seat.

Cromwell resumed the interrogation. 'You once mentioned something about the Queen making inappropriate comments about the King. Do you recall what they were?'

'Yes, Master Cromwell. I'm ashamed to say that the kitchens are ripe with gossip. Grooms from the royal apartments come and go all the time and trade their secrets for treats from the bakers.'

'And what is the Queen alleged to have said about our King?'

Heat rushed into Mawde's cheeks. 'I'm not comfortable repeating it in present company, master.'

'Come now, Mawde, you struggled to contain your glee when you shared this gem with me. It's imperative we document anything that might be relevant.' He stood and moved to stand behind Ralph. He waited for Mawde to look at him before discretely patting his jerkin.

Mawde imagined the stash of coins nestled in Cromwell's purse. At least the information he wanted now was gossip from the tongues of other servants and not something of her own fabrication. 'The Queen told a couple of her ladies that the King never satisfies her in matters of the bedchamber. She tries to tempt him with tricks learned at the French courts, but to no avail. Without his seed, she cannot provide an heir.'

A shadow crept across Sir John's face. 'A king unable to sire an heir is troublesome news indeed.' He turned towards Cromwell. 'That doesn't bode well for any future queen.'

Cromwell was quick to discount any suggested failing on the King's part. 'Sir John, the King *has* sired heirs, but the Queen failed to carry them to term. Therefore, the fault lies with her!'

'Perhaps.' Sir John fixed Mawde with a challenging stare. 'Are there grooms you can name who will corroborate what you say?'

'I'm not sure. The gossip reaches the confectionary later than everywhere else so I cannot name a direct witness to the claim. Although... no, it doesn't matter. It's inappropriate for me to draw my own conclusions.'

'Say it,' commanded Cromwell. 'Whatever's on your mind, share it. We will judge its relevance.'

'Perhaps the King suspected the Queen of consorting with other men and considered her unsuitable for bearing his heir. She might have become distasteful to him, so that he couldn't... well... you know...'

Sir John seemed pleased by her suggestion. 'Yes, yes, that would make sense. Do the rumours hint at her taking other men to her bed? Men whose names you can share?'

'Forgive me, but I'm a confectioner and far removed from the Queen's private chambers, although there is one incident that might be relevant.'

Cromwell's eyes were shining. 'Tell us more.'

'Several months ago, a musician came to the confectionary. He wanted us to make sweet treats for the Queen, to lift her spirits after she miscarried. He said he came on behalf of the King, but Widow Cornwallis was certain he came of his own accord. The way he made his request, I'm inclined to agree with her.'

'That's merely a woman's supposition, and not something we can use to strengthen our case,' Sir John said.

'You might not think so,' Mawde said, 'but it's what he asked for that made me wonder.'

'And what was that?' Cromwell asked.

'A love token. I made a small posy of flowers, and he was thrilled. Said it was exactly what he'd been hoping for.' The lies flowed too easily. Mawde knew she should stop, but something major was afoot, and it seemed to Mawde that she had an important part to play in whatever Cromwell and Sir John were plotting. If successful, her contribution might be further rewarded.

'His name?'

'Mark Smeaton.'

Cromwell beamed at Sir John. 'Now we have the foundation upon which to build a thorough investigation.'

But Mawde had more to say. 'Of course, sir, with the

Queen unable to birth living children since delivering Princess Elizabeth, one wonders if she used witchcraft or love potions when she first drew the King's eye. God may have denied her a living male child because He's angry and refuses to bless an unholy union that is the work of deceit and magic. That's not me suggesting that, you understand, I'm repeating what others have said.'

'Your statement is noted,' Cromwell said. 'So, Sir John, what do you say? Should we take the matter forward?'

Sir John stroked his beard between his thumb and fingertip. 'I believe we should. The deeper we dig, the more treasure we might find.'

Mawde felt a glow of pride. Whatever Cromwell and Sir John were planning, her revelations had fuelled their cause. 'Will that be all, Master Cromwell?'

'For now,' he replied. A subtle lift of his eyebrows told her to report to him once the household had retired for the night. Her heart lifted.

'Before you go, Mawde, you must make your mark on this statement.' Ralph pushed the large piece of parchment across the desk towards her. 'Shall I read it back to her first, Master Cromwell?'

Cromwell studied the elegant handwriting. 'No need. Sir John and I will read it through before adding our signatures.'

Mawde took the quill from Ralph and carefully drew the letter 'M' at the foot of the document.

'Leave us now,' Cromwell instructed. 'I will send for you if I need you again.'

CHAPTER FORTY-SIX
APRIL 1536

'His Majesty's raging.' Anthony was wide-eyed with excitement. 'I gave the comfits to an usher of the King's chamber, and I'd barely turned my back when the dish crashed against the wall. A groom came running after me. Gave me the dish, apologised for the dents and said it might be best not to send more comfits to the King today. He's refusing everything, including bread and ale. First time the groom's known the King to not eat something.'

'Is he sick?' Mawde asked.

'Heartsick, most likely. It's because of the Queen, isn't it? Someone told the King she used spells to make him fall in love with her and set Queen Katherine aside. She gave him love potions, too. Imagine the King being a victim of witchcraft! Course, once they were married, he wasn't enough for her. We've heard that rumour before, but now there's a witness who's come forward and sworn the Queen's had at least one man other than the King. They're saying all those lost babies weren't the King's after all, and that God was punishing Queen Anne for her infidelity.'

Widow Cornwallis sank onto a stool and grasped the

edge of the table. 'God have mercy on the Queen's soul,' she said. 'Who would make such cruel accusations?'

Mawde's blood pooled towards her feet. The confectionary seemed to spin around her, and she staggered backwards to lean against the wall.

'Gets worse.' Anthony was oblivious to the impact of his words. 'I've heard the Queen was plotting to murder the King.'

'Good Lord, no!' Widow Cornwallis pressed her hands to her cheeks. 'What would she stand to gain? She has no son for whom she would act as regent, and she'd lose her status as Queen of England. I don't believe for a moment she wanted to harm the King.'

'Maybe not,' Anthony said. 'But you can't deny she cuckolded him. Not when there's a witness.'

'A witness to what?' Mawde asked, recovering her senses.

'Remember you saw them kiss in the courtyard once? Well, this is even worse! Someone signed a statement saying they saw Queen Anne and Viscount Rochford sharing an intimate moment, and his hands went where only the King's hands should go. Her own brother!' Anthony's eager smile faded from his lips. 'The King's ordered a thorough investigation. If they prove she committed adultery, they'll burn her at the stake.'

Mawde felt her legs go weak. Noises ebbed away. Her vision greyed, then everything turned black.

'Mawde? Mawde, love. Open your eyes.' Widow Cornwallis's distant voice penetrated the fog.

Mawde felt a light tapping on her face. She opened her eyes and shivered as the chill from the flagstones cut through the layers of her clothes. The back of her head throbbed where it had struck the hard floor.

'Up you come, gently does it.' Widow Cornwallis

helped Mawde sit on a stool. She sent Anthony to fetch a cup of ale. 'You were out cold. Had us worried, you collapsing like that.'

Slowly, it all came back to Mawde. Standing in Cromwell's office, making accusations against the Queen. It was all her fault. She had unleashed the King's wrath. Worse still, she had endangered the Queen, and all for a small bag of coins. Mawde recalled the Queen's smile from the encounter in the stable yard. She was so full of joy, excited to see her brother and about the prospect of bearing the King's son. Her heart rose into her throat, threatening to choke her. She needed to speak to Cromwell and undo this nonsense. She had to save Queen Anne from disgrace. The only way to do that was to retract every exaggerated word that had tumbled from her lips.

'I have to go,' she said, rising unsteadily to her feet.

'You look pale, dear,' Widow Cornwallis said. 'Go home and rest.'

Mawde felt a rising sense of panic. Cromwell would punish her for her lies. Her words, her sworn statement, had caused a royal rift. She had to do something to stop the Queen from facing a death sentence based on lies and exaggerations.

Widow Cornwallis fussed around her. 'Anthony will walk you home in case you pass out again.'

'Can you spare us both?' Mawde muttered.

'We'll manage. Away with you now, and we'll see you on the morrow if you're feeling better.'

Outside in the spring sunshine, Mawde grabbed Anthony's arm. 'Please, Anthony, find Master Cromwell. I must speak with him at once.'

Anthony shook his head. 'Can't do that, Mawde, because he'll be with the King. He won't mind you going home to rest until you feel better, and he doesn't even need to know.'

'It's not that.' She tightened her grip. 'It's about the Queen. I need to tell him something before it's too late.'

'But Mawde, if he's in the King's Privy Chamber, he won't thank anyone for calling him away, especially with the King being in such a rage.'

'Please!' Mawde's voice was shrill and desperate. 'Help me, Anthony, I beg you! I've done a terrible thing.'

Anthony patted her hand. 'I don't like to see you look so wretched. Wait here. I'll send a page to ask Cromwell to come down.'

'Make sure he knows I wish to speak about the Queen!'

Anthony raised his hand in acknowledgement and hurried away. Mawde sat on a step. She grabbed a fistful of kirtle and twisted it this way and that. Greed had reduced her to a storyteller. A dangerous liar.

'What do you want?' Cromwell towered over her, large, dark and threatening.

She scrambled to her feet. 'Master Cromwell, I beg you to forgive me. I've been foolish and committed an atrocious sin.' She took a few gulped breaths. 'I don't know what to do.'

'For goodness' sake, stop snivelling. I've no time for this.' He turned as if to leave.

'Master!' She grabbed the bottom of his cloak and pulled herself up.

His angry glare forced her to back away. 'Forgive me,' she mumbled. 'I didn't mean...' She took a deep breath. 'I lied about Queen Anne.' She braced herself for Cromwell's angry backlash. It was not forthcoming. Puzzled, she continued. 'You recall that day you questioned me in front of Sir John Seymour and Ralph wrote my statements? I'm ashamed to confess that any truths I told were exaggerated, and the rest…'

Cromwell was unmoved.

'The more I lied, the more pleased you seemed to be. I knew you would reward me well, and that's why I did it! The musician didn't ask for a love token, but I made it look that way. And the Queen and her brother – they didn't kiss like lovers. It wasn't at all how I described. They did nothing wrong! Please stop this nonsense before it goes too far.'

A loud crash followed by vicious shouting came from an open window of one of the royal apartments.

Cromwell glanced towards the source of the noise. 'I must return to His Majesty. You may stop fretting because I have the situation under control.'

Mawde's shoulders sagged with relief. 'Oh, thank God.'

'The Queen's fate is decided. Opinion against her is so strong that nothing can save her now.'

'No! The Queen's done nothing wrong!'

'That's not the consensus.' Cromwell's lips lifted into a sneering smile. 'The musician you reported confessed to their affair, so there's no need to retract your statement. Let it stand and take pride in the knowledge you helped bring this unfortunate situation to an end.'

'But the other things I said – the sorcery, the potions, her brother…'

'The King often voiced concerns he was tricked into the marriage. Regarding her brother, investigations are ongoing. Enough of this, now. You're wasting my time.'

Cromwell hurried away, his limp causing an ungainly lurch to his stride.

Anthony returned to Mawde's side. 'You don't look so pale now. Feeling better?'

'A little. The musician, Mark Smeaton, confessed to a relationship with the Queen.'

'Course he did,' Anthony said, his voice thick with sarcasm.

'Why do you say it like that?'

'They tortured a confession out of him, didn't they? Cromwell and his cronies. Poor Smeaton – the infatuated fool must have thought confessing would save his life.'

A strong wave of nausea gripped Mawde. She bent forward, clutching her stomach.

'You look awful sick.' Anthony put his arm around her to support her. 'Let's get you home.'

Mawde tipped her coins onto the bed. It was a decent sum, but not enough to return to Roseland. With no warrant to travel, the journey was impossible anyway. She flung herself onto the mattress, causing the coins to jingle. Not so long ago, the small fortune would have brought great joy, but now there was only shame. Mawde felt dirty, defiled by blood money.

CHAPTER FORTY-SEVEN

MAY 1536

ANTHONY FLUNG open the door to the confectionary. 'You won't believe this!' Flushed from running, he put one hand against the wall and leaned forward to catch his breath. 'They arrested her!'

'Who?' Widow Cornwallis demanded.

'Queen Anne!'

Mawde stared down at the stained leather of her shoes.

'They're leaving for the Tower. If we hurry, we'll see them take her away.'

Master Dawes slipped off his apron. 'A queen arrested. That's not something you see every day.'

A large crowd packed the riverbank. Mawde squeezed her way to the front, reaching the edge of the jetty just as Queen Anne stepped into the royal barge. She was flanked by guards, and Cromwell followed close behind. He settled his wide frame on a bench directly behind the Queen and made a comment that triggered a laugh from his neighbour. Mawde hated him for that. How could he make light of such a serious occasion? Her eyes flicked back to the Queen. She looked dignified, but afraid.

The oarsmen pushed the boat away from the steps, allowing the barge to drift a little way before lowering their paddles into the water. When the command came, they raised and lowered the oars in unison to the slow rhythmic beat of a drum.

The Queen scanned the onlookers. Her gaze fixed on Mawde.

Mawde pressed her hands to her chest, trying to soothe her aching heart. 'Forgive me,' she mouthed.

The Queen puckered her brow for a moment before drawing her gaze away and studying the ripples that fanned out from the sides of the barge.

The disgraced Queen shrank into the distance, and the crowd dispersed. Servants returned to the confines of Greenwich Palace, scurrying about in silence, each lost in their own thoughts about what they had just witnessed. Mawde remained at the riverside, watching the barge slowly shrink from view. She turned and stared at Greenwich Palace. Sunlight glinted on the oriel windows, and the imposing red brick walls radiated warmth. In the orchard on the hill rising beyond the palace, apple trees were flowering with a spectacular display of white and pink blooms.

Mawde imagined the palace servants going about their business in a state of stunned silence. And it was all her fault.

CHAPTER FORTY-EIGHT

MAY 1536

THE PALE LIGHT of dawn crept through the thin drapes covering the window of Mawde's bedchamber.

Mawde's head throbbed and her eyes ached. Nightmares had broken her sleep every night since Queen Anne's arrest. Every time Mawde closed her eyes and drifted off to sleep, she imagined the Queen tied to a stake, calling Mawde's name and screaming as she burned. Her scream was a perfect match for Tamsin's, and it made Mawde's blood run cold. Every morning she had refused to rise, ignoring Widow Foxe's pounding on the door. Even Widow Cornwallis's pleas had gone unanswered when she had begged Mawde to let her in the evening before.

Mawde wrinkled her nose at the pungent odour rising from her sweat stained skin. Her uncombed hair drooped in tangles, and her skin itched from neglect. She caught her image staring back at her from the mirror and barely recognised herself. Her cheeks were sallow, and her flesh was wasting while her mind was sick with guilt.

She retrieved her stash of coins from their hiding place in the door frame and picked out the golden angel. It was a shimmering reminder of poor choices made and consequences endured. She placed the pouch on her bed and rested an angel on top, wondering how Widow Foxe would react when she discovered it later.

When Mawde stepped outside, the air felt damp and oppressive. Noxious fumes rose from the filthy gutter and rats feasted on vegetable peelings immersed in pisspot slops. The streets were empty, a lull before a storm when dock workers and merchants would sweep through in a swarm to begin their day at work. Mawde peeled away from the warren of narrow streets and climbed the steep hill rising behind the palace. Her chest heaved and her breaths came in snatched, unsatisfying gasps. She headed for an oak tree, standing tall and regal, its trunk thickened from many decades standing sentinel over Greenwich town. Mawde dropped to all fours and then settled on the mossy ground beneath the tree, her back pressed against the ribbed bark as she struggled to catch her breath.

Miniature figures darted about within the walled grounds of Greenwich Palace as servants rose from their slumbers and set about their morning tasks. Men and women streamed along the muddy road dissecting the palace grounds, servants merging with outsiders such as messenger boys, merchants and washerwomen. Mawde wondered if they were missing her in the confectionary. Unlikely, she thought, because they were used to the many occasions when she had been summoned to Austin Friars.

From a branch high above, a blackbird sang out with a confident, mellow voice. Mawde envied his simple life. She stared at the angel in her hand, a gift from Robert Perris that had failed to protect her from slipping into a lifestyle tainted by sin. She launched it into the distance, not caring where it fell. Her kirtle had folded back on itself, revealing the bottom of her shift which had started to fray at the hem. She picked a thread loose, and another, then tugged at the fabric, relishing the ripping sound as the cloth split in two.

Mawde tore at the linen, piling narrow strips on her lap. Drained from the effort and two weeks of not eating, she dropped her hands to her sides and gazed into the distance. The sun crept from beyond the horizon, a great fireball casting an angry glow over a world full of sinners.

Boats crowded the river, jostling for space. Watermen called to one another, the breeze reducing their booming voices to a distant feeble whimper. Greenwich was a boiling pot, vibrant and exciting, yet Mawde had a niggling thought that she should leave it all behind. She toyed with the linen strips nestling on her lap, weaving them together.

A painful cramp in her calf muscle forced Mawde to her feet. She stamped on the ground between the exposed tree roots to ease the discomfort, then rested her arms on a low-slung branch and stared across the river towards London.

Many years had passed since Mawde had climbed a tree. She sat in the crook of a strong, wide branch, sheltered from the wind and hidden from the sun. Leaves whispered. Branches creaked. She considered climbing higher, but the branches were thinner and she feared they might break.

The booming of cannons ricocheted from Tower Wharf, a triumphant proclamation that Anne Boleyn was dead.

Mawde stared at the noose she held in her hand, plaited from the shredded strips of her shift. Her grandmother once told her that her life would end with a cord around her neck. She grasped the branch above her head and shuffled out of her hiding place, freeing the makeshift rope after it snagged on the bark.

The sun was still climbing, the angry red blaze softening to a golden glow. Mawde's mind was made up. She dropped from the branch.

Her ankle twisted as she landed on the ground, making her cry out in pain. She rubbed the throbbing joint and gazed at the noose suspended high in the tree. How Grandmother would have gloated if her prediction had come true, but Mawde refused to give satisfaction to that mean woman's ghost. Mawde had been a victim for long enough – a victim of bullying; a victim of misfortune; a victim of greed. She withdrew the Madonna and Child carving from her pocket, kissed it, then held it firmly in her hand. This was a day for starting afresh and the day for becoming the person she wanted to be.

She was Mawde of Roseland, and she would be herself.

Mawde walked into the confectionary as if she hadn't missed a day. Her skin burned from a vigorous rubbing with a coarse cloth and her scalp tingled from a battle with a comb. She had swapped her soiled shift for a clean one, and felt stronger for following Widow Foxe's insistence on eating a chunk of bread dipped in honey and ale.

Widow Cornwallis greeted her with an affectionate smile. 'You're a welcome sight, Mawde. The King's appetite has returned, and we can't keep pace with his demands.'

'Surprising what a new love interest will do,' said Anthony. 'Can you believe he announced his betrothal the day after Queen Anne's execution? Rumour is—'

'I think we've had enough rumours to last us a lifetime, don't you?' Mawde picked up a comfit pan and set it over a box of coals.

Widow Cornwallis rested her hand on Mawde's shoulder and gave a gentle squeeze. 'I agree, Mawde. King Henry is back in good humour, so we can go about our business with contentment and good grace.'

Master Dawes entered the confectionary and removed Mawde's comfit pan from the heat. 'Sergeant Barker wishes to see you in his office right away.'

Mawde steeled herself. Explaining her prolonged absence would be the first of many obstacles she knew she would have to overcome. Anthony threw her a concerned glance. Widow Cornwallis murmured words of encouragement. Mawde approached Sergeant Barker's office, imagining what she might say. Whatever words she used, they would be nothing but the truth.

'Come in, Mawde.' Master Dawes gestured she should sit in a plain wooden chair facing his desk. He waited for her to settle before continuing. 'It's my duty to inform you that you are released from Master Cromwell's employ with immediate effect.'

Mawde clamped her lips together and stared towards a small window overlooking the stable yard. She had feared this might happen, but it was still hard to bear.

'I regret my absence, Master Dawes, and I apologise most humbly. I was taken unwell, but I'm better now. Please, I beg you, allow me to continue working here. I promise I won't let you down again.'

'I know that, Mawde.' He looked over her shoulder towards his office door, then added, 'I would if I had my way, but something prevents me from keeping you here.'

'Please, Master Dawes, there must be a way of letting me stay! I'll do anything, work anywhere – in the bakery if need be.'

'No, Mawde.' It was another man's voice. 'You're coming with me.'

Mawde whirled around in the chair. Her heat beat so fast she feared it would burst. Her pulse thrummed in her ears, drowning out the sound of the man's voice. She rose from her chair, afraid to believe her eyes. 'Nicholas?' Her fingers flew to the pendant that still hung around her neck.

'Yes, sweeting, it's me. I know my appearance has changed since we parted, but my love for you has not.'

Master Dawes left his office and closed the door behind him. Mawde stood still, lost for words, drunk on the vision of her true love. Wind and sun had lined and darkened his skin, and his hair was streaked with silver. But his eyes were the same, as blue as the sky on a summer's day, glistening with hope and promise. He opened his arms and cocked his head, and Mawde stepped into his embrace.

Mawde's joy soon evaporated, displaced by intense self-loathing.

Nicholas's face creased with concern. 'Mawde?' He reached for her hands.

'So much has happened since we parted at Powderham. You'll find me much changed.' Mawde fixed her gaze on his fingers, fearing she would lose him the moment he let go. 'I've done terrible things.' She looked into his eyes, reliving and regretting every poor decision. 'I will release you from your promise so you may find someone worthy of your love.'

'You are worthy, Mawde.' Nicholas drew her forward and kissed her on the lips. 'I'm sorry I failed to send you word all the years that I was gone. I was on the King's business, travelling up and down the country, always believing I'd be with you before too long.'

'But I broke our promise. I did not save myself for you.'

It was Nicholas's turn to hang his head. 'I didn't stay true either, but I swear I will be from now on.' He lifted his head and tilted Mawde's chin to make her look at him. 'My uncle sent word to me that Cromwell took you from Powderham. Cromwell's confectioner, bedfellow and spy! Your reputation travelled far. It had to be you, sweeting, because no other maid would have shown your courage. For all Cromwell's airs and graces and pompous superiority, he's fond of you. I played on that affection to persuade him to release you from his employ. It's time to put the past behind us, sweeting. I'm here to take you home.'

'Home?'

'I'm taking you to Roseland.'

'Roseland? How?' She was almost afraid to believe him.

Nicholas cupped her face in his hands and kissed her again on the lips. 'The King made me a yeoman and has promised me some land. I'm to oversee the construction of a castle in St Mawes and provide sustenance for those who will build it. I couldn't believe my luck when he told me. Our fortunes are changing, sweeting, now we are on the rise. The time has come at last for me to take you as my wife.'

Years of accumulated loss and regret ebbed away as Mawde made sense of the dramatic turn of events.

'I have warrants permitting us to travel,' Nicholas assured her, 'and we'll stop at Powderham on the way.'

'For Elsebeth?'

Nicholas grinned. 'Yes, for Elsebeth. And when the castle is complete, we'll stay on as farmers supplying both castle and village. I hope some of your family members will work alongside us, too.' He paused, waiting for Mawde's tears to ease. 'I need to hear it from your lips, sweeting. Tell me you love me, and you still want to be my wife?'

Mawde pressed her cheek against the soft leather of his jerkin. 'With all my heart, I love you, and I long to be your wife.' His heartbeat thrummed against her ear, pulsing with love and optimism. The bullying, the greed and the desperation were all in the past.

Nicholas had found her.

Nicholas loved her.

And Nicholas would take her home.

THANK YOU FOR READING THIS BOOK.

I hope you enjoyed reading about Mawde. If you did, and you can spare a minute or two, it would mean the world to me if you would leave an honest review on your favourite bookstore's website.

I'm currently working on the sequel to this story, and I hope to release it in 2023. Meanwhile, you might enjoy my other books:

Winds of Change
Running With The Wind
The Winter Years
The Second Mrs Thistlewood

Have you joined the
Allium Books Readers Club?

Members receive a monthly newsletter, advance notification of my new releases and a FREE downloadable short story. There's no catch to joining, and I'll never pass on your information to third parties. You can unsubscribe at any time. If you'd like to know more about this club and my other published books, visit my website at www.dion nehaynes.com.

SELECT BIBLIOGRAPHY

I have read many books about the Tudor era, but these are my favourites:

How To Be A Tudor by Ruth Goodman

Woodsmoke And Sage by Amy Licence

The Private Lives Of The Tudors by Tracy Borman

The Tudor Housewife by Alison Sim

The Lives Of Tudor Women by Elizabeth Norton

Thomas Cromwell by Robert Hutchinson

ACKNOWLEDGMENTS

My grandparents lived in a small cottage on the seafront of the Cornish village of St Mawes on the Roseland Peninsula. What their home lacked in size was compensated for with kindness, affection and a warm welcome for anyone who stepped over their threshold.

During the 1970s and 1980s, the village was a haven where I roamed free on land and sea, and enjoyed many adventures with family and friends. There are countless people who contributed to those magical times, the memories of which I shall treasure forever. Many family members and friends are no longer with us, but they remain forever in my heart. To the rest of you – and you all know who you are – a simple "thank you" is inadequate, so I dedicate this novel to you.

My thanks also go to Liz Monument (lizmonument.com) for her fabulous editorial feedback and advice, Helen Baggott (helenbaggott.co.uk) for her meticulous proofreading, and Dee Dee (deedeebookcovers) for creating the beautiful book cover design.

Thank you, dear reader, for choosing this novel. And thank you, Paul and Charlie, for your unwavering love and moral support.

Life is full of twists and turns and ups and downs, but may we always have the strength to accept adversity, adapt and move on.

Printed in Great Britain
by Amazon